She was going to have his baby.

The tender and passionate feelings Sam felt for her
at that moment sprang from the bottom of his soul.
He closed his eyes, certain she could read those
things in their depths and not at all sure he wanted
her to. He gathered her close, and the thought ran
through his mind again. *She's having my baby.*

All the time at the cabin, he had been wanting,
waiting. But he didn't want to wait any longer. He
wanted Kerry now with all the pent-up longing a
man could feel.

Beneath his fingertips she felt so fragile and
delicate. He explored her body, careful to avoid
the area where the baby was. He was reluctant
to touch her there, but she seemed to sense his
curiosity and moved his hand to her abdomen.

"That's what it feels like," she said softly. "Not too
scary, is it?"

Speechless, Sam shook his head. Beneath the palm
of his hand, floating in its own special world, was a
major miracle. His child.

Dear Reader,

Spring is coming with all its wonderful scents and colors, and here at Harlequin American Romance we've got a wonderful bouquet of romances to please your every whim!

Few women can refuse a good bargain, but what about a sexy rancher who needs a little help around the house? Wait till you hear the deal Megan Ford offers Rick Astin in Judy Christenberry's *The Great Texas Wedding Bargain*, the continuation of her beloved miniseries TOTS FOR TEXANS!

Spring is a time for new life, and no one blossoms more beautifully than a woman who's WITH CHILD.... In *That's Our Baby!*, the first book in this heartwarming new series, Pamela Browning travels to glorious Alaska to tell the story of an expectant mother and the secret father of her child.

Then we have two eligible bachelors whose fancies turn not lightly, but rather unexpectedly, to thoughts of love. Don't miss *The Cowboy and the Countess*, Darlene Scalera's tender story about a millionaire who has no time for love until a bump on the head brings his childhood sweetheart back into his life. And in Rita Herron's *His-and-Hers Twins*, single dad Zeke Blalock is showered with wife candidates when his little girls advertise for a mother...but only one special woman will do!

So this March, don't forget to stop and smell the roses— and enjoy all four of our wonderful Harlequin American Romance titles!

Happy reading!

Melissa Jeglinski
Associate Senior Editor

That's *Our* Baby!

PAMELA BROWNING

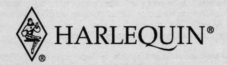

HARLEQUIN®

TORONTO • NEW YORK • LONDON
AMSTERDAM • PARIS • SYDNEY • HAMBURG
STOCKHOLM • ATHENS • TOKYO • MILAN • MADRID
PRAGUE • WARSAW • BUDAPEST • AUCKLAND

For the Friday-morning yoginis,
who could hardly believe it.

ISBN 0-373-16818-7

THAT'S *OUR* BABY!

Visit us at www.romance.net

Printed in U.S.A.

ABOUT THE AUTHOR

Pamela Browning is the award-winning author of thirty romance novels—many of which appeared on numerous bestseller lists. Her books consistently win high ratings from reviewers and readers alike. She makes her home in North Carolina.

Books by Pamela Browning

HARLEQUIN AMERICAN ROMANCE

Dear Reader,

What is a baby?

A baby is potential. In the grand scheme of things, babies embody our best hopes and dreams. The future newly seen through the eyes of a child seems brighter, shinier, more optimistic than we ever imagined.

A baby is connection to the past. When we hold our firstborn in our arms, we feel an outpouring of emotion such as we have never felt before, and we're forever enlightened when we realize that our parents felt the same way about us.

A baby is wonder, reminding us that our world abounds in miracles. We have only to gaze deep into a baby's eyes to know that life is meaningful and good and true.

A baby is joy. That first little smile, that first robust laugh, that gleeful chortle—these brighten our days and lighten our load. There is no happiness on earth like that of a child.

But most of all, a baby is love. Nothing in all the world compares to the love that children bring into our lives. Our love for our children makes us want to work hard for them, to strive and sacrifice and be all that we can for them, and because we do those things we become better people, with the ultimate and worthwhile result that we are better parents.

What is a baby? A simple question, but the answer is complex. Perhaps it is best answered by saying that a baby is everything. And even that falls short of the mark.

With love to you and your babies,

Pamela Browning

Chapter One

Somewhere over the interior of Alaska

Sam Harbeck would have given anything at the moment to be in sunny Key West bolting down margaritas and kicking back with friends. They'd invited; he'd refused. Which was why, instead of lounging around in swim trunks, he was capping off his first vacation in years by piloting a float-plane into a September snowstorm deep in the Alaskan wilderness.

Some vacation, he thought ruefully. A killer storm roaring out of nowhere, a decrepit plane hell-bent on shaking itself apart, a distasteful errand and, on top of all this, Kerry Anderson. She wasn't expecting him, and Sam didn't relish the encounter. Oh, she was gorgeous with that wild tumble of blond hair and those long shapely legs—not to mention thick-lashed gold-and-silver eyes whose unerring gaze knew how to pierce right through a man. But leaving out her spectacular good looks, there was something about Kerry that made Sam uncomfortable. And when she found out what he wanted from her, all hell would break loose.

Sam gripped sinewy fingers around the yoke of the Cessna 185 and forced himself to concentrate on the challenge of setting this baby down safely on Kitty Kill Lake.

If he was anywhere near it, that is. To the north, summits of the highest mountain range in North America shored up the sky—had to stay clear of them. Somewhere to the west, a vast frozen river ground toward the sea: Williwaw Glacier. Its icy tongue split the land, its meltwater fed the lake below as well as the Kilkit River. Silverthorne Lodge was at the juncture of lake and river—God's country.

But he didn't see the glacier, the lake or the lodge. All he saw was dreary gray clouds concealing the glorious scenery of what Sam considered the United States' last frontier. With its icy tundra, vast distances, untold natural resources, and teeming wildlife, Alaska was big, bold and unlike any other place in the world. Sam liked to think that he was like the land—rugged, brash and untamed. A lot of people would have agreed with him.

No point in trying the radio; too much static. He peered out the Cessna's window, searching for landmarks. A sudden blast of turbulence knocked the plane into a prolonged pitch and yaw. Cursing, Sam yanked back on the yoke to halt a sharp descent before he rammed in the power. Clouds fell away to reveal the snow-crested tops of trees and a dark slice of water. Ahead lay a curve of the river surmounted by a rocky bluff.

He fought to hold the plane level in the wind and tipped the nose up slightly as a swirl of snow across the windshield blurred his vision. Forget a clean approach; he'd have to make do with these less than ideal conditions. Adrenaline kicked in, the high he always got when faced with a dangerous and demanding task.

As he swooped low over the gray belly of the river looking for a patch free of rocks, he saw a downed tree spreading a tangle of limbs across the riverbank and into the water. He cursed again and tried to avoid the obstruction. Too soon he felt a thud of impact against the right float and strut. Something snapped, and a branch scraped across the top of the plane before the Cessna veered and hit the water with a sickening lurch.

It was a couple of minutes before Sam's head cleared. The Cessna was upright, at least, but the right wing leaned into a tangle of vegetation. The left float was in place on the water. He climbed out of the cockpit groggily, side-stepped along the length of the float, and jumped across to the rocky bank before easing down on his haunches to assess the problem.

The plane's right strut was broken, and its float had sheared off and lay on its side amid snow-covered boulders a few feet behind. The plane was skewed at an angle, its left wing canted in the air. Wait until he told his friend Vic Parnell that he'd damaged the plane. Vic admitted to a sentimental fondness for the Cessna, his first and only float-plane.

Sam straightened and brushed the snow from his shoulders before climbing back into the cockpit. He checked the Emergency Locator Transmitter, the ELT; evidently the plane hadn't impacted hard enough during the landing to trigger the signaling device automatically. The ELT would guide search planes to him if anyone was monitoring. He flipped the switch experimentally. Nothing happened. He tried again. Nothing. Great. Apparently the battery was dead.

Jeez, if he'd known this would be the result of doing Vic a favor, he never would have taken off this morning. Sam kept his own planes in excellent condition, and this particular friend wasn't ordinarily lax about safety precautions. However, Vic had been sick for over a year and was now recovering from an operation at his daughter's house in Anchorage. Sam checked the survival gear and discovered that there wasn't much. A roll of duct tape, a musty sleeping bag, a Mylar survival blanket, some canned food. No flare gun, no matches, no drinkable water.

Sam prided himself on being pretty good at flying by the seat of his pants, so not being able to use the plane's radio hadn't hampered him too seriously. As for the ELT's being out of commission, that was a blow. Now Sam regretted taking off at all today. He certainly hadn't expected a change in the weather, and snow didn't usually fall in this part of the Country until mid-October.

Sam pulled a compass from his pocket and studied it. If he was where he thought he was, Chickaback Creek was to his right. According to the direction of the river's flow and the compass reading, Williwaw Glacier lay to the north. Ditto Silverthorne Lodge...and Kerry Anderson.

There was nothing to do but strike out in that direction on foot. The Cessna, he noted glumly, wasn't going anywhere. At least not until he repaired that strut and float. Hell, he could probably do it with the aid of chewing gum and a few paper clips, and the thought made him smile. It was what his old buddy Doug Anderson might have said.

He and Doug had prided themselves on being cracker-jack fliers, and between them they thought they knew everything there was to know about airplanes. Except, sometimes, how to keep them in the air. Doug had died a year ago in a crash of the commuter plane he was piloting, leaving Kerry a widow and Sam with the possibility of becoming a father. But Sam was about to nix that option.

Sam saw now that ice was already forming along the river's shoreline; not a good sign. He quickly scribbled a note to leave in the plane in case anyone should happen along and wonder where he was; he listed his destination as Silverthorne Lodge. Then he shouldered his pack and survival gear, checking carefully to make sure that the forms he'd brought for Kerry to sign were safe in their waterproof pouch in the inside pocket of his parka. Yeah, they were there, all right. If everything had gone according to plan, they would have been signed, sealed and delivered to the sperm bank in Seattle within the next forty-eight hours. *It could still happen if the river doesn't freeze,* he thought to himself with a dark sense of foreboding.

His hunch told Sam that he'd arrive at Silverthorne Lodge shortly after dark. Despite the way this whole situation was shaping up, he couldn't help but grin as he thought of Kerry's reaction when she saw him, of all people. She'd never liked him, had considered him a bad influence. That alone was enough to spur him on across rugged terrain and through the blinding, blowing snow.

At Silverthorne

KERRY ANDERSON lay sprawled on the floor beneath the wildly swinging moose-antler chandelier and tried not to scream her frustration. Her finger, the left ring finger, was broken. She just knew it. Thank goodness she'd left Doug's wedding ring in the wall safe at her friend's house in Anchorage. There sure weren't any jewelers around this neck of the woods to cut it off after her finger swelled.

Talk about stupid! She hadn't been able to stand looking at the thick furring of dust on those moose antlers for one more minute, and against her better judgment, she'd climbed the first few rungs of a shaky ladder before it had toppled to the floor, taking her along with it. She'd better get an ice pack on her injured finger, and fast.

Kerry sat up and took stock of the rest of her. Fortunately her hand had broken her fall, and aside from a bruised hip, she was okay. But what if she wasn't okay? Something else could go wrong, and she'd never forgive herself if it did. Experimentally she smoothed her right hand, the uninjured one, over the slight curve of stomach and abdomen. Nothing hurt, nothing cramped, and she drew a deep breath of relief.

She had planned it all so carefully: She'd stayed in Seattle until she could take care of business that had been postponed for too long, then she'd retreated to the lodge. In the three months since she'd been there, she'd accomplished a lot in the refurbishing of the eighteen-room building, but it had taken much longer than she'd expected, mostly because she sometimes got hung up on details. Like dusty moose antlers.

But the moose antlers were, well, picturesque and would lend an air of rustic authenticity to the lodge. That's what tourists in Alaska paid good money for. And money was what Kerry needed at this point. Otherwise she'd never even contemplate opening her late husband's ancestral fishing-and-hunting retreat to the public.

She couldn't help sparing a thought for funny old Captain Crocker. He'd wanted her to leave with him on the last run of the *River Rover* over Labor Day weekend, and he'd called her a crazy *cheechako,* which was what Alaskans called someone new to the Country. The word came from the Chinook language, and it meant "tenderfoot."

Cheechako or no, Kerry had blithely waved him away from the dock anyway. If he were here, she would have grudgingly admitted that he'd been right. She should have left when she had the chance. No one with any sense, particularly a *cheechako,* would camp on the edge of an Alaskan glacier with winter coming on. Now, feeling the weight of responsibility settling squarely on her narrow shoulders, she wanted to cry. She couldn't, wouldn't fail.

As soon as she could perambulate, Kerry dusted herself off and headed back to Silverthorne's original homestead cabin, where she'd been living ever since she'd arrived. A light snow was sifting out of a milky gray sky, and the temperature had dropped drastically since lunchtime. It was only the middle of September, and it wasn't supposed to be snowing yet. She'd been prepared for lots of rain, since she knew that it rained overmuch in Alaska. But snow? No.

As if I don't have enough to worry about without bad weather, she told herself as she tried to ignore the stabs of pain darting up her arm. She was chilled to the bone and wondering if she'd made the worst mistake in her life when she'd told Captain Crocker to go back to Anchorage without her.

FOUR HOURS LATER, the pain in Kerry's finger was horrendous, but a broken finger wasn't her worst worry. The storm was.

The cabin was engulfed in a blinding snowstorm complete with a howling wind that shook it to its foundations. Kerry huddled drowsily on the couch nursing her finger with an ice pack, her favorite goose-down pillow cradling her head. She wished she had a first-aid kit, and somewhere upstairs was one of those medical advice books. But right now she didn't have the energy to climb the narrow ladder to the loft to get it. She was exhausted, and sometimes she felt so queasy. And if only her finger didn't hurt so much, she'd sleep. She closed her eyes, trying to drift away, making herself think of pleasant things, of happy times...

She awoke with a start. Her finger was swollen to twice its size, and the ice she'd packed around it had melted. No telling how long she had dozed; she glanced out the window and tried to figure out if the storm was letting up. No, it was as fierce as ever.

And then she saw it—a face at the window above the

couch. It wavered in the flickering light from the kerosene lamp on the table.

Kerry jumped up with a little shriek, clutching the pillow to her chest. Was she dreaming? She didn't think so. She must be having hallucinations from the pain. There could be no other explanation for such a frightening visage.

The face was distorted in the wavy glass and encircled by a big furry hood. The eyebrows bristled white with crusted snow. The nose was red from the cold, the jaw dark with stubble, and the mouth a wide gash uttering words that she couldn't hear for the lashing of wind-driven snow against the windowpane.

As she stared at the apparition, it moved toward the door. She was seized with sudden irrational fear. She was alone here and at the mercy of anyone who came along, and she'd thought she was protected by the surrounding wilderness, by the fact that the closest human beings lived sixty miles away. Yet here was this stranger who was now banging loudly on the door. She hadn't bolted it when she came in earlier; she had been in pain and thought there was no need.

Whoever it was scrabbling at the latch. In a panic now, Kerry threw her full weight, all one hundred and ten pounds of it, against the door.

Too late she realized that she should have armed herself with the poker from the fireplace. As the door swung open on rusty hinges, the sound of the wind was deafening. A snow-covered figure stumbled into the storm vestibule, the wind gusting hard against its broad back. Knowing that she had to protect herself from this unwelcome intruder, Kerry summoned all her strength and socked it as hard as she possibly could—

With the pillow. Which broke open and scattered feathers everywhere.

A cry of outrage drowned out even the howl of the wind.

"Hey, don't you know me? I'm Sam, Sam Harbeck!" The figure ripped off its hood, and Kerry's mouth dropped open in astonishment. She forgot, for the moment, her pain.

"Sam?" she said, her voice rising on an incredulous note. The intruder *couldn't* be Sam Harbeck.

But it was. In those crazily disoriented seconds, she couldn't imagine how Doug's best friend came to be tapping on her window here in the middle of the wilderness during a blinding snowstorm, but it was Sam, all right. How could she not have recognized his square, stubborn chin, that sharp, straight blade of a nose? Even now, with wet feathers plastered in his hair and all over his face, he couldn't be mistaken for anyone else.

A flurry of snow billowed into the room and mingled with the floating feathers on a burst of cold that almost knocked Kerry over. She dropped what remained of the pillow and struggled to slam the door, but the wind was too strong. Sam joined her in throwing his full weight against the heavy door, and together they managed to shut out the raging storm.

In the sudden hollow silence, Sam spat feathers out of his mouth, slung his backpack into a corner and peeled off his parka.

"What kind of welcome is this? I hammered on the door and yelled until I almost froze. Or is that what you had in mind?" His piercing blue gaze swept over her, taking in her mussed hair now frosted with feathers, the worn jeans, the red wool hiking socks with a hole in one toe. She stood gaping at him, unable to speak.

"You shouldn't have dressed up," he said, stomping clumps of snow off his boots and making a feathery mess on the floor. He threw the parka over a peg beside Kerry's coat and strode through a few still-fluttering feathers to the kitchen area where he helped himself to a towel from the shelf over the dry sink.

"*You* forgot to shave," Kerry snapped back, picking feathers from her hair, her sweater, her jeans. She felt perilously near tears; it was because her finger hurt and her favorite pillow was ruined. Or maybe it was because she'd been foolish enough to think that Sam Harbeck had the capacity to care about anyone but himself.

"I've been roughing it, camping out."

"In snow?" Kerry said, heavy on the sarcasm. She bent to pick up the pillow. Its case was wet, and feathers were still falling out.

"It wasn't snowing when I started," Sam said. He wiped his face with the towel and tossed it into a basket under the sink before peering into the cloudy mirror beside the back door and brushing feathers from his hair. In obvious distaste, he poked at a pot of red beans she'd left on the stove after lunch and dropped the spoon before looking her over again from head to toe.

It was a thorough inspection, his gaze lingering on her face before sweeping the rest of her slight frame. It unnerved her, that look. She felt as if she were standing in front of him buck naked. For something to do, she walked over to the wood box and shoved the sadly deflated pillow in between the logs. She didn't know what else to do with it.

"Whatever brings you to this neck of the woods?" she blurted. She held her injured finger in the palm of her other hand; it was throbbing painfully. Through her pain and astonishment, she had the idea that maybe Sam was checking on her out of a feeling of obligation to Doug. At that thought she felt a kind of absurd gratitude, but it evaporated as soon as Sam opened his mouth.

"Your friend Emma told me you'd written and said you

were staying on here after the last boat of the summer came through. I couldn't believe you could be so dumb. Why are you staying here in the cabin instead of the lodge?''

"It costs too much to run the electrical generator there, and the lodge is too big to heat. Anyway, the cabin is cozy. It suits me.''

"What ever possessed you to hang on at Silverthorne with winter coming on? With winter already here,'' he amended, with a meaningful look at the storm flailing outside the windows.

"I had lots of work to do. I was in the middle of painting the dining room because I was running behind schedule when the *River Rover* made its last run. Captain Crocker is sending his son-in-law Bert to pick me up in his plane in a couple of weeks when he flies to the Indian village on government business.'' She narrowed her eyes. "The captain didn't send you instead, did he?''

Sam's hair was coal-black and unruly, and now he furrowed a hand through it, which only made it wilder. "Hell, no. If anyone had asked me to fly all the way over here to pick up a *cheechako* woman who was enough of a nitwit not to head for civilization in the face of an Alaskan winter, I would have refused.'' Like Captain Crocker, he'd pronounced it "cheechaker.'' "Nope, it was my own fool decision to stop here. You should have left weeks ago. And if Bert's planning to fly to an Indian village, which one?''

"To Athinopa. Captain Crocker said Bert wouldn't mind stopping here.''

"He wouldn't. If he heard about you, that is.''

"Why wouldn't he?''

"Josiah Crocker habitually tosses his captain's hat onto his bedpost on the last day of August every year and goes on a six-month drunk, that's why. I wouldn't count on Joe to tell anyone anything.''

"How was I to know?" Kerry said, feeling deflated.

Sam evidently took this for a rhetorical question because he picked a few feathers from his shirt and changed the subject. "You're too thin. Don't you eat properly?"

"I try," she said evenly. For the first time she noticed that Sam Harbeck looked like a cross between Harrison Ford and George Clooney, heavy on the Harrison. He seemed to take up too much space in this small room; he filled it up. Kerry tried to inhale, but found that she couldn't breathe. She grabbed the back of a chair with her uninjured hand and closed her eyes against the bevy of black dots swarming behind her eyelids. Meanwhile her visitor was pacing like a caged animal. An *agitated* caged animal, who was incongruously wearing the ubiquitous Alaskan bush boots. Feathers fluttered lazily in the air like snowflakes.

"Worse September snowstorm I've seen in many years. I was halfway here when it hit. I ditched the plane at the bend in the river where it meets Chickaback Creek. Do you have anything to eat? Anything good?" He cast a disparaging look at the pot of beans.

"I—um, well, I made goulash yesterday out of the last of the beef and was going to heat it for dinner. Anyway, beans are very nutritious. I cooked them with wild onions and chili powder. What plane?"

"It's an aging Cessna 185 that I agreed to ferry back to Anchorage for a friend. Against my better judgment, by the way. Last week I had one of my pilots drop me off at Vic's camp, it's out Tolneeka way, and indulged in a few days of fishing. Where's the goulash?"

She ignored his question. "What happened to the Cessna?" she asked. She was still trying to figure out what Sam was doing here.

"It was an emergency landing, and the plane's not fly-able. I guess the damage could have been worse considering the conditions. Actually I didn't land far from here, but I had to walk most of the way against the wind. Is something wrong? You look like hell.'' He tucked his hands into his belt loops and scowled at her. His brows were still damp and stood out from his face; a small scar cut through the left one. His mouth turned down at the corners; it was too generous to be considered handsome. Even as she noted these irrelevant details, Kerry couldn't help thinking that there was something overwhelmingly, reassuringly masculine about him. She told herself that under the circumstances, she should be relieved to see another human being, any human being. Even Sam Harbeck. Even when he was saying uncomplimentary things.

''I thought rule number one was never to leave the plane if you go down.''

''Yeah, well, I've never been much for rules. I asked you if something was wrong.''

''I think I broke my finger,'' Kerry said with reluctance.

''Let's see.'' It wasn't a request, it was a command.

Reluctantly Kerry presented her hand, and Sam enveloped it in his larger ones as he studied it. He whistled. ''That's a lovely shade of violent.''

''Violent?''

''Violet. It's a joke, Kerry.''

''It hurts too much to laugh.''

She could tell he didn't like the looks of her injury. ''What have you been doing for it?'' he asked.

''Cold packs. I've been hoping it's only sprained.''

''It looks like more than a sprain, all right. What were you doing, smashing your fingers with a hammer? You have no business trying to renovate that big old lodge by yourself. You should have waited until next year when you could bring in a crew of workmen.''

''There's no money for workmen, and by next summer

I'll need paying guests. Doug didn't leave me in great financial shape, you know.'' She pulled her hand away from him, but he grabbed her wrist. His fingers were surprisingly gentle.

"Not so fast. Where does it hurt most?'' His voice had lost its challenge and its banter now. Also he had ignored the reference to her finances, which Kerry thought was probably just as well. She didn't want Sam Harbeck to pity her for her financial difficulties; everyone knew that he had built the small bush-flying service that he'd inherited from his father into Harbeck Air, Alaska's biggest charter airline. Sam was worth millions of dollars. His remarkable success only underscored her late husband's recklessness with money.

"I think my finger's broken in the end segment. That's where it hurts most. Hey, careful! Your hands are cold.''

"I'll spare you the usual comeback.'' His eyes now were surprisingly mischievous, a pale sparkling blue.

"'Cold hands, warm heart?' It's not necessarily true.''

Sam ordinarily seemed to enjoy sparring with her, but now he was all business. "What's true is that we'd better do something about this finger. Usually doctors don't treat fractures in the end segment of the finger unless they involve the joint. Think the joint's fractured?''

Against her better judgment, Kerry tried to wiggle her swollen finger. "It hurts so much that it's hard to tell. I may have just jammed it. My hand took a blow when I broke my fall.''

"You're lucky it's your left hand.''

Kerry shook her head. "Not so lucky. I'm left-handed.''

"Well, what I'm going to do is tape your ring finger to the middle one. It won't hurt so much if it's immobilized.''

"Wouldn't a splint be better?

"There are pros and cons. A splint decreases pain, but

may increase joint stiffness after it's healed. If we leave your finger as it is, the pain may last longer and chances are you'll end up with a stiff joint anyway. Taping it to the adjoining finger is a good compromise.''

"How do you know so much about this?" she asked, watching him as he dug a first-aid kit out of his pack and withdrew a thick roll of gauze.

"I had a broken finger once from a sled accident. The doctor explained the alternative treatments to me."

His touch was sure and gentle as he bound her ring and middle fingers together with gauze, and he stood so close that his face was only inches from hers. She inhaled the welcome warm male scent of him, a combination of leather, wood smoke, musk and something indefinably exciting. He smelled of the outdoors, of melted snow and a raw wind and, too, of the river.

What he was doing to her finger was painful, and she forced herself not to flinch. Instead she would trust, and that wasn't easy. She had come to depend on no one but herself long before Doug died. Even as she was thinking how nice it might be to be comforted and cosseted, to have someone to take care of her, Sam's eyes met hers.

She instantly felt a jolt. Not just a mental one, but a physical one, too, as if a current of electricity pulsed from one to the other. Where it originated, in her or in him, Kerry couldn't have said, nor did she know if it was conducted from his hand to hers or over the brilliantly charged space between them. It unnerved her and made her want to yank her fingers away, and yet she couldn't move. Couldn't stop looking at him, into him, wondering if he too felt something. Felt—what? They had never much liked each other.

This reality check gave her the strength to look away. It was too intimate, that blistering brief moment of eye contact and this electrifying physical closeness. While she was contemplating her own embarrassment, Sam dropped the adhesive tape into her free hand.

"Here, hold this," he said abruptly. He ripped a piece off the roll and wound it around her fingers. If he noticed anything amiss, he gave no sign.

"What medicine are you taking for the pain?" he asked.

"None," she replied, striving to keep her tone even. "I didn't bring any, and there weren't any medical supplies here." Did she sound normal? No. But maybe she sounded normal enough to fool him.

"I'll see if I have something." Sam rummaged in the first-aid kit and produced a small white envelope. "It's not much, but it'll have to do." Sam shook out two acetaminophen. "Take them," he said. "You'll be more comfortable after it kicks in."

Without comment, Kerry picked up the glass of water she'd set on the table next to the couch and swallowed the pills. She definitely did not feel like herself. The day had been a strain, and she'd been working hard for weeks with no respite. And here was Sam, and she didn't know why he was here, and her finger hurt worse than anything she could imagine.

"Didn't you hear what I said?" Sam was wrinkling his forehead at her. He really had such a noble forehead, so wide. And the way that one curly lock of hair fell across it was charming.

Charming? Sam Harbeck was anything but charming. *I may have broken my finger, but falling off a ladder hasn't made me lose my mind,* she thought just as Sam grasped her around the shoulders. She struggled to push him away, but he said, "You look a little woozy. Here, let's ease you down on the couch," all the while holding her so close that she actually felt the muscles ripple across his chest.

"Now sit down and put your feet up," he said close to her ear.

"I'm all right, leave me alone," she replied weakly.

He snorted. "I'm not going to have you dropping in your tracks, at least not until I clean the water and feathers off the floor."

"I'm all right," she repeated, but he knelt beside her and studied her while his face kaleidoscoped into several Sams, all of them wearing the same expression of concern.

"I'm going to pull this blanket up over you, and you can lie back and watch me work." Sam settled the striped wool blanket across her as Kerry allowed herself to sink back on the couch cushions.

"How do you feel?" he asked. Absently he reached over and plucked a feather from her hair; he sat looking at it thoughtfully.

"Lousy," she mumbled. She wondered if Sam was aware of how endearing he was when he was being kind.

"Great. We should have that finger x-rayed, you know. But the nearest x-ray machine is in Anchorage, over three hundred miles away." He tucked the feather in his pocket.

"Believe me, the same thought has occurred to me. Go away, Sam. Let me suffer in peace." This dramatic utterance brought a derisive hoot from Sam.

He stood up. "As long as you can talk, I know you're fine," he said dryly.

How could she have found his behavior endearing only moments ago? He was making fun of her. "Go on," she said, pushing at his knee. His jeans were wet from being out in the snow.

After one last exasperated glance at her over his shoulder, Sam went to the supply closet and dug around amid the welter of old brooms, battered skis and bent buckets until he produced a mop.

"Too bad there's no electricity in the cabin. A vacuum cleaner would come in handy for these feathers."

"D'you know how to use that?" Kerry said thickly as he began to wield the mop.

Sam paused and indulged in an amused chuckle. "My first job at my Dad's airport was janitor," he said.

"Oh," she said, but she couldn't help recalling the time she and Doug had flown into that very airport and visited Sam in his plush office, where he was ensconced behind an enormous mahogany desk while he fielded telephone calls from all over the world. Afterward they'd glided in Sam's Mercedes sedan to his elegant house in exclusive Turn Again by the Sea. The house was an architectural marvel overlooking an arm of Cook Inlet, where his house-man served them a gourmet's dinner of grilled Alaskan King salmon and wild rice sauted with roasted pine nuts.

It was hard to reconcile that image of Sam with the slightly rakish and unshaven man who was so vigorously mopping the wide planks of the cabin floor and stirring up drying feathers. She watched him through half-closed eyes as he worked, admiring in spite of herself the swift power of his movements and his attention to the task. When he had finished mopping and stowed the mop in the closet, he said, "That's about the best I can do, so now I'm going to shuck these wet clothes. Close your eyes."

One thing about Sam Harbeck—he certainly knew how to get a girl's attention. Kerry roused herself to object, pushing herself to a half-sitting position and regarding Sam with what she hoped would pass for outrage.

"You could step out to the shed to change," she pointed out. "Or go up in the loft." Those were the only two possibilities for privacy. The cabin consisted of only one twelve by eighteen-foot room with a loft built above the kitchen section.

"I'm not going anywhere. The shed is too cold and the loft ceiling is only five feet high and slanted, which would require that I change clothes in a crouch."

"What's wrong with changing clothes in a crouch?" Kerry said for the sake of getting an argument going.

"Since I'm over six feet tall, I'd end up with a crick in my neck or worse. It's your choice. You can watch me as I expose my shivering male body to your eyes—or not. I'll leave it up to you." Sam was maddeningly arrogant, but that was nothing new.

The worst thing was that Kerry couldn't think of anything at all to say in response. She caught only a glimpse of that devil-may-care grin of Sam's as he turned and reached into his pack to withdraw neatly folded jeans. As if to underscore his own outrageousness, he tossed a pair of black male briefs to the floor where they lay in all their skimpy glory.

"I don't want to see anything shivering or naked," Kerry blurted with all the conviction she could muster at the moment, and Sam laughed when he saw where she was looking.

"I thought so. Don't worry, I'll sound the all clear when I'm decent." He was already unbuttoning his shirt.

Kerry closed her eyes, tight. She heard the clomp of Sam's boots as they fell to the floor followed by the whisper of sodden jeans against flesh and the dull muffled thud as they fell. Telltale sounds reported that Sam was pawing through his pack; he tossed some things onto the floor, humming to himself.

"I could have sworn I stuck a wool flannel shirt in here," Sam mused. More digging. More humming. At last Kerry couldn't stand it anymore and opened her eyes to a slit so that she could peer from beneath her eyelashes for a peek.

He stood in the middle of the cabin facing her, light from

the kerosene lamp playing over his well-muscled body. She'd never considered Sam Harbeck good-looking; he was too rawboned and rugged for her taste. But it was all she could do not to gasp at the magnificence of his commanding physique.

His shoulders were broader than she'd remembered. Not that she ever had reason to think about them, but if she had, she'd have assumed that they'd be average. They weren't. And their width emphasized a tapering torso thickly furred with springy black hair all the way down past his navel to a taut, rock-hard abdomen. And below that...

She closed her eyes again, and fast. Generally speaking, she wasn't the least bit interested in men's anatomies, and certainly not in Sam Harbeck's. Yet the image of that stray lock of black hair falling over his forehead, the lamplight shading the hollows and curves of his utterly masculine body, seemed burned upon the inside of her eyelids. The shape of him, the details of him, wouldn't go away.

Sam's fresh clothes weren't the only thing that was dry; her mouth might run a close second. She swallowed hard, but didn't dare peek. Her memory of the way he'd looked was bad enough.

"Mission accomplished," Sam said after what seemed like an eternity. "I'm ready to stand inspection."

She didn't look. She didn't want to encounter those keen blue eyes, sharp as daggers. She didn't want him to discover in her own eyes what she was afraid he'd detect. She'd never liked Sam, and she wouldn't give him anything he could use against her.

"I'm really very tired," she said, which was true.

"You might as well go ahead and relax. I'm going to pitch a couple more logs into the stove and nab some chow."

"Mmm," Kerry replied, hoping she sounded sleepy. She

needed time to figure out Sam's motive for being here, and yet she could hardly think. Not only was she still in pain, but she knew now that she shouldn't have looked at him undressed. Doug had been dead for over a year, and she tried not to dwell on how much she missed the sexual aspect of marriage. Seeing Sam had made her think about it again, and life was hard enough without lingering on thoughts about all she didn't have.

Sam, by this time, had discovered the pot of goulash and was stirring it on the stove. He seemed at home in a kitchen and found dishes, flatware and mugs without having to ask where they were. Of course he'd be comfortable here, she thought. Sam and Doug had come here many times together, usually for their ridiculous once-a-year, no-women-allowed male bonding experience.

Kerry had never figured out why, the whole time they'd been married, Doug had felt that he had to leave her behind while he disappeared into the wilderness every year to squander a whole week's precious vacation. She'd always thought it was so he could grow a beard and refuse to take a bath for seven days but, even so, she still didn't understand how beard stubble and the lack of bathing promoted male friendship.

She opened her eyes and saw that the pot on the stove was steaming alarmingly. "Careful, or you'll burn that goulash," she warned.

"Nah," Sam said, not seeming to notice her waspish tone. He slid the pot from the burner and ladled the hot meat and noodles onto two plates.

"I didn't say I want any," she told him.

"Doesn't matter. You've got to eat. If you don't feel like sitting at the table, I'll bring this over to the couch, and you can eat there."

"With one hand mostly out of commission? No thanks.

I'll join you at the table—if you'll remember that I'm a lefty and ignore my clumsy attempts to eat with my right hand. And don't expect brilliant conversation. It's been a long day.''

"I don't expect conversation at all. Come to think of it, last time I sat down to dinner with you, you got up, flounced into the bedroom and slammed the door. It pretty much ended small talk." He shot her a look out of the corners of his eyes.

She didn't like that look, but countering it was far from her first priority. She stood up, gingerly shifted from one foot to the other to see if her knees worked, and when they did, she wobbled over to sit at the table. In the process she tried to make up her mind if Sam's last accusation merited a response. Finally she said as coolly as she could, "The incident you're referring to happened four years ago, and you had come to visit Doug and me in Seattle. And you took the money I'd been saving for a bang-up anniversary celebration weekend and wouldn't give it back."

Sam leaned over the table, his eyes dancing. "I won that money fair and square from you and Doug in a poker game after both of you insisted that you could beat me. A bet," he said pointedly, "is a bet." He went back to the stove and brought her a plate of goulash.

"A bet may be a bet, but because of it Doug and I had to stay home for our wedding anniversary, when I'd been counting on a lovely weekend in the Napa Valley complete with a room at a picturesque inn overlooking the vineyards, complementary wine and a heart-shaped Jacuzzi. Some friend you were, Sam."

"*You* were the one who turned down the chance to play strip poker." He yanked out his chair and sat, regarding her with uplifted brows.

This made her indignant. "We were joking about it, sure, but neither Doug nor I would have—"

"That's why we played for money instead. I hate sore losers." Sam shrugged and dug into the goulash. "Say, this is good."

If there was one thing she couldn't stand, it was Sam's cockiness. He thought he was God's gift to women. No, to the whole world. She forgot to concentrate on eating, and noodles slipped from her fork. Then she lost her grip and the fork fell to the floor with a clatter. Sam raised his eyebrows and went on eating.

She pushed away from the table and stood up. "I don't think I'm hungry," she said.

He stared at her blankly. "What is this, some kind of grandstanding for attention? I'll pick up the fork. Also the noodles. So sit back down." He got up and cleaned up the mess.

"Grandstanding? Is that what you think I'm like?"

"You don't need to get all upset," Sam said in a reasoning tone. "Come on, sit down, you're making me uncomfortable looking down my throat while I eat. There's nowhere to go anyway." He sat down again.

In the past, Doug had acted as a buffer between Sam and Kerry. Suddenly Kerry missed Doug so much that tears welled in her eyes. She wanted nothing so much as to scramble up the ladder to the loft and curl up on the narrow cot there, preferably in the fetal position. But Sam would probably call such an exit grandstanding. She sat.

"There's nowhere to go, all right. That's nothing I didn't already know," she said heavily. Tears blurred her vision, and she blinked them away, but not before Sam skewered her with a keen but not unsympathetic look.

"Why don't you go stay with your parents in La Jolla?"

"They offered to send me a ticket, but I had work to do here."

He started to scoff at that, but she interrupted. She'd already lowered her guard. She saw no point in lying and, moreover, she thought Sam might as well know how things stood. "My lease on the Seattle house expired, and coming to Silverthorne gave me a place to stay over the summer. I'd already had the idea of opening the lodge to the public. I'm counting on this place to provide me with an income next year and I'm going to need every penny of it."

After a long silence Sam cleared his throat and said slowly, "I advised Doug not to invest in that avocado farm near San Diego. He wouldn't listen."

Kerry managed a shrug. "Both of us trusted friends who painted a too-bright picture of how well it would pay off. By the time we pulled out of the venture, our money was gone."

"I thought you'd managed to save some before he died."

"We had other expenses," Kerry said, thinking of the pricey fertility workup that she and Doug had undergone when she didn't get pregnant on schedule as they had hoped and planned. All their remaining funds after the avocado-farm disaster had gone to pay the clinic.

She drew a deep breath. "Anyway, Doug and I thought we'd have time to rebuild a nest egg, but then he died. I paid off our debts with most of the insurance money, and there's not much left over. Silverthorne Lodge is one of the few assets I have left. Either I make it pay or I sell it."

"Opening it to tourists is another gamble," Sam pointed out.

Kerry's chin shot up. "I'll make it work. I will!"

Sam grinned. "I'm not saying you won't. But you can't stay here now. It's too late in the year to be up here in the wilderness."

"I still have to strip the wax from the floors in the dining room, I wanted to put the finishing touches on the upstairs bedrooms so there won't be anything to do but make the beds when I come back in June, and—"

"You're leaving when I do. I thought I made it clear that you can't count on Bert. How much work can you get done with a broken finger anyway?"

"A lot," Kerry said hotly. As she spoke her finger began to throb again. "Anyway, I thought you said the Cessna's not flyable."

"I can fix it."

"If you think I'm flying out of here in a plane that's missing a strut and a float, you've got another think coming."

"Is that so?" Sam leveled his fork at her. "Well, let me tell you this. I don't want to be responsible for what happens to you if Bert doesn't show up."

"You could talk to him when you get to Anchorage, remind him to stop for me."

"And what if the weather is so bad he can't make it for weeks? Don't be ridiculous."

"I'm not any such thing!" Kerry shoved back from the table and winced when her finger hit the edge. She gripped her smarting finger and glared at him. "Why repair the plane at all? Someone's got to come looking for you, don't they? When you don't show up back in Anchorage on time?"

Sam stood abruptly and stalked to the window. He stared out at the blackness beyond the pane; it rattled with the force of heavy gusts. Windblown snowdrifts furled around the tree trunks outside, and the view of the river was obscured by eddying snow.

"I didn't file a flight plan, Kerry. Nobody knows that I left Vic's camp and came here."

Kerry froze. "And you think *I* do dumb things? Listen, Sam, everyone knows you're supposed to file flight plans. Including you." She paused as their situation sank in. "You're telling me that no one is going to be looking for you. They'll think you're still at the camp."

"For a while, at least. And the Cessna's ELT isn't working. Its battery is dead."

She closed her eyes for a moment, then opened them. "Aren't ELTs supposed to be checked every so often to make sure they're in operating condition?"

"Every two years. Vic keeps the plane at his camp and evidently hasn't paid much attention to safety since he's been going round and round with this illness of his. I didn't know that when I agreed to fly the plane to Anchorage for him."

"How about the radio?"

"It's not much use with the mountains blocking transmission. I'll try it again tomorrow."

Kerry didn't think Sam sounded too hopeful. "Well," she said lamely, "maybe the radio's signal will at least reach Athinopa. They could relay the message to the rescue people."

Sam was silent. "Another thing we don't know is what this weather will do," he said after a time, his words carefully measured. "If the river freezes, no float plane will be able to get in or out of here until after the ice breaks up in the summer. The same thing goes for a boat."

"The only way in and out of this place in the winter is by dogsled or helicopter, and those possibilities are closed to us until Search-and-Rescue gets on the case, right?"

"Right. As soon as the weather clears, I'll start repairing the plane. It's our best hope."

"How much do you have to do to it?"

"I told you. Repair the strut, attach the float."

"That sounds like more than you can do with two-inch duct tape."

"Doug kept a good set of tools in the shed."

"They're still there, but repairing a strut and attaching a float sounds like a serious job."

Sam turned back toward her, his gaze level. She thought she detected a glint of worry behind his eyes.

"The thing I'm most concerned about is the weather. There are ice crystals already forming along the riverbank. If the river freezes solid before we get airborne, we're stuck here. Maybe for a long time."

Kerry felt a sharp stab of foreboding. "How long does it usually take for the river to freeze?"

His short laugh was entirely without humor. He gestured with a curt nod at the blustery scene on the other side of the window, and his expression was grim.

"Depends. I'd say there's a good possibility that within a day or so we'll be able to stroll all the way to Anchorage right down the middle of the river, wouldn't you?"

Chapter Two

Sam hated the way Kerry's face fell when he said that. She looked like a kid who'd just had her candy yanked away by a big, bad playground bully.

"Couldn't you put skis on the plane? Take off from the river ice?"

"I don't have skis for this plane. That was another of Vic's oversights."

"So what happens if we have to stay here?" She remained unruffled, but he sensed an underlying tension, as if she were hanging onto what he might say as a lifeline out of this situation. One part of him, the Sam he wanted to be, longed to touch her shoulder and tell her that everything was going to be all right. The other part of him, the Sam he was, knew that he didn't dare touch her. And so he found a way to put space between them.

"Well now," he said, moving away so that he could no longer see the silvery motes in her golden eyes, "I'd say we'd get to know each other a whole lot better than we do." It was a statement meant to raise the barriers between them. And it worked.

"That," she replied in a tone heavily infused with irony, "does not reassure me."

She didn't laugh, but he wished she had. He'd begun to

sense that Kerry was different from the way she'd been in the past—more sober, more serious. Maybe it was because of her widowhood, maybe because of financial problems, maybe because of the pain from her broken finger. As for himself, he was worried about the plane and the river, more worried than he cared to let her know, but any thoughts he might have entertained about bringing a sense of lightheartedness to this situation evaporated. Kerry stood staring bleakly out the window, pale and tight-lipped.

"I assume you've got some food around here, enough to last for a while," he said. He strode to the cabinets ranging along one wall and started hurling doors open.

"A bit of powdered milk. Packets of hot chocolate mix. Freeze-dried chicken stew. A few cans of soup. Canned chili and some other stuff. Is there more food somewhere? In the cache below the trapdoor in the kitchen maybe?"

Mutely she shook her head.

He walked back to where she stood, balancing his hands on his hips and staring down at her. "That's barely enough for one person for two more weeks. If Bert didn't show up on time, exactly what did you plan to eat?"

"I expected him to be here on schedule," she said with admirable dignity. She lifted her chin and treated him to that flint-eyed gaze. "Anyway," she said, "I thought I could fish. I've fished in the river and the creek and the lake before."

He could barely contain his scorn. "With a broken finger?"

"My finger wasn't broken to begin with."

"What would you do if I hadn't come along? If Bert were never told you're waiting here for him? Of all the tomfool things to do, woman, this takes the cake. And sitting here with a broken finger to boot."

She caught her lower lip between her teeth and glared at

him for a moment. "We've been through all this before, Sam. I already know you think I'm an idiot, thank you very much, but actually I don't think you're much smarter than I am."

"If I hadn't come along—"

"If you hadn't come along, I'd be in deep trouble, okay? Does it make you feel better to hear me admit it?"

"Damn straight," he said. But he felt no satisfaction when she whirled and marched to the back door.

With one last furious look back at him, she flung a thick woolen shawl around her shoulders and slammed out into the night. Sam recalled that the storage shed that served as an outhouse was partly protected by a breezeway. It wouldn't be pleasant going out there in weather like this, but she'd be all right.

At least that's what he thought in the beginning. He started cleaning up the dinner dishes, scraping scraps into a bin, sluicing water over the plates from a pitcher that he filled from a wooden barrel beside the back door, all the while listening for sounds of trouble outside. The kitchen window overlooked the breezeway, and he looked out to see if anything was amiss, but the night was pitch dark and thick with windblown snow. He could barely make out the outline of the shed at the end of the breezeway, but where was Kerry? He worked with one ear cocked to the keening of the wind. By the time all the dishes were put away on their designated shelf, he was feeling edgy. She shouldn't have gone out by herself. How long could anyone spend in an outhouse, anyway?

Too long, he stewed as he unpacked his things and stashed them in the closet beside hers. It wasn't a big closet, and he didn't think she'd like him taking up much space, so he crammed his few shirts and extra pair of jeans into the far corner.

A flutter of cream-colored lace snagged his wristwatch, and he paused to disentangle it. The lace edged the sleeve of a silky scoop-necked gown. It was lined in flannel and buttoned up the front, not quite granny-style but almost. Granny or not, he had a vision of Kerry wearing it. She'd look ethereal and graceful, the lace trailing along those dainty hands, the scooped neck revealing a bit of cleavage. No, a lot of cleavage. Kerry was well endowed. He'd never really noticed that about her before.

The back door catapulted open, and Kerry rode in on a wedge of snowflakes. Guiltily he dropped the sleeve of her nightgown and hoped she wouldn't notice.

"Whew! I don't think the weather's anywhere near letting up!" she said, seemingly in better humor than when she'd left. She doffed the shawl and draped it over a chair near the stove to dry.

"You shouldn't have gone out in the storm."

She spared him a hard look. "A human body has certain needs. It was necessary."

He realized that if he hadn't been there, if she hadn't needed privacy, she would have taken care of those needs inside. He knew for a fact that there was an ancient chamber pot stored under the eaves upstairs.

"If it's still storming next time you go to the shed, let me know. I'll go with you and wait outside. You shouldn't go out alone."

"I've been going to the shed alone for the past three months and have never had a problem. I think I can still manage it for the next couple of days." She took in the neat kitchen. "Thanks for cleaning up," she murmured grudgingly.

"No thanks are necessary," he said. She'd tucked the light sweater she wore into her jeans, and her breasts strained against the fuzzy fabric. The color was a luscious cherry red, and he found himself studying the curves of her breasts in expectance of seeing the outline of a nipple. He thought he detected a puckering of the fabric, and his unbidden thought was of Kerry's nipples erect from the cold, shifting tantalizingly against the soft knit.

The thought made him swallow hard past the lump in his throat, and he clamped his lips tight against the wave of desire that swept over him. Which only reminded him that yes, he did have lips, and that so did she, and that they were exactly the same shade of red as her sweater, and that it would be oh so easy to kiss her and let his lips follow the sweet line of her neck all the way down to the swelling of her breast.

This was going much too far. "I'd better check the shed and see what tools we have," he said, his tone intentionally brusque. He grabbed his parka and pushed past her toward the door.

As he braved the icy barrage that greeted him in the breezeway, he found himself wishing again that he'd accepted his friends' invitation and hightailed it for Key West last week. He could sure use a margarita right about now.

WHEN SAM WALKED BACK in the cabin ten minutes later lugging a two-by-four and Doug's old toolbox, he startled Kerry so much that she spilled hot chocolate all over the countertop in the kitchen.

Sam dropped the lumber and the toolbox and grabbed a roll of paper towels. "You didn't burn yourself, did you?"

"No," she said, tearing off a wad of towels and blotting at the dark-brown liquid inching across the counter and dripping down the front of the cabinets. "I can't do anything right lately. Not even make hot chocolate from a mix," she said.

He spared her a glance. "Maybe you'd better leave cooking chores to me until you can manage with your finger a little better.''

''I feel like such a doofus,'' she said unhappily.

He ignored this. ''There are spatters on your sweater,'' he pointed out.

She looked down at the brown blotches spread across her midsection. ''I'll go change,'' she said, reaching behind her with both hands and fumbling awkwardly with several tiny buttons at the neck. She muttered impatiently and turned her back toward him. ''Would you mind?'' she said.

She lifted her hair out of the way, exposing the pale skin at the nape of her neck, and, acting as if he did this all the time, Sam reached up and unbuttoned the buttons one by one. His fingers grazed her soft flesh, and he thought he felt a shudder run through her. Or maybe she was only shivering. The cabin was well-chinked, but all this going in and out of doors had lowered the air temperature in the cabin considerably.

Well, it was time to change the focus here. He was getting much too rattled over this. Over her.

''Do you mind if I build a fire in the fireplace?'' he said.

She didn't speak, only shook her head, fluttering into motion the loose tendrils wisping around her neck. Sam found himself wanting to push her hands away so that the weight of her hair would swing across her shoulders, brushing against his hands, tangling in his fingers. It shone in the dim lamplight, a marvelous wealth of hair. Her ear peeped through the edges of it, and he wanted nothing so much in that moment as to nibble on the lobe and keep going until he came across something more substantial and equally delectable.

As soon as he finished with the buttons, she said, ''Thanks,'' her voice murmuring so softly that he could hardly hear her.

"Be careful climbing the ladder," he said, deliberately trying not to stare at her breasts.

"I guess I do seem accident-prone," she replied with a rueful laugh, but he noticed she didn't look at him as she took off lickety-split for the ladder.

The boards above his head creaked as Kerry moved around the loft, and Sam imagined her there, lifting the lid of the big old trunk nestled close to the eaves, tugging the sweater over her head to reveal a lacy bra. But maybe Kerry didn't go in for lacy underwear. Maybe she wore plain white cotton. Or maybe she didn't wear any.

When Kerry came back down again she had donned a somewhat less provocative plaid flannel shirt of Doug's, and Sam was sitting on the raised stone hearth and building a fire in the fireplace.

"Is the finger feeling any better?" he asked, keeping his tone neutral.

"I'm not sure. Maybe I'm getting used to it," she said.

She walked to the sink and dipped water from the barrel into a large chipped enamel dishpan. He watched her as she dumped detergent into the water and began to swish the red sweater around in the suds.

"I would have done that if you'd asked me," he said, fanning the growing flames.

Her expression was skeptical. "It never occurred to me to suggest it," she said. She poked at the sweater; he jabbed at the fire. When he'd revved the flames to his satisfaction, he noticed that Kerry was having a hard time rinsing and wringing as she tried to spare her bum finger.

"Here," he said, rising to his feet. "If you absolutely must do that, I'd better help."

She didn't move when he approached, just stood there ineptly stirring the sweater around in a few inches of water.

Her bottom lip was held firmly between her teeth, and he thought that she looked as if she were going to cry.

He couldn't stand it. Kerry was supposed to be all bite and fizz, not soft and squishy and the kind of woman who would cry, for Pete's sake. Her present state was so different from her usual persona that he felt at a loss to deal with her.

Well, that wasn't entirely true. He'd deal with her the same way he always had when he felt threatened by her. He had to get her back up, had to rile her.

"Look at your bandage," he said. "You've gotten it all wet."

"Yeah, but I know where I can get another one." She moved sideways, and he took over.

"If you're lucky. Say, was it absolutely necessary to do this tonight?" he said.

"It's a new sweater. I've only worn it a few times." While he wrung it out, Kerry produced a clean towel and silently accepted the dripping bundle from him, rolling it awkwardly into the terry cloth.

Impatient with her, with her failure to lash out at him, Sam said, "Give it to me." He blotted at the sweater, then unrolled the towel. "Dry enough?"

"Sure. Here, you can spread it on this paper on the table." He did, and edging past him in the narrow space, she moved in to shape the sweater into its proper form.

"All right, looks like I'd better rebind those fingers, only don't think you can get away with this too many times," Sam said when she had finished.

"So what else is there to do besides this?" Kerry affected a bored tone of voice and presented her fingers as he unrolled lengths of gauze.

"I don't know. Play tiddledywinks. Engage in intelligent conversation. Reminisce." He bent close. Her hair smelled fragrant and outdoorsy, redolent of balsam and pine. He wondered what she used to wash it up here at the cabin. Rainwater perhaps.

"*Reminisce,*" Kerry echoed, clearly taken aback. "Just what would you and I reminisce about?"

"Old times. Good times."

"If we'd had any, that is. Ouch, you're winding that too tightly."

He released some of the pressure. "Reminisce—that's what Doug and I used to do here at the cabin. We'd fry us a panful of salmon, kick back and examine our experiences in the clear light of reason."

"You did?" Kerry sounded surprised.

"We sure did."

"Did you ever talk about Sybilla?"

Sam cocked his head at her and tried not to laugh. "Nope. Never."

"Well, I sure had to witness a lot of rib-poking and eye-rolling every time her name was mentioned."

"Doug liked to rag you about her." Sam remained non-committal because of all things, Sybilla was one thing he didn't want to talk about. His lips would remain sealed about that little caper.

Kerry watched him work, silent for a time. "If there's one thing I hope to find out before the last trump sounds, it's about Sybilla," she said, seeming much too hopeful.

Sam finished the job quickly and more sloppily than he would have liked, mostly because he couldn't keep his mind on what he was doing. "I'm not telling you about Sybilla," he said firmly. "No way."

Kerry looked sulky, annoyed. "Why not? It was a long time ago."

"When Doug and I were stationed in Germany with the

Air Force, to be exact. Too long ago to remotely interest anyone.''

"Me," Kerry said stubbornly. "It interests me."

"What interests *me* is that you'd better not get those fingers wet again tonight. Doctor's orders." It also interested him that when Kerry became petulant, her lips curved into the most mesmerizing pout. An eminently kissable pout. And right now the strain of pretending that he wasn't becoming attracted to her was beginning to make him slightly crazy.

While he was making himself think about this, Kerry held her hand up and waggled her fingers experimentally, then winced with the effort.

"Time for another pill," he said, falsely jolly. He handed her one, and she swallowed it.

"Want me to give the hot chocolate another try?" he asked.

"Might as well. If you're not up to talking about Sybilla."

"I already told you I'm not." Wishing she'd shut up about Sybilla, Sam pulled out packets of hot-chocolate mix and filled the old coffeepot with water to heat on the stove; he ignored Kerry, who sat down and pulled her legs up so that she was sitting cross-legged on the old green pullout couch that had been in the cabin ever since he could remember. She stared into the growing flames and looked pensive.

"That hot chocolate's going to taste pretty good," she said as he poured it into two mugs and carried one back to her. She scooted over to make room for him, a movement that in anyone else Sam might have considered a sign of companionship. In this case, however, there was nowhere else to sit unless you could count a saggy old hassock and a hard backless wooden bench on the other side of the

room. So sitting beside her really meant nothing. He tried
to remind himself of that.

Beside him, Kerry blew on her hot chocolate to cool it;
he drank his immediately. The fire crackled and spit, a
whirl of sparks flitting up the stone chimney like so many
manic fireflies.

"What are you going to do with that lumber you brought
in?" she asked.

He had laid the two-by-four along one wall, one end of
it resting on the colorful rag rug covering part of the floor.
"That's what I'll need to fix the plane."

She lowered her cup. "No way," she said.

He laughed at the way she looked when she said it. She
had a funny way of quirking her upper lip in disbelief; it
was a trait that had once annoyed him.

"It'll work. Here, let me show you," he said. He reached
over to the upended varnished keg that served as an end
table and picked up the pencil and paper that were there.
A dog-eared magazine served as a lapboard.

As Kerry leaned close, warming her hands around the
hot mug, her injured finger and the one that supported it
stuck out at an odd angle. Her knee brushed his acciden-
tally. She jumped away like a scared rabbit, which was how
he knew that she'd felt something, too. He wondered if
what she felt remotely resembled the sudden shock of
awareness that had whipped through him fast as lightning.

Sam wasn't accustomed to such bodily phenomena in his
daily life. He knew he was attractive to women and had
even become smug about it, taking what they offered and
refusing to give much of himself in return. But he'd certainly never, even at his most receptive, felt anything that
remotely resembled a lightning strike.

And maybe he hadn't really felt one now.

He made himself bend over the paper, deliberately keeping his distance. "This is the plane," he said, sketching it roughly, "and this is the float and strut that are still there. Here's the shorn-off strut. I can cut the lumber to the right size with a saw I found in the shed and bolt it onto the shaft. After that I'll figure out a way to affix the float, and we'll be out of here."

"It sounds too simple," she said. Her eyelashes cast long shadows on her cheeks.

"It isn't hard. Of course, I'll have to assess damage to the float and the rest of the plane."

"And the river had better not freeze," Kerry said. She had bundled her hair into a ribbon on the side of her head that faced away from him, exposing the curvy line of her jaw. She had ridiculously high cheekbones, the kind any model would die for. He had the urge to reach over and cup her cheek in his palm, to caress her smooth skin. It would feel like flower petals. Hibiscus blossoms, like they grew in Key West.

Get a grip, Harbeck, Sam told himself. He couldn't imagine why Kerry was so attractive to him. True, he'd recently broken up with Marcia, his girlfriend for the past six months, so maybe he was feeling the excitement of being free. Usually the women found him, however. He didn't have to go looking for them.

And he hadn't been looking for Kerry.

Well, he might as well face it: He'd sought her out because he wanted her to sign those forms. And that was supposed to be the end of any association between them. So why was he thinking he might call her when they both got back to Anchorage?

He wouldn't. She wouldn't want to hear from him. Not after he revealed the secret that he and Doug had kept from her.

Agitated, he stood up and went to his parka, removing a

United States Geological Service map from the inside pocket. His fingers brushed the waterproof pouch containing the papers he'd brought for Kerry to sign, and he hesitated. He had the reckless thought that maybe it would be better to get the whole thing over with now. Maybe she'd sign without making any problem tonight before he managed to rub her the wrong way again. Before—anything. Suddenly he realized what might happen here in this cabin while they were together. The thought brought a buzzing to his ears and dryness to his mouth.

He hadn't heard her getting up from the couch.

"What are you doing?" she said, close behind him. She was peering over his shoulder.

"Getting out my charts. I thought you'd like to see how we stand," he told her, turning the coat so she couldn't see the pouch in the pocket. He felt her close behind him, so close that her breath was warm upon his cheek. He glanced around and saw that her lips were slightly parted, her eyes wide and curious. In the dim lamplight her pupils were large and luminous, and in that moment Sam thought he could have drowned in their depths.

By now his heart was pounding, and he told himself it was out of fear of discovery. He didn't want her to catch him with those papers. But why? Hadn't he come here for the express purpose of getting Kerry's signature on the dotted line? Why didn't he slap the papers down on the table and whip out his pen?

Why indeed? He knew the reason, and now it ate at him, stirred up his gut, filled him full of regrets.

Sam had serious misgivings about surprising Kerry with those papers after being around her and seeing how vulnerable she was, and how valiant. He didn't think he could bear to witness the cold fury he knew his revelation would bring.

And her fury would only be part of it. It was sure to be followed by hurt and disappointment when she digested the fact that he, Sam Harbeck, had shamefully conspired with her late husband to betray her.

Chapter Three

Shaken by the realization that he cared, truly cared, what Kerry Anderson thought of him, Sam needed a few moments to gather his thoughts and pull himself together. He brushed past Kerry and busied himself by tugging the hassock over to the couch and spreading the map open on it. Kerry followed, perching beside him on the couch and leaning forward, her shoulders hunched, her hair tumbling forward in a froth of golden curls.

"All right, Harbeck, I'm looking. You want to explain?" Her eyebrows lifted slightly as she spoke. They were like softly curved birds' wings, those brows, lending thoughtful expression to a face that was already almost too perfect.

Sam cleared his throat. He wished he'd never come here. He wished he'd never agreed to the crazy scheme that he and Doug had cooked up in this very cabin. And at the moment he wished with all his heart that he'd never met Kerry.

But he had, and he might as well act as if nothing was wrong.

He drew a deep steadying breath. "Here's Williwaw Glacier," he told her, tracing its ribboning track on the chart with a blunt forefinger, "and here's the bend in the Kilkit where I left the plane. This cabin is a couple of miles away from there. It won't take long to walk to the plane if the weather's good.''

"We can start early in the morning," Kerry said, glancing over at him. Her eyes reflected the warm glow from the fireplace, and he distractedly noticed a pulse throbbing in the hollow of her neck. The collar of her shirt parted to reveal a dusky shadow—cleavage, and he was achingly aware that the shirt she was wearing molded itself to her curves.

He made himself look back at the map. "There's no need for you to go with me," he said. "I can handle the repairs myself."

Kerry regarded him steadily. "I want to help. If it hadn't been for me, you wouldn't be in this situation."

At that false pronouncement, guilt settled over Sam like a cold, wet blanket. Of course he hadn't come here to check on her; the papers he wanted her to sign had been paramount in his mind. He knew he ought to steer her in another direction.

"So," she went on, oblivious to his jumbled thoughts as she got up and headed for the kitchen, "since you're here, the least I can do is get us both another cup of hot chocolate." She moved closer and poured more hot chocolate from the kettle into his cup.

She went on talking over her shoulder as she returned the kettle to the kitchen. "After we get up in the morning, we'll hike to the plane, and you'll get started on the repairs. I'll be your helper and your gofer."

He shifted uncomfortably in his seat. "Repairing the Cessna isn't going to be a picnic, you know."

"I believe you." She settled herself on the small backless bench across the room and regarded him over the rim of her mug. "Two people can work faster than one. You know, Sam, I'm counting on you to get us out of here."

Sam knew she was. That was the worst of it. He finished off his hot chocolate and tried to think past the knowledge that he was a cad and a jerk. Or was he? His intentions had been good at the start of everything. It wasn't his fault the plan had gone awry.

Kerry, who couldn't possibly be aware of what he was thinking, offered a tentative smile. "I'd better get to bed if we're starting out early."

It was a handy escape and he took it. "I'm going to turn in, too. It's been a long day. Are the sheets for the couch still in that chest?" He indicated a dresser that had been shoved against the far wall.

Kerry shook her head. She went to the old wardrobe beside the ladder to the loft and opened the drawer in the bottom of it. "I had to move the sheets to make room for some of my clothes." She tossed him two sheets, a top and a bottom one, and a heavy wool blanket. "There are pillows behind the couch," she told him. She caught herself up short and cast a glance at her old pillow, still stuffed into the wood box.

"I guess I'll need one of those pillows myself," she said sheepishly.

"I'll get it," he said, but she reached the couch at the same time he did. He didn't mean to, but he bumped into her.

Kerry let out a sharp cry, and Sam realized that he must have hit her finger.

"It's all right," she said, but her voice quavered.

His heart went out to her. It must be hard to be Kerry Anderson right now. She'd lost her husband, faced up to financial problems and set out in a bold new direction—all in the past year. He didn't want to add any more problems to the ones she already had. Life for her must be difficult enough. And if he waited until they got out of here to unload those papers on her, the ride wouldn't be as bumpy, and he wasn't only thinking of their mode of travel.

"Good night, Sam," Kerry said softly.

He was unable to take his eyes off the sway of her body as she climbed the narrow ladder. She turned to look at him over the low loft railing. "I'll set the alarm for sunrise. That'll give us all the daylight hours to work on the plane," she said. Then she disappeared into the darkness beyond.

Sam pulled out the folding bed, made it up with the sheets and settled into it. Was he doing the right thing by not confronting Kerry with those papers right now? And what if he did and the resultant resentment made it impossible for them to cooperate well enough to ensure their mutual survival? In his anguish, he wished with all his heart that this was one of those black-and-white situations in which proper conduct was clear. There was nothing clear about any of this, least of all his conscience.

As he punched his pillow into submission, he heard Kerry rustling about upstairs and wondered if she was getting undressed. With one finger out of commission, sleeping in her clothes would be easier for her than trying to take everything off and shimmying into pajamas or a nightgown.

On the other hand, maybe she slept in the nude.

AFTER SHE WAS SNUG in her solitary bed, Kerry lay close under the rafters of the loft listening to Sam sleep. It hadn't taken him long to drop off. He made noises while he slept, although it wasn't snoring exactly. More like "snoofling," which was something less than a snore but more than a deep breath. There probably wasn't any such a word in the dictionary, but there should be.

I wonder if he ever snores, she thought sleepily. Doug used to snore, and even though other wives complained about their husbands' snoring, Kerry had always found it reassuring to know that he was right there beside her. Maybe that came from his being absent so often, on one of his frequent overnight flights somewhere.

She couldn't help thinking about Doug. Tonight Sam had brought out feelings that Kerry hadn't known she could have anymore. She'd felt protected by Sam, and cared for, which was silly considering the fact that they didn't like each other much.

But still… She'd been startled to discover a confusing and totally out-of-line sexual attraction working between them, and she couldn't imagine where that came from. She was pregnant and hadn't known she was capable of sexual feelings. Was this normal? Was it commonplace? With no man in her life at present, she'd expected her sexuality to have settled into a dormant stage, and the possibility of feeling desirable to any member of the male sex had seemed remote.

She wished now that she could discuss this with Emma, her friend in Anchorage, or her sister Charlene, but Charlene was single and wouldn't know anything about having babies anyway. Charlene did, however, understand male-female relationships. Charlene could have a field day with what was going on between her and Sam, and certainly Charlene would know if what Sam was exhibiting was sincere interest in her as a human being, concern over his best friend's widow's welfare or something else entirely.

And if it was something else entirely, then why was it happening?

That was the last thought to escape Kerry's consciousness before she fell soundly asleep.

WHEN SHE WOKE UP before the alarm the next morning, dragging open eyelids that felt stone-heavy with sleep, she felt sore all over. Her hip hurt where she'd bruised it the day before, and her shoulder was stiff. Her finger felt okay until she tried to move it, and then she realized all over again that she'd really and truly broken it.

Bedsprings creaked in the cabin below, and she thought, "Who's that?" And then she remembered: *Sam.* Memories of the night before flooded her consciousness.

Sam. Sam Harbeck was here.

Her finger ached. Sam had really bumped it hard last night while they were trying to get the pillows from behind the couch. And he'd looked so contrite after it happened. For a moment she'd thought he might offer to kiss it and make it well.

Ha! No chance of that. He still didn't like her, and she didn't like him. The best they could hope for was a period of cooperation after which they would each go their separate ways.

"Yo! Kerry!"

She sprang bolt upright in bed. She hadn't realized that Sam was already awake.

"I'm up," she called into the hollow predawn darkness. "I'll be down in a minute." She reached for the saltines she kept nearby as an antidote to morning sickness.

"No rush, I've been awake for a while, waiting for the alarm to go off. I think I'll light a lantern. It's mighty dark down here."

She heard him striking a match, which was followed by the flare of the lamp wick. She squinted at the clock and saw that it still had a half hour to go before the alarm. As she punched the alarm button down, she swung her feet over the side of the bed. The floor was cold, and as she groped around in the dark with her feet for her slippers, she heard the back door slam. No surprise; Sam was heading for the shed.

Downstairs, she gingerly started assembling the ingredients for breakfast, treating her sore finger with respect all the while. Sam had removed the slop bucket from below the sink, which she appreciated because she didn't like walking into the woods to empty it. Also, he must have stoked the cook stove earlier, because the coals were hot. A cursory check through the window at the spruce wood neatly stacked in the breezeway showed enough to last another two weeks, or at least it would have lasted that long before the weather turned unseasonably cold.

Surely the river wouldn't freeze in September—or would it? As the wife of a pilot and as a former flight attendant, she knew enough about bizarre weather patterns to be wary. While she folded blueberries into the flapjack batter, she wondered what was taking Sam so long. If he'd only gone to the shed, he should be back by this time. She wished he'd hurry. She wanted to use the shed herself. Pressure on her bladder from the growing baby made frequent trips to the facilities absolutely necessary.

She tossed strips of bacon in a skillet and wrinkled her nose at the greasy odor, which was unfortunately making her stomach feel unsteady. Still no Sam; where was he? Her stomach was churning. She kept swallowing, willing the nausea to stop, and finally she munched on a couple more saltines.

After she'd laid the cooked bacon to drain on a bed of folded paper towels, she didn't think she could stand the bacon odor any longer so she wrapped herself in her shawl and ventured out into the breezeway. The morning felt cold and crisp, and the sun reflected off billowing drifts of snow deposited by the storm of the night before. When she knocked at the door of the shed, Sam didn't answer. Then she saw his footprints leading off through the new snow toward the river. So she was free to use the shed, which she did with much relief.

Back in the cabin, she walked through to the front door and opened it to let fresh air blow some of the bacon odor out. A stand of birches stood between her and the river, and she saw a startled deer dart back into the forested slope at the foot of the mountain. She often saw wildlife at Silverthorne; it was one of the many things she loved about the place. But this morning, the only wildlife she wanted to see was Sam Harbeck. He had been gone too long, to her way of thinking.

SAM HAD LEFT to give Kerry privacy. And to give himself a chance to think things over. That pouch containing the incriminating papers was burning a hole in his pocket.

A rocky moraine, left long ago as Williwaw Glacier retreated, covered the bank of the river. The water, opaque with glacial till, was cold, but still moving freely. So maybe there was hope that the river wouldn't freeze after all, despite the shelf of ice that now lined the bank. Yet he knew all too well that freeze-up could occur very quickly. First small wrinkles of scum ice would appear on the water's surface, then more wrinkles, then the wrinkles would join and become hard. He'd seen it happen in a matter of hours.

He made himself stop thinking about it and stood for a moment, bowled over as always by the grandeur of the towering mountaintops and the craggy ice wall of the glacier. The glacier's passage had crushed centuries'-old trees against the rocks and boulders along the glacier's banks, pulverizing them as it ground relentlessly forward, and he marveled at how much the ice had moved since his last visit. Well, so had they all—Doug was gone, Kerry was a widow, and at the moment he was missing his friend very much.

"Halloo! Sam!" The sound of his name startled him out of his reverie.

He saw her through the trees, a small figure wearing bright colors.

Kerry.

What was going on between him and this woman? Her voice put him in mind of things he'd rather not contemplate. Or that he would like to contemplate. He was contemplating them even now, and why? His hormones had surged into overdrive from the first minute she'd hauled off and brained him with her pillow.

He felt a grin spreading over his face as he thought about how funny she'd looked, all spooked, but feisty. Kerry got her back up much too easily, but he had to admit she was an interesting woman. Most women weren't, at least not to him. And his response to Kerry was totally unexpected. Unnecessary. And unforgivable. He had no business getting the hots for his best buddy's wife.

Widow, he reminded himself, for all the good it did.

"Sam?"

"I'm on my way," he said, turning around and plowing back up the bank toward the cabin.

Kerry waited outside for him, fully dressed in jeans and a lumberjack's red plaid jacket, her hair in two braids tied with incongruous blue satin ribbons. She looked...different. Not like the Kerry who had been Doug's disapproving wife, not like the wounded Kerry he'd found here yesterday.

"I made breakfast," she said without preamble.

"Good," he said, stepping past her into the cabin, forgetting to knock the snow off his boots. Too late he remembered, but by that time she was sweeping past him and asking if he'd like scrambled eggs along with the flapjacks and bacon reposing on a large platter near the stove.

"Not fresh eggs," she hastened to add. "They're powdered. I've learned to do a pretty good job with them, though.''

"Eggs would be good," he said. "We need to bolster ourselves for a long walk and a lot of hard work."

She didn't say anything, but busied herself at the stove. He saw that she'd already brought in the slop bucket that he'd emptied earlier. It impressed him that she was so efficient, and he admired the way she moved around the kitchen, graceful but focused on her task. When the eggs were ready, she carried them over to the table, where he sat drinking coffee from a big cracked blue mug that had always been his when he stayed here.

"You make good coffee," he said.

"Doug taught me how."

"No way. Yours is much better. Doug's coffee always tasted like runoff from a moose wallow."

She looked like she wanted to smile. Instead she set the platter of eggs down.

"Aren't you going to eat?" he asked sharply.

"I—well, I ate something earlier," she said. She shoveled flapjacks from the platter to his plate—six of them.

He looked at the large stack of flapjacks in front of him. "Blueberry flapjacks," he said, pleased. "My favorite."

"It was a good summer for blueberries. The patch behind the lodge was full of them."

She busied herself at the stove while he got down to the business of eating. "You should have eggs," he said conversationally as he wolfed them down. He'd certainly eaten worse powdered eggs, and this surprised him. Kerry had never seemed like the kind of woman who would enjoy roughing it, much less know how to navigate her way around a kitchen.

"More bacon?" He looked up to see a strange and unfathomable expression cross Kerry's face even as she held the bacon toward him.

"Thanks, this is a great breakfast," he said as she all but dropped the platter on the table. Her face had a peculiar color to it, a greenish tinge.

"Are you—" he began, knowing in that moment that something was wrong. But he'd hardly uttered the words when she blurted, "Excuse me," and darted quick as all get-out out the back door. She didn't shut it after her, either. He heard the shed door slam and got up to push the back door shut, thinking in his annoyance that only a fool *cheechako* would fail to shut a door in this kind of cold without regard to how much cabin heat she was wasting.

The sounds coming from the shed were unmistakable. Kerry was upchucking with great fervor.

The realization totally unnerved Sam, and he stepped outside into the cold air. He didn't know whether to make his presence outside the shed known or if he should speak to Kerry or what exactly his behavior should be. She might prefer to be private about this. He was sure that she'd be embarrassed to know he was listening, but she sounded really sick.

He settled on clearing his throat, although he doubted she could hear him.

But Kerry, mortified, did hear him, and that didn't make this any easier. Morning sickness was the one thing about having a baby that she hated, burdened as she'd been with the symptom almost since the first week of her pregnancy. Now Sam Harbeck, the last person to whom she wanted to show any weakness, was shifting from one foot to the other only a door away while she reversed a breakfast of five saltines and a flapjack.

Unsteadily, she groped in her pocket for a tissue and

wished for a giant swig of mouthwash. Sam, of course, was still cooling his heels in the breezeway.

When she was ready, she opened the door and tried for nonchalance, as if vomiting were no big deal. Truth was, she was embarrassed beyond talk. If forced to explain, she'd pray for instant annihilation from whatever source: an asteroid, being kidnapped by elves...

"Are you okay?" Sam asked. Anxious lines radiated out from his eyes, and a furrow of concern bisected his forehead.

"I—um, well, it's just a slight upset," she said. If she looked the way she usually looked after one of these episodes, her face was milk-white. Snow-white. Snow seemed like an inspired idea at the moment, so she reached down and grabbed a handful, which she then used to wipe her face. Sam stared at her, his mouth hanging open.

"You aren't coming down with some kind of virus or something, are you?" he asked sharply.

"No, I don't think so. Maybe I ate too much goulash last night." It had been heavily seasoned, and he might buy this explanation.

"I ate goulash, too, and my stomach is fine," he said, sounding perplexed.

"Then I probably shouldn't have taken a pain pill on an empty stomach," she said. She sidestepped past him, and he followed her into the house. The heavy odor of bacon dredged up an urge to throw up again, but there was nothing left in her stomach. For which, Kerry reminded herself with the steely resolve that had brought her this far, she might as well be thankful.

"Maybe you'd better take it easy," he said. "Stick around the cabin while I take a look at the plane."

"Don't be silly. The two of us are more likely to get the plane airworthy than one of us, even if the one of us is you. And didn't you tell me that time is of the essence? That we need to get out of here before the river freezes? I'm going with you, Sam. No argument.''

Sam knew better than to buck Kerry when she'd put her mind to something.

''Well then, you'd better put on a warm jacket and a good pair of boots. And I'll clean up the kitchen. How's your finger?''

''Sore.''

''Let me see.''

She held her hand toward him, and he inspected it carefully. ''There's not as much swelling as I expected. Come over here and I'll change the binding.''

Kerry followed obediently. She remained quiet while he administered gauze and adhesive tape.

''There,'' he said as he finished. ''How does that feel?''

''Fine,'' Kerry said, wiggling her fingers experimentally. He noticed that she winced, but she didn't complain.

''Good. We'll apply snow packs during the day, and that should help bring down the swelling even more.''

Kerry dug in the closet and pulled out a quilted down coat, bright red. When she put it on, she looked like a kid with those pigtails. It would be good if he could think of her as a kid, Sam thought. That would keep him from noticing the sensual lines of her lips.

''I threw a light lunch together,'' she said. ''Hot chocolate in a thermos. A can of macaroni and cheese. Also, dried fruit—apples and peaches.''

While she was talking, Sam arranged Doug's tools in his pack. Kerry handed him the bag containing their lunch, and he stashed it on top. Then he slipped his arms through the straps of the pack and hoisted it onto his back. Kerry helped him adjust it.

When they left the cabin, he was surprised when Kerry locked the door and hid the key under a rock.

"Way up here in the wilderness, it's usual for people to leave their cabins unlocked in case somebody in an emergency situation happens along and needs food and shelter. If the place is locked, it's considered all right to break in. So who do you think you're keeping out?" he said. He couldn't help laughing at her.

She flushed, but took the jibe in stride. "It's a habit, I guess. Old habits die hard, you know."

He did know. The reason he wanted to keep needling her was that annoying Kerry had been his habit in the old days. And yet somehow it seemed inappropriate now.

The cabin was situated on a knoll overlooking a small bowl of a lake that had been named Kitty Kill Lake by Klondikers during the Alaska gold rush. The lake fed the Kilkit River, which emptied into the Gulf of Alaska. In the distance, the icy summits of the highest mountain range in North America glittered in the sun. Above, the sky was azure and unmarred by clouds. The path to the river was narrow and steep, but not long, and Kerry followed Sam to the trail that skirted its edge.

They found themselves wading through drifts of ankle-deep snow across a landscape blanketed in pristine white. The wide terminus of Williwaw Glacier rose a good five hundred feet over the lake, a huge frozen wall glimmering pale turquoise-blue in the sunshine. As they walked they heard a shudder and a groan from the direction of the glacier, and they whipped their heads around as a small jagged iceberg leaned forward and tumbled off its perpendicular face, sending up a frothy splash from the lake below. Kerry stopped to watch for a moment. Sam watched, too. He didn't speak and neither did she, but he didn't have to hear her say the words to know that she was spellbound by the beauty of their surroundings.

Without a word, they resumed walking. The snow made their journey hard going, and more than once Sam looked back at Kerry to see if she was having trouble keeping up. She had apparently decided to make her way a bit easier by placing her feet squarely in the hollows of his footsteps, concentrating with great determination on what she was doing. To make it easier for her, he shortened his stride.

By this time, the tip of Kerry's nose had pinkened from the cold, and her braids with their blue ribbons bobbed against her shoulders with each step. *Braids,* he thought in amusement.

The next time he looked back, he saw that the tips of her ears were red. "You'd better pull the hood of the coat up," he said gruffly.

"What difference could it possibly make to you whether I wear a hood or not?"

"I don't want to have to thaw you out if you get frostbite."

"Oh, I'm all kinds of fun, aren't I, Harbeck?"

For some reason it irritated him for her to call him by his last name. "My name's Sam," he said.

"Mine's Kerry. *You* never call *me* anything."

He stopped and looked back. She had missed one of his footprints and was floundering toward a snowbank. She looked plain tuckered out.

"Time for a rest," he said. For the heck of it, trying out the way her name sounded on his lips, he added, "Kerry."

She rolled her eyes and bent over to brush the snow off a fallen tree. When she sat, she let all her weight down at once, which was how he knew she was more tired than she let on. After he removed his pack, he went over to the log and lifted one leg up on it. He leaned on his knee with one elbow and bent down to study her face more closely.

"You're exhausted, aren't you?"

She shook her head in vehement denial. "I—"

"Do you want to go back to the cabin? I'll walk you back, take care of things at the plane by myself."

"No! I'm keeping up, aren't I?" She didn't dare let on that she was having a problem walking in the snow, that every step made her finger throb. She knew she should have eaten more at breakfast, but there was no way she could have with her stomach roiling as it had been. She shifted position on the log, wincing as her bruised hip came in contact with a burl in the wood.

Sam sat beside her, determined that he would let Kerry rest until she was ready to move on. The last thing he needed was a sick woman to hold him back. The thought made him feel small, petty and self-serving. Was he? Well, maybe. Or maybe he was only jamming thoughts into his mind every which way so he wouldn't have to think about Kerry's effect on him.

It seemed important to stem the awkwardness between them by saying something, anything. "I remember the first time I ever came up here," he said. "Doug and I were on leave from the Air Force, and he said he had this place. I was curious, and we came and canoed and fished and enjoyed some great R and R."

"That must have been the first of your male-bonding retreats," Kerry said wryly.

"Yep. It was. We decided to make a habit of it after the first one went so well. I thought I'd never seen more beautiful scenery, although I was born and raised in the Country and I'm used to spectacular."

"The first time I came up here was on our honeymoon," she said.

He shot a quick look at her. She didn't look sad, only subdued.

"Does it bother you to talk about Doug?" he asked.

She shrugged lightly. "No. I miss him, that's all."

"So do I."

She blinked, then smiled slightly. "I only hope he would approve of what I'm doing to keep the lodge in the family."

"What family? There's only you."

She looked at him penetratingly and stood abruptly, avoiding his eyes. "I feel better now. Let's get a move on."

While she stuffed her braids under her hood, he wondered what had brought that on. Well, maybe Kerry really didn't want to talk about Doug, but hadn't wanted to say so. This irked him, since he considered himself a straightforward guy, and he'd rather Kerry would tell him if she didn't want to talk about her husband, his buddy. But okay, if that was how she felt, fine. They might as well continue on their way.

Kerry stood shifting from one foot to the other and blowing out a mist of vapor in the cold air as he hefted his pack. Wordlessly he took the lead, and she fell in behind him. "Any time you want to stop, Kerry, holler. I don't mind a rest now and then," he called over his shoulder.

"Right," she said, close behind him. He didn't turn around to look at her because he knew exactly what he'd see: Kerry plodding pluckily along, a stoic expression on her face, and those remarkable eyes throwing the challenge right back at him.

They stopped only one more time before they reached the plane. It had settled more solidly into the mud at the river's edge and was covered by a mantle of snow. Even if someone had flown overhead, they probably wouldn't have been able to distinguish the Cessna from the snow-covered landscape.

Kerry stood with her hands on her hips, surveying the damage. She made no comment, but Sam doubted it was because she was being tactful. It was much more likely that she didn't know what to say. He slipped off his pack, unzipped his coat and took in the situation. *Not good,* he thought. *But fixable.*

Kerry scooped a handful of snow into a plastic bag that she produced from her coat pocket and iced her finger with it while studying the plane. "Wow, Sam, do you think you're going to be able to fix this by yourself?"

He made himself sound confident. "Sure do. You have doubts?"

There it was again, that wry little quirk to her lip. "Gosh, no, Sam, far be it from me to cast doubt. However, I see a float that appears not to be part of the plane anymore and a place where the strut should be. It seems to me that we need an aircraft factory in this neck of the woods, but golly gee, I don't think we're going to get one before the river freezes over, and that's a real shame."

This lengthy speech made him grin wickedly and say, "You've got it pegged, all right. And remember, you and I get to spend the winter in the cabin if none of this works. Now that would be the real shame, don't you think?"

Kerry only heaved a sigh and blew the air out of her mouth, ruffling her bangs.

Sam checked the ELT to see if the battery had somehow regained power. It hadn't. He tried the radio, but managed to raise only static. It was what he'd expected—too many tall mountains around for transmission.

While he was inside the plane, Kerry took it upon herself to tackle the encroaching branches; she started pulling the larger ones away and tossing them alongside the river. She worked awkwardly because of her broken finger. Well, Sam thought as he watched, nobody could accuse Kerry Anderson of being lazy.

After he'd checked whatever he could inside the plane, Sam unfolded himself from the cabin and walked the float until he could wipe the windshield clear of snow. From where she worked alongside, Kerry made a face at him.

"I'll be ready for a hot drink soon," he told her.

She paused and shook her braids back. "Me too," she said.

Sam jumped down for a close look at the propeller. To his dismay, something had gouged a good-sized chip out of the aluminum, maybe one of the tree branches he'd sideswiped on the way down. He hadn't noticed the ding yesterday, but then he'd been in a hurry to be on his way.

Kerry stopped working when she saw that he was pulling tools out of his pack.

"What are you going to do?"

"File that ding out of the propeller."

"Is that necessary?"

"You'd better believe it. It has to be balanced or it won't work properly."

"Major job?"

"Major enough, but it won't take too long." He picked up the tools he needed and walked back to the plane.

"How is it you know so much about plane repair?"

"A bush pilot has to. You can get stuck out here in the woods, and if you can't repair your plane, you're dead." He concentrated on unscrewing the spinner—the nose cone in layman's terms—and removing the bolts that held the prop in place.

"Now what are you doing?"

He had the prop off, and picking his way carefully through the maze of boulders on shore, found the rock he wanted. It was pointed on top, and he centered the prop on it so that the point was through the hole.

He looked up as Kerry approached. "See this chip on one side? I'll have to file away as much metal on the other side for it to balance." He selected a file and began work, gauging carefully so as not to take off too much metal.

Kerry settled down on a nearby boulder, icing her sore finger while she watched. "Have you been in many tight situations?"

"Not lately. But when I was a kid and my dad was teaching me to fly, I was kind of reckless." He concentrated on the prop, selecting another file, working quickly.

"You want to explain that?"

"I had to gain respect for the weather, for the Country, for the plane. I learned it by getting myself in and out of some hairy situations. I remember once when I had to set down on a glacier with skis on the landing gear instead of wheels. The engine wouldn't start, and I had to figure out if I should walk out of there or stay with the plane until someone came to get me."

"What did you do?"

"Stayed with the plane, and the engine started later on. Just luck, I guess. But that wasn't the worst. Once when I was flying supplies to a family in the bush, I had to make an emergency landing on a remote frozen mountain lake, and the ice was too thin. I didn't have any choice, mind you, but no sooner had I climbed out of the plane than the plane broke through the ice and sank. There I was in the middle of the lake and having to walk across that same ice to the shore. I walked very carefully." He laughed at the memory, but it hadn't been funny at the time. The plane had been salvaged, lifted out by helicopter, and his father had been livid.

"That's some story," Kerry said.

Sam lifted a shoulder and let it fall. "I chose my flights more carefully after that. As my dad used to say, there may be old pilots and there may be bold pilots, but you'll never see any old bold pilots."

He glanced at Kerry for her reaction. She looked somber, worried and in that instant it hit him that perhaps he'd been insensitive. Her husband had died in a plane crash, after all.

He cleared his throat. "Look, Kerry, maybe I shouldn't be talking about flying disasters. Under the circumstances, I mean."

"I was a flight attendant," she said tightly. "I understand the risks. But now," and she shook her head, "it's different."

He hated to see her looking so down. He tried to think of a way to cheer her up. "You know what?" he said after a time. "I'll see if I can't provide our lunch myself. I've got a pair of hip waders and a fishing pole in the plane."

Her smile was faint, but it was a smile nonetheless. "You're on. We can save the other stuff for later if we want it."

Later, when it was time for a break, Sam pulled on his waders and cast a lure into nearby Chickaback Creek, twitching the lure through the water as his mouth watered with the thought of fresh fish for lunch. It only took a few casts before the tip of the rod bowed toward the water with a strike. Playing the fight out of the fish required some skill, but in a matter of minutes he'd landed a fine, fat trout.

Kerry built a fire while he dressed the fish, and after they'd cooked half of it, they wolfed it down while sitting on one of the boulders. Overhead the sun was shining brightly, and some of the snow had melted. A few red squirrels scampered up and down nearby tree trunks in a mad race to store nuts in the face of an early winter, and a flock of ptarmigan wheeled up out of a nearby patch of weeds.

"Look," Sam said, pointing to a cliff above the river, and Kerry glanced up to see two magnificent Dall rams, snow-white and with massive curling horns, looking down into the valley. They seemed to be hanging from a precarious ledge, almost motionless. As Sam and Kerry watched, the sheep suddenly turned and bounded away, as surefooted as they were agile.

"Those are full-curl rams, moving down to lower elevations because of the cold," Sam said.

"Full-curl? What does that mean?"

"They're older rams, so old that their horns have grown large enough to make a complete curl. Their ewes are well camouflaged. Can you see them?"

Kerry shook her head, and Sam pointed. She spotted a group of females, their wool so white that they blended into the snowy background. As if they knew they were being observed, the ewes suddenly came to life and took off, graceful but quick.

"That," Kerry said with conviction, "is one of the scenes that makes me want to live here."

She spoke with such intensity that Sam swiveled to look at her more closely.

"I never pegged you for a nature freak," he said.

"Freak? Is that the word for it? I don't think so."

"All right, I agree. Maybe I should have called you a nature lover."

"I like that better," she said. "And I never was all that appreciative of nature until I came here. Just think, I haven't seen a car in three months. Three months! In Seattle, I thought fresh air smelled like exhaust fumes. Now that I'm accustomed to living amid the most spectacular scenery in the world—"

"The most spectacular? Are you sure of that?" He was teasing her because she seemed so focused and so intense.

"I've been all over the world in my job and I think this is the best. The greatest. The most magnificent." She threw out her arms as if to encompass the river, the mountains, the sky. "I don't have Doug, but I have this to remember him by. I'll never sell this property if I can help it."

She was beautiful in that moment, and he could think of nothing to say but, "Good for you." He meant it.

She stood up and dusted her hands off. "Well, I'm cleaning up. What's the next step?"

As a native Alaskan, he'd learned to keep one eye on the sky around the time that he'd cut his first teeth, and he didn't like the way cumulus clouds were piling up to the west of them. "I was going to stay here and put the prop back on, but I don't like the way those clouds look."

"What's the problem? They're white, fluffy and beautiful. Mashed potatoes clouds."

"They may not stay that way. We'd better head back."

"You mean it?"

"Yeah, I don't trust the weather at this time of year. We're close to the fall equinox, and that's a time when a rain squall can strike out of nowhere."

"All right, Sam. You're the pilot-in-command, and I know better than to buck orders."

"First we're going to spread a tarpaulin in case anyone happens to fly over. It'll draw attention to the downed plane," Sam said. He brought a bright-orange tarp from the cockpit, and they spread it folded so that it pointed toward Silverthorne.

"On the off chance that Search-and-Rescue would be flying over, this would be enough to alert them to the fact that they need to mount a search," he told Kerry as he secured the corners of the tarp with several large rocks.

"They'd already know that if you'd filed a flight plan," she pointed out.

"You don't have to keep reminding me," he said, but she only tightened her lips and turned away.

The clouds grew more numerous and darker as they plowed their way back toward the cabin. They hardly spoke, although a couple of times Sam warned Kerry about a boulder beneath the snow or a slippery section of path. They were about a half mile from the cabin when they felt the first few spits of rain. Soon rain streamed down Sam's face, stung his eyes and made it hard to see Kerry when he turned to check on her progress, but she was there, all right, trudging along like a trouper.

"We're going to have to hurry," he urged. "The rain could get a lot worse."

"I'm walking as fast as I can," she said, but her voice lacked oomph, if not conviction.

Nevertheless, after that exchange he checked on her more frequently. Every time he glanced back, she appeared wetter and more forlorn; although she'd pulled the hood up, her bangs were soaked and stuck to her forehead. By the time they were a quarter of a mile from the cabin, he detected a thin white line around her lips, a sure sign of strain.

Sam waited until she caught up with him and reached for her hand. "Come on," he said encouragingly. "It's only a little farther."

Kerry didn't speak, which was a certain measure of how exhausted she must be. And she didn't pull her hand away. He felt the coldness of her fingers right through her glove at first, but they warmed up as he propelled her along. As the lodge and the smaller cabin on this side of it came into view, the sky started to rain hail upon them, great big chunks of it rattling against the tree trunks, bouncing up among the rocks, burying themselves in the snow drifted around the cabin.

"Good thing you left the key out. I'd hate to have to take time out to break in," he shouted over the rising fury of the storm. He meant for this to be funny, but it fell flat.

"Hurry," she shouted back, slapping her arms against her chest to keep warm as he dug the key out from under its rock and fitted it into the lock.

They both practically fell into the cabin. After she took off her boots and lined them up on the black rubber mat inside the vestibule, she steadied herself against the wall. When Sam offered to help her with her coat, she shook her head and started for the kitchen, unzipping it on the way. Sam removed his parka slowly, hearing the crackle of those papers he'd brought for her to sign and hoping she wouldn't comment on it. Kerry didn't seem to notice. She was putting on a pot of water to boil.

"I'll make tea," she said. Her voice was heavy, tired.

"That sounds great. And I'll get a fire going. Amazing how warm it stayed in here, though, isn't it?"

"I—I—"

He stared at her across the narrow room, taking in the way she was gripping the post between the kitchen area and the rest of the cabin.

"Kerry? Are you okay?"

But he'd barely said the words when a strange look came over her face and her hands slithered slowly down the post, and in slow motion she crumpled to the floor.

Chapter Four

Exactly what Sam was mumbling when she regained consciousness, Kerry couldn't quite figure out, since it was obscured by a furious buzzing in her ears. She thought she might have heard something about the foolishness of *chee-chakos*.

"Sam?" she said, but it came out so faintly that she had to repeat the word. "Sam?"

"You gave me a scare, Kerry. You fainted." His eyes were full of concern.

She forced herself to sit up, bracing herself against the pillar. "I have never fainted in my life," she said muzzily.

"Well, you have now. Relax," he said as she started to get up, "you're not going anywhere." He helped her out of her coat.

Kerry prudently decided to be reasonable and settled back against the pillar. "How long was I out?"

"A few minutes, that's all. I thought you looked peaked all day. I think you're getting the flu."

Not the flu, Kerry thought to herself. She had to admit she was worried about the way she felt. She had gone to a lot of trouble to get pregnant and she didn't want to do anything that would cause her to miscarry. Even the thought brought tears to her eyes. She wanted this baby.

Though it wasn't technically Doug's child that she carried in her womb, legally it was his baby. And this new little being was the only part of her life with him, the only human tie to him that she had left. *She wanted* this baby. She would have given her life to protect it.

"I think I want to lie down on the couch," she said, wishing her mouth didn't feel as if it were full of cotton.

"Okay, but don't move. I'll carry you," Sam said, and he swooped her off the uneven plank floor as if she were a doll, depositing her on the couch and even settling the blanket over her feet.

She barely had a chance to marvel—again—at this solicitous side of Sam before the whistle on the tea kettle sounded, startling both of them.

"Don't move," Sam repeated sternly. He went to the stove and rattled around a bit while Kerry closed her eyes and took stock of herself. One broken finger. One stomach, always slightly queasy. One bruised hip, one bruised shoulder—and now she'd fainted.

"I'll bring you some tea," Sam said, sparing her another watchful glance.

"Okay. Tea's in a canister on the shelf. Sugar, too. No lemon. Canned milk if you want it." The words took such an effort that she rested her head on the couch back and caught her breath. She spread her hands protectively over her abdomen. She wanted the baby to know that she wouldn't do anything to put it at risk. But walking to and from the plane today shouldn't have been a risk, considering that she walked every day. Maybe it was the fact that she was so tired. So very tired. She thought she could sleep and sleep and sleep.

In fact she dozed off for a moment before Sam brought the tea. "I found honey and put some in it. Instead of sugar," he said. He was looking down at her with a mixture of puzzlement and anxiety, and she saw that he wanted her approval.

She didn't mind giving it. She was glad she wasn't alone. By this time she didn't feel like drinking anything, but she took a sip anyway. "It's good," she said.

He seemed encouraged by this. "What I think you need is a little pick-me-up after being out in the cold," he said. He wheeled and walked over to the long cabinet along one wall of the cabin and opened it. Kerry didn't understand what he meant until he brought a bottle of brandy over and began to unscrew the top.

"No!" Kerry exclaimed sharply.

"It'll bring the roses back to your cheeks, get your circulation going," he explained, but Kerry knew that alcohol wouldn't be good for the baby.

"Please, Sam, I can't. I mean, I don't like brandy," she said. She didn't want to tell him about the baby. She didn't want to feel the force of his disapproval when he found out that she had gone ahead with the artificial insemination even after Doug was dead. Sam would think she was nuts and would have no qualms about saying so.

Slowly Sam withdrew the bottle, which had been poised over her cup, gave a light shrug and went to the kitchen, where he poured himself a hearty dose. He regarded her from across the room as he swirled the amber liquid around in a glass.

"What's the weather doing?" she asked, not only because she was curious, but because the weather held the key to whether they'd get out of there or not.

Sam went to the window. "It's stopped hailing, but I saw some hailstones the size of chicken eggs. I'm glad we're not out in this mess." He sipped reflectively at the brandy, keeping his back to her.

"Me too. It was smart of you to know when to leave the

plane today, Sam.'' She meant this to be a compliment, as sincere as she could make it.

"I've had a lot of experience with Alaskan weather." *And a lot of experience period,* he thought to himself. It was one of the things Doug used to tease him about, his penchant for beautiful women. And yet all that experience seemed unimportant when he was around this one woman. He couldn't explain the phenomenon. He didn't know why Kerry made him feel so protective, so confused and so hell-bent on pleasing her.

At the same time he realized that she didn't expect to be pleased. She expected to be treated as his equal. It was almost as if she wanted him to think of her as one of the boys, giving her no special consideration. Which was ridiculous. She had a broken finger, was clearly sick and she must weigh only a hundred pounds.

When he ambled back over to where she lay, he saw that she had fallen asleep. Her hands were curled beneath her chin, her broken finger and the one next to it held separate from the others at an awkward angle. One of her braids had come out of its ribbon, and the damp hair spilled over her cheek. Her bangs had dried stiffly, and the spiky ends gave her a kind of a pixie look. She looked like a child, not a woman at all.

He went to build up the fire, thinking about Doug and how he would feel if he knew that Sam and his wife were alone in the cabin. He thought Doug would be shocked if he knew that Sam was speculating about Kerry in a sexual way. But he also thought Doug would be grateful to know that Sam was taking care of her and would never hurt her, not in a million years.

For some reason, he thought about the Dall rams they'd seen earlier in the day. He knew that the rams fought each other for dominance of the ewes. Sam wished it were that simple with Kerry. There was no one to fight for her favor but Kerry herself. And, of course, Doug's ghost.

It was a beautiful bright day at the beach in Santa Monica, and Doug raced across the wide sand ahead of Kerry into the water.

"Can't catch me!" he shouted over his shoulder as he struck out toward the horizon.

"Wait!" Kerry called. She was a good swimmer, but not as good as Doug. They'd always joked that she couldn't swim as fast as he did because her size-five feet were too small; she claimed that his big size elevens were more like flippers than feet.

Today she swam hard, kicking with all her might, but it still wasn't fast enough to catch her husband. Kerry could feel him in the water ahead of her, his feet stirring up bubbles that floated past her when she opened her eyes under water. And soon she didn't feel like swimming anymore. She was tired, so tired. And Doug wouldn't wait. He just kept on swimming.

Soon she couldn't even feel him ahead of her, and she lolled over on her back to stare up into the endless blue sky. She had left the beach with its scents of suntan lotion and hot sun on sand far behind, and she couldn't even hear the clear high voices of children calling to each other as they tossed a Frisbee. All was calm and quiet, and she was floating in the middle of the ocean, suspended on the waves, the sun beating down on her in all its warmth. She felt happy, the way it had been those first years she and Doug were married.

"Kerry?"

She opened her eyes to see Doug treading water beside her. "I thought I'd better come back, see how you were doing," he said.

She stared at him. She hadn't expected to find him there. She'd almost forgotten that he was ahead of her, swimming.

For some reason her arms and legs wouldn't move. She didn't have to tread water to keep afloat. She was surrounded by blue sky, blue water and blue eyes. Doug's eyes.

"I'm okay," she said, gazing deep into those eyes that she had loved so well.

"That's what I thought. I did some stupid things, Kerry."

She didn't know what he meant at first, but it suddenly dawned on her that he must be referring to their ill-fated investment in the avocado farm.

"It's all right, Doug. I can earn more money. The lodge—"

"The lodge will be a big success. Pay attention to what Sam says. If I'd listened to him before we invested in avocados, you'd be ahead right now. But I mean when I was flying. I got overconfident. I shouldn't have flown into that mountain. I'm sorry, Kerry."

Her mouth seemed thick, and she couldn't get the words out. "I—I—"

"I love you, Kerry. Everything will be all right."

"The baby. Do you know about the baby?"

"You did the right thing. Goodbye, Kerry."

She suddenly felt herself sinking, and she reached for Doug. Her hands touched his face, slid down to his chest, grappled for his arms but couldn't find them. She wanted him to hold her up because she didn't want to drown. But his eyes seemed to merge with the deep blue sea, and then she couldn't see him at all....

Salt water dripped down her face, and she heard Doug calling her name. She opened her eyes fully expecting to see him, to find herself warm and safe in his arms, but the blue eyes she saw weren't Doug's. They were Sam's.

"Kerry," he said, shaking her slightly.

She reached up and slid her arms around his neck. "Oh, Sam, Sam," she said, not realizing that she was crying and that the salt water on her face was not the sea but tears.

"You were dreaming," he said. "I had to wake you up." He looked so shaken that her heart went out to him. His arms were around her, too, holding her so close that she could hear his heartbeat.

Her own heart was hammering, and she thought he must notice. Aghast at how needy she must seem to him, she pushed him away.

"What happened?" Sam said. "I was rummaging in the bookcase looking for something to read when you cried out."

"I was dreaming," she said helplessly. "Dreaming about Doug."

Sam still held both her hands firmly in his, but he let one go so he could dig in his pocket for a bandanna. He gently wiped her eyes with a corner of it. "Want to tell me about it?" His voice was gentle.

As he stuffed the bandanna back in his pocket, Sam moved away slightly and eased himself down on the hassock. She wished he were still holding her in his arms. But then she didn't, because she thought about Doug and how she had almost touched him; it seemed wrong to be wanting another man's arms around her.

Her voice was shaky. "Doug and I were swimming off Santa Monica, where he used to like to surf. Do you remember?"

"I remember," Sam said. It was one of the first places the two of them had gone together after mustering out of the Air Force on the same day all those years ago. They'd borrowed a couple of surfboards and had a great time that afternoon, surfing, lying on the beach and planning their future careers. They'd both grown up in Alaska, but Doug had a job with a commuter airline based in Seattle and dreamed of moving on to a larger airline. Sam was going back to Alaska and was determined to make something of his father's flagging bush-flying business. That was the day that he and Doug had decided to take a vacation together every year so their friendship would never die.

Kerry was talking, telling him about her dream. "Well, it was like Doug was really there. In the water, I mean. And he talked to me. It seemed so real, Sam."

She looked so devastated that all Sam could say was, "I'm sorry."

"I thought I was getting over it. Losing him, I mean." She sounded heartbreakingly bewildered.

Sam leaned forward, elbows on his knees. He stared into the flames in the fireplace.

"You probably never will get over it, Kerry. It's impossible to lose your husband and just forget that it happened."

She settled back against the pillow and pulled the blanket up higher. She looked delicate and fragile, though Sam knew she was neither. "I know. They say time heals, but I wonder why it takes so long."

"I can't begin to know what you feel about losing Doug. But he was my best friend. I—I miss him very much."

He thought she seemed surprised. "I guess I never realized that. I mean, I realized, but—" and she stopped talking. "I don't know," she said after a moment. "I probably didn't think that your grief was anything like mine. Now I think they're one and the same. Two different perspectives, but my grief isn't any more real than yours. If that makes sense." She stared mutely up at him, her eyes searching his face.

"It makes sense, all right. One of the reasons I went to Vic's place to be alone for a while was that I'd never quite

come to terms with what life without Doug would be like."
He'd never told anyone this. He hadn't wanted to.

"And that's one reason I'm here at Silverthorne. Not
only to open it for tourists, but to be in a place that meant
a lot to Doug and to see if I could feel him here."

"Do you?"

"Sometimes. For instance, in the dream I had."

"I wish I could have a dream like that," Sam said. He
meant it. Somehow he would draw comfort from talking to
Doug in a dream. He might even be able to reach a place
of peace if he could only talk to Doug one last time.

He stood abruptly and went into the kitchen. "I think
I'll make chowder out of the rest of that trout," he said.

"I'm not hungry."

"Let's hope you will be. We both need to eat properly,
keep our strength up." He tried to make his voice jovial,
but in his opinion he failed.

While Kerry rested, he fried a couple of slices of salt
pork with onions and put the mixture in a pot with the trout
and the one potato he'd found in the cache under the
kitchen floor. He added a generous dose of evaporated milk,
and when the chowder was done he opened a can of stewed
tomatoes to go with it. From time to time he glanced over
at Kerry, who stared at the rafters and didn't speak.

He brought her a bowl of chowder, for which she
thanked him. "Sorry about the ambience," he joked, ges-
turing with his spoon at the cabin. "Usually I treat my dates
to a decent dinner in a nice restaurant."

"Your, um, dates," Kerry said, thinking that she was
hardly his date. It was a slip of the tongue, nothing more,
and there was no point in calling Sam's attention to it, since
he was wolfing down food from the bowl in his lap and
didn't seem to realize that he'd made her feel extremely
uncomfortable. "Do you have a girlfriend?" She was cu-

rious about Sam's personal life. Maybe she shouldn't ever
ask. But there wasn't much for them to talk about.

"I did, but we broke up recently. Her name was Marcia
and there were no hard feelings. Last I heard she was in
the Lower Forty-eight living with a race-car driver. I guess
she likes men who indulge in dangerous occupations." He
laughed, and Kerry decided that the breakup hadn't affected
Sam much.

She picked at her tomatoes, shoving them around so it
would look as if she'd eaten more than she actually had.
She didn't want to have to make a precipitous run for the
shed if her stomach started to act up.

"Is your occupation all that dangerous? You don't fly
much anymore, do you?"

"Only when I undertake some nutso favor like flying
Vic's plane back to Anchorage." Sam set his bowl on the
table beside the couch and got up to stir the fire into more
activity. The flames leaped up, illuminating his face for a
moment before they subsided; in that brief span of time
Kerry detected that Sam was still more concerned about
their plight than he had been letting on.

When he came back to the couch, he yanked a pillow
out from behind it and tossed it on the floor. Then he lowered himself to it and leaned back against the couch arm,
staring thoughtfully into the flames.

Kerry didn't speak for a long time, but she couldn't eat
any more. "Tell me," she said after a time, "about the last
time you and Doug came up here to Silverthorne."

He shot her a quick glance, and she didn't understand
why he looked so wary at first. Or maybe she'd been mistaken. Maybe it was just the way the firelight reflected in
his eyes.

"Well," Sam said, and then there was a long pause. "It
was like every other time in a way. We arrived, threw ou

stuff all around the cabin, slept late the first morning, went fishing all the first day. We talked over old times, laughed and joked and had a great time. And we promised we'd meet back here in a year like we always did, and then we didn't.''

Something about the quiet way Sam spoke lulled Kerry into a sense of well-being; maybe it was hearing him talk about that time as if it had just happened.

"It's hard to believe Doug is really gone, isn't it, Sam?'' she said softly. Especially after today's dream. Especially when he was so fresh in her memory and in Sam's.

"Yes, it is,'' Sam replied.

"Did he ever talk to you about us? About our life together?''

In the past few moments, Sam had been feeling really close to Kerry and to Doug. But he didn't want to talk about the two of them together. He didn't speak, wishing she hadn't asked.

"Did he, Sam?''

He swiveled his head and saw that she was staring at him intently, perhaps hoping for more solace than he had to give. And considering what Doug had told him about his life with Kerry, about their inability to make a baby and Doug's despair over Kerry's unhappiness about it, Sam couldn't tell her what they'd discussed without exposing Doug's part in the resultant scheme.

"He talked about how well-suited the two of you were,'' Sam said finally. It was the truth. Doug had loved Kerry with all his heart.

"I don't think we could have been any more happily married. No, that's not right. Perhaps we could have been even happier if we'd had a child.''

There it was, the situation he didn't want to talk about. It was amazing how Kerry had homed in on the one thing that Sam positively couldn't discuss with her until he was ready to fess up to the plan he and Doug had concocted, the plan that had brought him here to get Kerry's signature on those papers.

He couldn't deal with this. Abruptly Sam stood up and faked a yawn, which wasn't too hard considering what a long and tiring day it had been.

"If you don't mind, Kerry, I think you'd better sleep down here. I can bunk in the loft like I have many times before."

"No, I can sleep there," she said, sitting up.

Sam reached down and gently pressed her back onto the couch. "We can't have you passing out while you're climbing that ladder. It's better if I go. Besides, I want to keep an eye on you, make sure that fainting spell was only a fluke." He took their plates into the kitchen and brought the kerosene lantern over to the couch. He set it where she could reach it easily.

As he turned to go, Kerry said, "What's the plan for morning?"

"Depends on whether the storm's let up by then." Kerry's eyes were wide in the light from the lantern, and they looked golden. Like molten gold. He wanted to lean down and kiss her on the forehead, a kind of supplication or benediction or something but, of course, he didn't do any such thing.

"Good night, Sam," she said as he climbed the ladder, so softly that at first he thought her voice was only the whisper of the wind outside.

"Good night," he said, and he groped around in the dim light of the loft until his knees made contact with the edge of the narrow cot where Kerry usually slept. He stretched out on it, his feet dangling off the end. He fell asleep almost instantly, heady with the essence of her on the pillow where she'd laid her head last night.

WHEN KERRY WOKE UP, she heard the rattle of rain on the roof and thought, *Oh no! We won't be able to work on the plane today!*

On the other hand, she wasn't entirely unhappy about the weather. She wanted to help Sam, but didn't want to be a detriment as he worked to get the plane airworthy again—and she didn't think she'd been too helpful yesterday.

Under the blanket she folded her hands over her belly. *I will take care of you,* she silently promised the baby. *I won't let anything happen to you.* Her bruised shoulder hardly hurt at all today, and neither did her hip. Her finger was sore when she inadvertently moved it, but it had settled into a kind of dull ache. Even her stomach was behaving. Funny how that worked; some days she was sick as a dog, other times she felt entirely normal.

She plucked at her clothes with distaste at the thought of sleeping in the same grubby outfit she'd been wearing yesterday. She sat up and tiptoed across the floor in time to Sam's "snoofling" in the loft. It was the kind of day, dank and damp, that was meant to be spent in bed. She'd let him sleep.

When she came back from the shed, she lit one lantern for the kitchen and one to put on the table near the couch. She reached into the wood box and chucked a couple of small logs into the kitchen stove, closing the door quietly so as not to wake Sam. Then she dipped water out of the barrel to heat on the stove for her bath.

Bathing in the cabin was a cramped affair in an old miner's tub, a relic of times past. She hoped Sam would stay asleep until she'd finished; she didn't want him coming down the ladder and stumbling in on her morning ablutions.

Well, if she heard him waking up, she'd have to holler out and tell him to stay where he was.

She slipped a warm velour robe from the wardrobe nearby and undressed quietly, smoothing her hands down over her abdomen. It was slightly rounded with her pregnancy, and she thought it probably wouldn't be long before she started to show. She smiled at the thought; the growing baby within her was tangible proof of the faith that she and Doug had had in their relationship. Despite the hardships, the lack of money toward the end, despite everything, they had been partners for life. They'd longed for this baby. She was sad that Doug would never see it, but then, she would have it to remember him by. Even if it wasn't actually his baby, it was his in spirit. That's what he'd always said.

Once she was sitting in the steaming three inches of water in the bottom of the tub, she soaped herself quickly and economically, and it was all she could do not to hum while she bathed. She felt happy within herself and luminous with her secret, the secret of the baby.

When she had finished bathing, she dried herself on the rough terry cloth towel that she kept in the kitchen for that purpose and wrapped herself in her warm robe. She put on a clean pair of wool socks and padded soundlessly around the cabin. Outside the sky was gray and the cloud cover seemed impenetrable. She felt a pang as she realized that no planes would be likely to fly over today, which certainly decreased the likelihood that they would be found by chance. Funny, but during the summer planes flew over frequently, bringing tourists on sightseeing trips to Williwaw Glacier or on fishing expeditions. She'd grown so accustomed to seeing and hearing them that she'd taken them for granted. But now she realized that chances were that no plane would venture in this direction for weeks or possibly even months.

Well, she was counting on Sam—he was resourceful and capable, and Doug had called him one helluva good pilot. If anyone could fly them out of here, Sam Harbeck could.

So her best bet was to keep him well fed and to help him as much as possible, and to that end she slapped the frying pan on the stove. Suddenly the snoofling overhead stopped.

"Kerry?" She thought she sensed a note of panic in Sam's voice.

She stepped out from under the overhang of the loft so she could look up. Sam leaned over the railing above, his hair sticking out in wild-man fashion. His clothes were rumpled, and he needed a shave.

"Yes?" She looked up at him inquiringly.

An expression of relief swept across his features followed by a kind of wry sheepishness. "When you weren't on the couch, I thought something might have happened. Are you all right?"

"Very much all right. I'm cooking breakfast."

She smiled; she couldn't help it. Sam looked so little-boyish, so appealing in that moment.

"Oh. I guess I'd better come down."

When she next looked around, Sam stood yawning in the middle of the cabin floor. As she returned her attention to her cooking, he moved closer, scrutinizing her with an intensity that she found extremely uncomfortable. He stood behind her, and she felt his gaze on the back of her head.

"You're really all right this morning? No hint of dizziness?"

"I'm *fine*," she said, stressing the word and wishing he'd go sit down at the table.

"You gave me a scare yesterday."

She spared him a quick glance. His forehead was wrinkled into a slight frown, and he continued to stare at her in that appraising way of his. It made her nerves jangle, that look.

"Well, this morning everything is great. I'm raring to go," she said. "Well, as raring as possible when it looks as if we're not going anywhere," she amended. She gestured with a nod of her head at the window, which presented a vista of gently falling rain and an eddying mist that completely obscured the view of Williwaw Glacier and everything else.

Sam's gaze followed hers for a moment and then his eyes lit on the half-full bathtub in the kitchen.

"You've already had your bath," he said. An unnecessary statement, since it was obvious. Maybe he was as uneasy with this whole situation as she was. This perception made it hard for her to continue looking nonchalant. She felt the slow heat of a blush rise along the outside of her neck and wondered why she felt so flustered. It wasn't as if he'd watched while she was in the tub.

"Well, I'd better take one, too," he said. "After breakfast, maybe."

She made herself concentrate on lining up slabs of bacon in the frying pan. "Okay," she said, but the image of Sam Harbeck standing stark naked in the middle of the cabin the night before last sprang unbidden into mind.

"Do I smell coffee?"

"Yes, help yourself."

He found his favorite mug, the one with the crack, and poured a cupful from the battered coffeepot. He stood nursing it for a moment between his two hands, inhaling the rich aroma before he treated himself to a long satisfying swallow.

"Want me to do anything?" he asked.

She was acutely aware that her robe gapped open where it overlapped and that one of her socks was almost worn through at the heel. "Sit down at the table," she said, flipping sizzling slices of bacon with a fork. When he lifted one eyebrow as if he might say something sarcastic, she added, "Please."

Sam didn't speak, but sat down, still looking at her and not saying anything. She almost wished he would. She was accustomed to their usual back-and-forth teasing; where had it gone?

She thought it might be a good idea to get an exchange going, but try as she might, she couldn't think of anything with exactly the right amount of verve. And Sam didn't help. He sat quietly, hands folded on top of the table. She wished he'd disparage her sock with the almost-hole in the heel. She wished he'd comment that the bathtub in the middle of the floor got in the way.

"I think I'll go out for a minute," he said suddenly, and he stood up and pushed his chair back so hard that it almost tipped over. She didn't have a chance to get two words out before he clomped across the floor, past her and out the back door, and she heard the shed door slam as he entered.

She poured herself a cup of coffee, wondering why things were so tense between them and hoping that her morning sickness was gone for good.

JEEZ, IT WAS HARD being around Kerry. She was so calm, so sweet, and he was a jerk. A disgusting, creepy, degenerate jerk.

Well, maybe not all that creepy. But he was degenerate or he wouldn't be thinking about sleeping with his best friend's wife.

Widow, reminded a voice inside Sam's head. But it didn't help.

Under normal circumstances he would have run like mad from Kerry Anderson. He would have put as much space between them as was humanly possible. But these circumstances were anything but normal. He'd dreamed about her last night. About the way he had felt when he saw her crumpled on the floor. About the softly woozy focus of her gold-and-silver eyes when she finally opened them. About how he would have given almost anything to touch his fingers to her cheek to reassure himself that she was all right, really all right.

And he couldn't get away from her in this place. Worse, he didn't want to. In fact, it was all he could do to keep his hands to himself.

Get a grip, Harbeck, he warned himself. *Stay on the straight and narrow. Walk away from this whole scene.*

But he couldn't, that was the thing. He and Kerry were stuck here. Together. And if she found out about those papers, they'd be at each other's throats. Okay, so he'd move slowly, figure out how to proceed. That's what Doug would have counseled.

When he came back into the kitchen bearing logs for the stove as a kind of peace offering for leaving so abruptly, Kerry glanced around with that quick smile of hers.

"Thanks," she said. Her teeth were straight and exceptionally white, and he thought he saw the tip of her tongue before she turned around again to shove the bacon around the frying pan. She had piled her hair into a loose knot, making him think how much he wanted to press his lips to the soft white skin of her nape.

He stowed the logs in the wood box beside the stove. "Might as well empty this, too," he said gruffly, and he carried the battered zinc bathtub outside and tipped it so that the water flowed away with the rainwater that was still coming down.

This time when he came back in, Kerry was sitting at the table in front of a platter of bacon and scrambled eggs.

She'd helped herself to the food, and Sam was pleased to see that she was eating. Well, nibbling anyway. The dark circles he'd noticed below her eyes last night had faded.

She had spread a crossword puzzle magazine open beside her plate. He sat down across from her and started to eat, not speaking.

"What's a four-letter word for *marooned?*"

"Hell."

"Very funny." She thought for a moment, then filled in the squares.

"What is it?"

"L,E,F,T," she said without looking up.

He ate in silence for several more minutes, then got up from the table. He washed his plate in the pan of dishwater in the sink and said, "Mind if I shave?"

She spared him a glance. "Not at all."

He found the enamel pan he'd used the other night and heated water for his bath and shave in the two large pots she'd used earlier. She kept working on the puzzle while he shaved, and she didn't look up when he asked, "Where will you be while I'm bathing?"

"Upstairs," she said as she filled in a set of letters.

He managed to grunt at this. When he was through shaving, he made a show of pouring the heated water into the tub, thinking that Kerry would get the hint.

Instead she went right on working the crossword puzzle.

Sam cleared his throat. "I've filled the bathtub," he said.

Kerry had this vague way of looking up from what she was doing, something he'd noticed long ago, and it was a characteristic that had never seemed particularly attractive until now. Today he was struck by the slightly out-of-focus look in her eyes as she drew herself back from wherever she'd been—in this case the crossword puzzle—and made herself concentrate on whatever was at hand. In this case, him.

"Oh," she said, jumping up from the chair. "I'll just run upstairs and get dressed," and she dropped the magazine. Pieces of paper flew out of it as it fell, scattering across the floor.

One of them landed at Sam's feet. As Kerry bent to pick up the others, he retrieved this one. It was covered with Kerry's handwriting in graceful loops and curls.

He didn't mean to be nosy, but he couldn't help but read what she'd written on the paper.

Douglas Lytton Anderson, Junior
Daniel Lytton Anderson
Brett Douglas Anderson
Amy Anderson
Aimee Anderson
Amelia Catherine Anderson
Alissa Kerry Anderson
Aliss—

He didn't finish reading the list because Kerry, her cheeks turning a becoming shade of pink, snatched it from his hands. She stuffed it between the magazine's pages and said curtly, "Thanks. I'm awfully clumsy since I broke my finger." And before he could say anything, she was heading toward the ladder, clasping her long robe carefully around her as best she could while climbing the rungs.

Sam, pondering her obvious embarrassment, retreated to the kitchen, figuring that comment was unnecessary. He sensed that she hadn't wanted him to see the papers; he had not mistaken the two spots of color on her cheeks.

After undressing and lowering himself naked into the tub, he took his time bathing while he thought about the list of names he'd seen. They were baby names. He had no doubt of it.

The reason Sam knew this was that Marcia, his former girlfriend, had been on what he'd thought of as a baby campaign before she decamped for the Lower Forty-eight.

"I want a baby," Marcia used to tell him plaintively as they lay in bed together on Sunday mornings. She'd sing at him from the shower, "Let's have a boy for you, a girl for me, oh how happy we could be." And she'd bought him cutesy greeting cards and inked in her own messages, informing him yet again how much she wanted to bear his child.

But he hadn't wanted to marry Marcia, which to him seemed a prerequisite to having a baby. And Marcia wouldn't take no for an answer. She'd taken to strewing slips of paper around the house with "Samuel Clay Harbeck, Junior" written on them. And then he'd started to notice other names—Mary Marcia Harbeck, Jennifer Anne Harbeck—jotted on the back of dry-cleaning receipts, shopping lists, in the margins of the newspaper. There was no Mary Marcia Harbeck or Jennifer Anne Harbeck. It wouldn't have taken a rocket scientist to figure out that these were the names of the babies that Marcia hoped to have with him.

So they'd broken up in the usual way. Sam had it down to a science, breaking up with women. He was ingeniously adept at sabotaging his own relationships, which in this case meant that he'd met an old girlfriend for a drink at a place where Marcia would be sure to run into them. End of relationship, end of Marcia.

Marcia would have had another whole fit in addition to the one she'd had if she'd realized Sam had foolishly contrived to father a child, though not in the usual way. Marcia had never learned, thank goodness, of those vials at the sperm bank in Seattle.

And neither had Kerry. Yet.

"Sam? Are you through bathing?"

Kerry's voice cut into his thoughts, and Sam hollered back, "Almost." He supposed it wasn't so unusual that Kerry would be harboring lists of baby names. She had, as he knew better than anyone, intended to have a baby with Doug.

"I didn't hear anything, so I thought you must have finished."

Sam stood up, letting most of the water drain off into the tub before toweling himself dry. He stepped out of the tub before realizing that he'd have to go out into the open area of the cabin to get clean clothes, and then he would be visible to Kerry if she was standing at the loft railing.

"Cover your eyes if you're looking," he called out.

"I'm not looking," she said. "I'm waiting patiently on my cot trying to think of the word that Lewis Carroll invented in *Alice in Wonderland.* The clue says it's a combination of snort and chuckle, and all I can think of is *snorkle.*"

"Try *chortle,*" he told her as he grabbed a clean pair of jeans out of his pack.

"Great!" A pause while she filled in the word. Then a cautious, "Are you dressed yet?"

"No, but feel free to have a look if you like." He pulled on his jeans.

"Thanks, I'll pass. I'd probably only chortle anyway," Kerry shot back, and this seemed so much more like the old Kerry that Sam almost chortled himself.

"All right," he said as he shrugged into a turtleneck, "I'm decent."

Kerry came down the ladder, crossword puzzle in hand.

"I finished it," she said. "And now I have to figure out what to do the rest of the day." She moved to the window and stared out at the rain gushing down past the window from the slanted roof; there were no gutters.

"You know," she said suddenly, "I have work to do at the lodge. I think I'll go over there, clean up the mess I made when I fell after dusting the chandelier, see what else I can do."

"With a broken finger?" Sam knew he sounded skeptical.

She turned to glare at him. "If I can help with plane repair, I can certainly sweep and dust and maybe even paint."

Sam knew from the fiery look in her eyes that he was beaten. "I'll go with you," he said.

"You don't have to." She went and pulled a flannel-lined rain slicker from the wardrobe. He saw that lacy nightgown again and wondered when she wore it. He hadn't looked, but then again he hadn't noticed any pajamas or other nightwear in the loft. Which only reinforced his belief—hope?—that Kerry Anderson slept in the nude, which was how Sam thought everyone should sleep.

He helped her with her raincoat, sliding it across her shoulders as she inserted her arms in the sleeves. She flipped her hair out from under the collar so that it fell across her shoulders in a glorious tangle of gleaming gold. His hands moved slowly down to her upper arms and stayed there while he inhaled the scent of her. He didn't even realize that they held her until she broke away.

Shaken at the shamelessness of his longing to touch her, Sam fumbled with his parka. He jammed his hands deep into the pockets so he wouldn't be tempted.

"Well, now where's my umbrella?" Kerry was saying

briskly. Too briskly, it seemed to him. She assiduously avoided Sam's eyes.

Kerry knew that she had to chatter in order to regain control. The way he had held onto her for that all-too-short moment had sent her senses reeling. There had been something very sensual about it, something confusing, and she had wanted to lean into him, to feel those arms encircling her, those hands—

Those hands. They'd better stay in his pockets, right where they were.

I'm making things up, she thought distractedly. *I've been living alone for too long.*

But she hadn't been alone all this time, at least not in her mind. She had the baby, a little human being who had been abstract, but was now becoming more real to her every day. She would be glad when the baby had grown enough that it showed; it seemed strange to be harboring new life in her body and stranger yet that no one knew about it. She shot a look in Sam's direction. He wasn't looking at her. So was he avoiding her eyes the same way she was avoiding his?

"Ready?" Sam didn't want to open the door until they were ready to go out.

"Ready," she said, and, still not looking at each other, they hurried out into the gray, wet day.

The path to the lodge was sodden and mushy from all the rain. Little patches of snow remained on the ground, but most had washed away.

"I think it's warming up," Kerry said hopefully.

"I wouldn't bet on it." Sam hooked a hand under Kerry's elbow to guide her over a slippery spot as they reached the overhang in front of the lodge's big double door, but he let go as soon as they reached the doorstep.

"I can't wait to show you what I've done," Kerry said

as she swung the door open. "You'll hardly recognize the place."

She was right. Inside the great hall Sam let out a long low whistle. The lodge had always been cavernous and dark, its chinked walls studded with many game trophies, including a huge mounted ram's head, several salmon and an enormous stuffed bear that looked as if it were still alive. But now the big room was bright and light and, as much as it could be on this dark and rainy day, cheerful.

"You've done a fantastic job in here," he told Kerry.

"I tried. I love this place, all of it, every board, nail, shingle and shutter." She felt justifiably proud of herself.

"What happened to all the dead animals?"

"Captain Crocker was only too happy to haul the moose heads away, and I told him to sell old Abijah to anyone who would pay. I'll donate the proceeds to an animal shelter."

"Abijah?"

"That's the name I gave to the bear. Doug's grandfather shot him and had him mounted. The first time I ever saw the thing lurking in a dark corner, I screamed at the top of my lungs. Trophy hunting is a travesty in my opinion. We should appreciate animals when they're alive, not when they're dead. Although I doubt if there's much to appreciate about a live grizzly. You know, the thought of meeting up with one terrifies me."

"I didn't know you were afraid of anything," he said, teasing her.

"I'm afraid of bears. Even teddy bears."

"A little fear is a good thing, because bears are around here for sure. If you come upon a grizzly, you need to remember that the best thing to do is remain motionless."

"Oh, like I really could. I'd be scared spitless and running for cover so fast that I'd be a blur on the landscape."

"You should carry pepper spray. That'll stop a bear."

"I didn't know that."

"Remind me and I'll buy you a case of it before next summer."

"Will do." Kerry picked up a broom and started sweeping the floor.

"Well," Sam said, rubbing his hands together. "I might as well start a fire in here." He busied himself with kindling, tinder and matches.

When the fire was roaring and its welcome warmth radiating into the room, Kerry went into the adjoining storeroom and returned with a basket full of brass fixtures. She sat on a settee that had been draped with a quilt made of velvet scraps. "You don't have to stay, Sam. I'm going to polish these and then I thought I'd try to scrub the fireplace stones." She gestured toward the smoke-blackened fireplace surround.

"I can do that if you'd like," Sam offered.

"Sam, you don't have to—"

"I know I don't. But it's work that needs to be done, and I have nothing else to do. Where's the bucket?"

Soon they were working in amicable harmony. Outside, rain still beat against the panes of the windows; inside, the temperature was approaching toasty, at least near the fireplace. Kerry had exchanged her raincoat for a wrap that she always kept in the lodge for days when the chill didn't leave the air. It was a fleecy, multicolored garment that was more than a sweater but less than a jacket. Sam kept looking down at her from his position on the ladder so often that she finally made a face at him.

"If you don't pay attention to what you're doing, you might go bust like I did. We don't need any more broken fingers around here. And what are you looking at, anyway?" she asked.

He stopped to dip the scrub brush into the water. "Oh, I was merely admiring the way your hair looks in the fire-light," he said offhandedly.

She blinked. "That's not what I expected you to say," she told him.

"And what did you expect?" He resumed working so he wouldn't have to look at her.

"I thought you were going to tell me that I wasn't using the proper technique in polishing this doorknob. Or that I had spinach between my teeth. Or that—"

"Is that how you think I am? Always finding fault?"

She went on polishing. "Kind of."

"And what if I told you that I'm not usually that way at all? That it was the way I've always dealt with you, but that most people find me nonabrasive?"

She raised her eyebrows. "Then I would ask you why you choose to be so, well, pugnacious with me?"

"Pugnacious, huh? I can see you've been doing lots of crossword puzzles." He grinned that handsome jaunty grin at her.

"You know what I mean."

He took his time answering. "I think it has something to do with the relationship Doug and I shared."

"Really?" She stopped polishing and stared at him.

"I always kind of resented your coming between us, Kerry."

There was no hint of a joke in those words; he was dead serious.

Kerry suddenly tossed aside the polishing rag. She drew her knees up and circled her arms around them.

"I didn't even come on the scene until six years ago, when you and Doug hardly saw each other anymore," she said.

"Didn't matter."

The silence grew between them.

"Would you care to explain that?"

Sam eased himself down on the top platform of the ladder.

"I guess it was petty and stupid," he said slowly. "But Doug and I were buddies. When we got together for our annual vacation, we always talked about guy things. And then one year when we came to the cabin, Doug only wanted to talk about you."

Kerry stared up at him. "He did?"

Sam nodded. "Suddenly it was Kerry this, Kerry that. Kerry likes cats. Kerry wears really high heels. Kerry hates surfing, Kerry's going to Europe, Kerry, Kerry, Kerry. Nothing I could say or do was more important than what Kerry said and did. And I was—well, lost. I felt as if I was hanging out there in the wind somewhere while you and Doug were safe and warm inside."

"Safe and warm inside what, Harbeck?"

"Your relationship."

"Oh."

Sam descended the rungs of the ladder and moved it over another two feet. Then he climbed back up on it and resumed washing.

"I didn't know you two emoted when you got together," Kerry said slowly, feeling her way around this whole new aspect.

"'Emoted?'"

"Exhibited emotions. It's not a guy thing."

Sam raised his eyebrows and kept on scrubbing. "Emotion is a human thing. Guys are humans. Believe it or not."

Kerry laughed. "Well, yeah, but you know what I thought happened during those vacations? I thought you and Doug went around unshaven for a week and told each other crude jokes and made rude noises. I thought you drank way too much beer. And I know for a fact you played poker.''

Sam chuckled. "Well, we did. But Doug talked about you a lot in between the crude jokes and rude noises. I was sure that no human being could be as perfect as he thought you were.''

A wistful smile tugged at the corners of Kerry's mouth. "If it's any consolation, I'm not that perfect. Probably.''

"You're—'' Sam started to say something, then stopped.

"I'm what?''

"I was going to agree with that part about your not being perfect,'' he said slowly. "But I don't think I can.''

Kerry picked up her polishing rag and got back to business while she tried to assimilate this and figure out what Sam meant.

"Would you mind clarifying that?'' she said cautiously.

"You—well, Kerry, you're more than I thought.''

"You've known me for years, Sam. Have you reached some new mind-boggling revelation?'' She slanted him a cagey look out of the corners of her eyes.

"Maybe I have. You've proven to be more pleasant, more thoughtful and more energetic than I ever guessed.''

"Not that you spent a lot of time thinking about this,'' she said. "Not that it ever crossed your mind that you *should* be thinking about it.''

"You're probably right. But I told you, I admire what you've done with the lodge. I'd like to see the rest of it.''

"You're on, but not until we've eaten something. I brought a can of tuna and some crackers, so what do you say we break for food and then take the grand tour?''

Sam spared a few more swipes for the fireplace before descending the ladder. "How does that look?'' he asked, surveying the work he'd done.

"Better. Now if I only had something wonderful to hang

over the mantel, I'd be happy." Kerry spread a blanket on the floor in front of the fireplace and tugged the ring-top off the tuna.

"How about some of that old artwork stored in the attic?"

Kerry was surprised. "There's artwork up there?"

"Sure, a bunch of paintings in a closet. I saw them when Doug and I were searching all over for his old tackle box one summer."

"They must have been left here by Doug's grandmother. She was an artist and a teacher, and she dreamed of converting the lodge an artists' colony."

"Is she the one who died young?" Sam asked.

"Yes, Elise Anderson was on her way to becoming famous when she married Doug's grandfather and he sequestered her here six months out of the year. Elise died bearing Doug's father, and the second wife burned most of the paintings she left. I didn't know any had escaped. I don't think Doug did, either."

"Doug didn't see the paintings. I was the one who checked out the closets." Sam lowered himself to sit beside her on the blanket.

Kerry passed him tuna on a cracker and said, "You know, Sam, I didn't think we could coexist here for the few days it would take to make the plane flyable, but now I think there's hope. You're more than I expected, too."

In that moment there was a flash of something between them, though Kerry was hard put to know what exactly it was. Camaraderie? Understanding? She wasn't sure. She only knew that she was completely comfortable sitting on a blanket with Sam Harbeck and that maybe, just maybe, it was time to give him credit for being all that Doug had claimed he was. A fine person, Doug had said. A good friend. A helluva nice guy.

When they had finished eating, Kerry preceded Sam up the stairs to the attic. They wended their way toward the closet at one end through a welter of old mirrors, a discarded dressmaker's dummy and several baskets full of bric-a-brac. After a futile attempt to budge the door, Sam had to coax it open with a karate chop slightly to the south of center.

"Looks as if the pictures are still here," Sam said.

"Wow," Kerry said, peering around him. "Paintings. Lots of them." He stepped inside the closet to tug one out of the stack, passing it over to her. "This one's marvelous. Look, Sam, it's the glacier."

The painting was signed with Elise Anderson's name and was a landscape that captured the grandeur of the glacier and the mountains beyond.

"She's got the color of the ice just right," Sam said.

"Yes, and there are more. Oh, look at this one." It was a painting in the primitive style and was of Silverthorne Lodge, with people waving from windows, fishing in the creek, walking their children alongside the river.

Kerry straightened. "These are about to see the light of day. The one of the glacier will be perfect over the mantel."

As she turned around, her eyes met Sam's, and whatever he was thinking, she was sure it wasn't about the paintings. Something in his eyes tipped her off, warned her that she'd better get out of there, and fast.

The closet's dimensions seemed to have shifted, grown smaller. They were standing hip to hip, close enough to feel the warmth from each other's bodies. Kerry told herself that she should slide past Sam to the door, but something stopped her, and it wasn't only the lack of maneuvering room. She knew she couldn't get out of the closet without some portion of her anatomy coming into contact with his.

He turned first, but not toward the door. He swiveled so that he faced her, and suddenly she couldn't breathe. Her heart started dancing around in her chest, a wild jackhammer rhythm, and in the gloom the dust motes floating between them seemed to sparkle.

"We really should take some of these paintings downstairs," she said, but the words came out in a squeak.

Sam stared at her, his eyes half-lidded, the pupils dark. "Let's don't do that yet," he said, and his fingertips came up and caressed her cheek. She swallowed, incapable of movement, thought or speech.

Then the unthinkable happened. Sam curled a hand around her waist and diminished the space between them, his face close, his breath mingling with hers. And then it was their lips that were mingling, curving to fit as though made for each other, and Kerry was helpless to stop him. She resisted as long as she could, but when he deepened the kiss, she opened to him, let him in, hating herself for her weakness but unable to fight it. She melted against him, as his mouth plundered hers, her arms finding their way around his neck, her eyes closing so that all she could see was the warm, soft darkness, and so all she could feel was Sam's mouth on hers.

It was only one kiss, but it seemed to last an eternity, and when it was over she knew it hadn't lasted nearly long enough.

Her eyes flew open, startled, and she was afraid to think what would happen next. She was so close to Sam that she saw in bewilderment that his eyes had glazed over, that some resolve had chilled whatever it was that had made him kiss her so thoroughly and completely.

He took a firm step backward and away from her, or at least as far as he could in that cramped space.

"I'll take the big picture of the glacier downstairs," he

said. While she scrunched herself tightly into the corner of the closet, he lifted it and started for the stairs, leaving Kerry alone with only the hammer of her heartbeat to keep her company. She touched a hand to her lips, which felt bruised, and it came away wet. She closed her eyes and tried to believe that the kiss hadn't happened. But it had. And she hadn't stopped him.

She thought, *Now what?*

Chapter Five

The rain had tapered to a drizzle, or as Captain Crocker called it, a mizzle. When Kerry got back to the cabin, Sam wasn't there, but the sound of an ax striking wood told her where he was.

She peeked into the breezeway from the kitchen window. Sam was splitting logs, making the chips fly, and he'd already added considerably to the stack of firewood. He'd taken off his coat and was working in his shirtsleeves, the muscles in his back rippling beneath the knit of his turtleneck, and he couldn't see her watching him; he stood with his back to her.

Well, no point in disturbing him. Things could not be the same between them after that kiss. Sam had flung down a gauntlet of sorts, a challenge, and she couldn't accept it. She should tell him the truth, that she was going to have Doug's baby. *Not really Doug's baby,* she reminded herself, but that was the way she thought of it.

Distractedly, with frequent glances out the window at Sam as he worked, she put on soup to cook for dinner and tried to read a magazine. But the magazine was two years old, and Kerry wasn't interested in reading about "Forty Ways To Make Your Man More Fun in Bed." When the noise from the breezeway finally stopped, she waited nervously for Sam to come in, but he didn't. Finally she went and looked. He'd left spruce logs neatly stacked and was nowhere in sight.

It was still raining. Where would he go? You'd think he'd have let her know if he'd decided to take a walk.

Through the trees she could barely see the lodge, but she spied a light in one of the windows. That must mean that Sam had gone over there.

Naturally the thought occurred to her that Sam, too, was edgy about what to say to her after their kiss. Well, he wouldn't have to say anything, she thought. All he'd have to do is act as if it never happened. That was what she planned to do. That's all there was to do. They were required by circumstances to share this small space until they were able to get out of here, and then they'd never have to see each other again.

That would be just fine with her. If anyone should be upset about that ill-timed moment in the attic closet, it was her. She was the one who should be in the lodge sulking, not Sam. Had she invited him, by any stretch of anyone's imagination, to kiss her? Of course not. She'd been minding her own business, not asking for his help, not even wanting him around. He'd moved in on her plan for the day and made a nuisance of himself.

The more she thought about Sam the more annoyed she became. She went to check on the soup, tossed in a hunk of salt pork. Too bad there was no one around to eat the soup. Too bad she'd made it in the first place. She should have made Sam eat another can of tuna tonight. She slammed around the kitchen, deriving a certain satisfaction out of creating a lot of noise.

"What's going on in here?" Sam came in the door, stomping his feet on the threshold to shake off the wet leaves and bark chips from his boots.

"Nothing. Nothing is going on. I'm making soup, that's all. And my finger hurts. And I wish I were back in Anchorage at Emma's house, not here where planes don't fly and I have to worry about bears, thanks to your unhelpful warning. Besides, I hate this god-awful weather."

Sam rubbed the back of his neck and appeared bemused. "I didn't realize I'd scared you about the bears."

"I am *not* scared. I'm going to be cautious, that's all." She ran out of words looking at Sam, whose hair was damp with the rain. She realized that she had never noticed the faint web of creases at the corners of his eyes before. She had never noticed how long his eyelashes were, either.

Sam hung his parka on its peg. "Look, Kerry, if you're angry about what happened back at the lodge—"

"Angry? I don't think so. I wish it hadn't happened, that's all."

"Was it so awful?" His eyes twinkled for an instant.

"Yes. I mean no. Oh, I don't know what I mean," she said.

"I thought it was pretty spectacular."

"You would, just to be contrary," she retorted.

He moved closer and smiled his most infuriating grin. "If you want to know my opinion—"

"I don't."

"You're not as angry at me for kissing you as you're angry with yourself for kissing me back. And with such enthusiasm, too."

"Why, of all the cheeky comments, that one takes the cake."

He tossed off a shrug and moved away, picking up the crossword puzzle magazine. "Mind if I have a try at this?"

"What*ever*," she said waspishly as she dried her hands on a towel. She wished she didn't have to talk with Sam, although it didn't seem as if talking with him was presently one of the options. He had sat on the couch, taking up too much room. He could have left room for her. Where did he expect her to sit? On the hassock? On the backless bench? On a hard kitchen chair?

None of those choices had any appeal whatsoever. "I think I'll take a nap. Nothing else to do," she said.

She'd thought that this might wake Sam up to the fact that he needed to make room for her on the couch, but all he said was, "You're right about that." Then he looked up. "Too bad we don't have music. Not that a radio would work here, but tapes or a CD player might be nice."

She matched his cool tone. "Oh, I think there's a portable stereo over in the lodge. It may not have batteries, though."

"If I start getting cabin fever, I may go check it out." He was impressively polite. Annoyingly polite. She hated him.

Kerry made her way up the ladder and she knew he watched her all the way up. Well, let him. She didn't care. If he got a kick out of watching pregnant women climb ladders, that was perfectly all right with her.

Except that Sam didn't know she was pregnant. The thought deflated her anger, at least the part of it that was directed at Sam. She still hated herself, though, for not knowing how to handle this situation.

She settled herself on the cot, contemplating her limited options. Maybe she'd tell Sam about the baby. Or maybe she wouldn't. Right now her finger hurt, and she was so tired she couldn't think straight.

She closed her eyes and fell asleep listening to the light patter of rain on the tin roof.

As soon as he was sure Kerry was asleep, Sam got up and quietly let himself out of the cabin. He didn't think he'd ever felt more restless or cooped up.

Not that he particularly enjoyed strolling around in inclement weather. Or that a nap wouldn't be a great idea. But he didn't think he could be around Kerry right now.

When he stepped outside, he realized that the rain was mixed with sleet that was becoming even more plentiful. The river seen through the trees was a somber gray-green, swirling and shadowed in the cool mist. Glumly, Sam wandered down to the dock, checked the status of the ice on the shore and noted in dismay that there was a good deal more ice than yesterday. He could see little chunks of it floating down the river.

Jeez, what a predicament. He hadn't bargained for this. Or for Kerry, her eyes so soft upon him, her body so—

Stop it, he warned himself. *So she has a great body. That's nothing new.*

It wasn't as if he hadn't been aware of her as long as he'd known her. He'd agreed with Doug that Kerry was drop-dead gorgeous. Doug had always said she was smart, too, and he hadn't been wrong. It had taken Sam a long time to admit that Kerry was both beautiful and intelligent, but he was admitting it now. She was also a very good kisser.

So what was he going to do about it? She was legally free, and so was he. Under other circumstances, a sojourn with such a woman in this wilderness hideaway would be a boon, a gift, a sumptuous pleasure. However, this wasn't just any woman. This was his best friend's wife.

Widow. Kerry was no longer a wife.

Did she feel anything for him? If the way she'd returned his kiss was any measure, she did. He didn't think their attraction was all physical, either. They'd made some pretty good headway at communication earlier today, and yesterday, too. He wouldn't have admitted to Kerry before this that he'd been, well, jealous of her where Doug was concerned. It had taken a heap of gumption to tell her that.

By the time he headed back toward the cabin, Sam was chilled to the bone, but he knew what he should do. If he had the sense God gave to a goose, he'd get those papers in the waterproof pouch out of the way before proceeding. But in this instance, it wasn't his brain that ruled, or any other organ either. It was the way he felt about her, pure and simple.

Except that there wasn't anything pure about the thoughts he was having about Kerry Anderson, his best friend's wife.

Widow, he reminded himself.

He should tell her about those papers. Then maybe he'd feel better about this whole thing.

KERRY WOKE UP after a long nap and ventured downstairs to find Sam still on the couch. He was reading an adventure paperback, one of the ones that Doug had kept around. He looked up when he saw her.

"How was the nap?"

"Great. I highly recommend napping." She spoke diffidently and went immediately to the kitchen, where she ladled the steaming soup into bowls. Because she regretted having mean thoughts about him, she took one to Sam and sat down beside him on the couch.

He ate a few spoonfuls and said, "The soup is good, Kerry."

"Thanks. I see you found something to read." This seemed like a safe topic.

"Yeah, it's a book I started when I was here last time."

"Mmm." She paused. "You know, Sam, you're welcome to use this cabin whenever you like," she said. She hadn't thought about this beforehand, but said it as soon as the thought came to mind.

"Why, Kerry, that's sweet of you," he said, sounding surprised.

"Well, Doug would approve."

"I'd like to come for the fishing once in a while. Maybe even spend some time here when the lodge is open in the summer. Would you mind?"

She shook her head. "Of course not. You'll get to—" She caught herself up short. She had been about to say that he'd be able to get to know the baby.

He regarded her inquiringly, and she backtracked, thinking fast. "You'll get to see the picture when it's hung over the mantel," she said lamely.

"The picture. Yes."

Oh, why had she mentioned the picture? So soon after the fact, he would recall as well as she did those moments in the closet when she'd kissed him so enthusiastically. Of all the things she could have talked about, this was the worst.

She rose abruptly and carried her bowl back into the kitchen, where she made herself find things to do, thinking all the while of how pliant his lips were and how skillfully he'd used them to make her want to kiss him again and again and—

Sam cleared his throat. "Kerry, there's ice floating in the river."

Well, that interrupted her train of thought, a train that could go nowhere. She pulled herself back from a dangerous trip and said, "And?"

"I thought you'd want to know." Sam looked preoccupied, serious.

Kerry walked slowly to the kitchen window and looked

out at the thermometer. "Why, the temperature's down to thirty degrees," she said in alarm.

"It's starting to snow," Sam added.

She whirled around and went to look out the front windows. Unlike the kitchen window, which was sheltered by the breezeway, these windows were unprotected. Sure enough, large flakes of snow were intermixed with the sleet. Tree trunks were encased in ice.

"How long will it take until freeze-up?" she asked.

"Depends," Sam said. He came up behind her and stood so close that she thought she could feel his breath on the back of her neck.

"So maybe the snow will stop tonight and we'll be able to work on the plane tomorrow?"

"I'm not sure I'd want you to attempt it after what happened last time when we came back. You frightened me, keeling over like that."

"I was tired. That's all." She bit the words off sharply.

He grasped her shoulders gently and turned her around to face him. He watched her face as he spoke. "No need to snap at me. I only want you to come out of this experience without any injury, minor or otherwise."

She cleared her throat, willing herself to remain calm. "Well, I seem to have broken my finger already."

"How is it feeling?"

"I think I must have hurt it somehow in the lodge today."

"I have a few of those pills left."

"I'm trying not to take them unless I need them."

Sam didn't speak, just looked down at her, the pupils of his eyes wide. His eyes were the pale green-blue of the glacier; well, maybe not that pale, but almost, and they were anything but cold in this moment. She forced her gaze downward and found herself captivated by the neatly honed edge of his chin. Oh God, she had to move, get away, but she was unable to move so much as a muscle. She wondered abstractedly what would happen if she lowered her head and nestled it in the hollow of his shoulder. She wondered how he'd react if she brushed her lips against the pulse point throbbing in his jaw.

His eyes were clear, direct. Their pupils widened slightly when she mustered the determination to take a step sideways, but he took one too. She moved the other way, and so did he.

She tipped her head, raising her brows in question. He shook his head. "Kerry—" He found her hands, gripped them tightly.

"Don't," she said, regretting the word even as she spoke it. "Not again."

His hands dropped away and disappointment leaped in his eyes. And maybe, understanding.

She brushed past him. "I should go upstairs."

His arm flew out to stop her, whipped her around. There was something hard in the set of his jaw, grim in the tightness of his lips. "I won't do anything you don't want me to do," he said.

Her chin shot up. "That's—that's noble of you."

"I'm not trying to be noble. I feel anything but noble, if you want to know the truth."

Mutely her gaze sought and held his. "The truth? Maybe we'd both be better off if we didn't say too much, Sam."

"I'm not sure of that. I have something I want to tell you, Kerry."

"And if I don't want to hear it?"

He seemed surprised, and she stepped away, inserting a safe distance between them.

"It's something that needs to be said."

Her eyes were sorrowful yet held a spark of defiance. "Nothing needs to be said. Nothing, Sam."

Sam was nonplused at this development. He'd summoned all his courage, had decided to tell her about those papers in the pouch, and she'd misunderstood completely. Worst of all, he didn't have any idea how to correct the situation. He didn't want to embarrass her. If he brought up those papers now, if she found out that he'd been going to talk about the business of the sperm bank rather than make a play for her, she'd feel like a fool. Maybe it was better to let her go on thinking what she already was thinking.

And maybe not. If he let her believe that he'd been about to refer to the almost palpable sexual tension that hung in the air between them even now, that tension would only increase.

She lifted her head, and her eyes were moist.

He shifted toward her. It was impossible not to. He wanted to comfort her, to reassure her that everything was going to be okay—the plane, her emotions, the papers he wanted her to sign. It was the wrong thing to do.

Panic rose in her eyes, and he knew she was thinking about the kiss in the closet. He was thinking of it, too. Hell, it was impossible not to.

"I'm going to the shed," she said all in a rush, and she was across the floor faster than the eye could blink, ripping her shawl off the hook, hurtling out into the snow and the sleet.

In the silence she left behind, Sam rocked back on his heels. He heaved a sigh. All right, so she was conflicted about his feelings for her. Or maybe her feelings for him. She wasn't ready for any of this, that was clear now, and he was supremely aware that he'd rushed her. But how could he not?

He could no longer keep his affection from shimmering in his eyes, nor could he shake the notion that he could have a future with this woman. He was beginning to understand how lucky Doug had been to have a wife like Kerry. She was spunky, smart and functioned well in a crisis. It struck him that his own life would be a whole lot more interesting if he'd been able to find a life partner like her to help him out in the crunches. To come home from a challenging day at work to find Kerry waiting for him, her eyes sparkling, her face upturned toward his—it seemed like a vision of paradise. He scarcely dared to hope that it could really happen.

Maybe it couldn't. And certainly the time to talk about it was not now, not here. He'd have to give her time. He'd have to give her space, and maybe over a period of weeks or months she'd understand that he wasn't trying to take Doug's place in her life or her heart, that he was trying to carve out a niche for himself.

He knew he couldn't be heavy-handed about making her understand what he wanted and he knew he'd better back off. He especially didn't want to be here when she came back in, when it would seem entirely natural to take her in his arms and hold her until she understood where he was coming from.

He found a small pad of paper and a pencil. "Gone to the lodge to look for that tape player," he wrote. He left the pad on the table, where she would be sure to see it, and put on his coat. He fished the flashlight he'd seen earlier off the shelf of the closet, trying not to notice Kerry's nightgown or to smell the fresh sweet fragrance of her that wafted from its folds.

He left then, closing the door softly after himself, squaring his shoulders and trudging through the snow and sleet toward the black shape of the lodge, the flashlight beam bobbing ahead of him as he walked.

KERRY LEANED AGAINST the door of the shed listening to the hammer of sleet on the roof. Her stomach was churning, but this time it wasn't morning sickness.

She'd stopped Sam just in time. Once his feelings or hers were out in the open, she would no longer be able to ignore her response to him, nor his to her. And ignoring it seemed like the only way to deal with it.

This wasn't the way it had been with any of the other men who had shown interest in her since Doug died. It had, after all, been over a year, and there'd been men that she'd halfheartedly started seeing. She'd always called off these relationships, if that was what you could call them, before the question of intimacy arose. She'd felt as if she was babysitting with two or three of these guys; their immaturity had been a big turnoff. The others had expected her to act as if she'd been anointed because they deigned to take her out. If that was what dating was like, she'd figured, why bother? And later she'd had her own agenda—to bear the child that she and Doug had planned.

But this thing with Sam was nothing like those other sort-of relationships. The knowledge that she desired him was a blow to her self-image of hardworking widow soon to become self-sacrificing mom. The truth was that her yearning for Sam made her feel selfish. She wanted Sam Harbeck, and she wanted him for herself.

For months now she'd focused all her energy on getting the lodge up and running as a paying venture so that she could keep it in the family, for Doug's sake and the sake of their unborn child, and she'd pressed ahead with having the baby even though this might not be the best time in her life to take on more responsibility. She had worked so hard, felt so alone, and now here was Sam, something just for her. Something special, something real, something that had walked out of the wilderness and presented itself like a gift.

But she couldn't make herself accept it.

She was pregnant with Doug's child. She was honor-bound to do the best she could for this baby. And starting a relationship with Sam Harbeck wouldn't be in the baby's best interest or in hers.

But what would be wrong with a little fling? You're stranded in this cabin and you both could use the comfort. No one would ever know.

The voice of reason prevailed. She wouldn't listen to those insistent thoughts; they could very well lead her into trouble.

Because it wasn't true that no one would know if she allowed something to happen between her and Sam. Some-one would know.

She would. And Sam would.

"KERRY?"

When Sam returned from the lodge, Kerry wasn't in front of the fire or in the kitchen area, either.

He heard a rustling above. "I'm up here," she called down in a muffled voice.

"Are you all right?"

"I'm fine. I'm going to sleep."

This shouldn't have surprised him and it didn't. "Then I'll see you in the morning," he said heavily.

"Good night," she said. He heard the springs of the cot squeak as she turned over.

"Good night, Kerry."

He shrugged out of his coat and hung it up. He was too keyed up from thinking about Kerry to go to sleep right away.

He found a deck of cards where he knew they'd be, in a drawer of the wardrobe, and he began to deal a game of solitaire. The slickness of the cards in his hands took him back to the last time he'd been here and playing poker with Doug. It had been during one of those card games that Doug had spilled his guts about his inability to father a child.

Sam, by that time, knew at the week's outset that he'd have to listen to Doug's continuing praise for Kerry, not to mention how happily married they were, and he'd resigned himself to it. So when Doug became serious and started talking about their fertility problems, Sam had been surprised. He hadn't thought that the two of them had any problems they couldn't solve. They seemed like such a golden couple. But according to Doug, the one thing they wanted most, they couldn't have: a child.

And it was Doug's fault.

"Oh, we've had all the tests known to medical science," Doug had confided on that summer night over a year ago. "And there's nothing, absolutely nothing, wrong with Kerry. All her equipment is in great working order. But mine..." and Doug's voice trailed away as he stared down at the cards on the table.

Sam hadn't been sure he wanted to hear any confidences of this nature. He'd prefer to think that all was heavenly in the Anderson paradise. He got up to get another beer and offered Doug one as well. Doug accepted and leaned back in his chair, contemplating the two empty beer cans already in front of him.

"You two would be wonderful parents," Sam said, stalling for time while he tried to think of a way to console his friend.

"Yeah. Kerry'd be a fantastic mother. But I'm not ever going to be a father, Sam."

"What do you mean?"

Doug shifted in his seat. "Our infertility doctor recently found anomalies in my sperm. It's impossible for me to impregnate my wife."

A long silence, then, "Doug, I'm sorry. I mean it, man."

"Yeah, well, I'm sorry, too. Do you know what it means to love a woman so much that you'd do anything in the world for her, but the one thing she wants, you can't give her?" The anguish in Doug's eyes was heart-wrenching.

Sam leaned forward on his elbows. "Well, hey, isn't there something you can do about it?"

"The doctor tells us that artificial insemination is the way to go." Doug looked troubled.

Sam took a long pull on his beer. "That way Kerry gets the baby she wants doesn't she? Go for it." Made sense to him; why not?

Doug, visibly agitated, got up and crossed to the open front door. He stared out at the glacier.

"Kerry's all gung ho. But I don't like it, Sam. I don't like it at all." Doug turned troubled eyes upon him and shook his head. "I can't do it."

"Aw, come on, what's the problem?" Sam stood and went to stand beside Doug, clapping him on the shoulder as a sign of support.

"Kerry wants to schedule an appointment at the sperm bank soon, and I've been dragging my feet. I don't want her to know this, Sam, but the idea of rearing another man's child, a man I don't know, has no appeal to me. I have serious reservations, but I've never told her that. If I refuse to go through with this, it will break Kerry's heart."

Sam understood Doug's dilemma. Or at least he believed he did. He thought that if he were in the same situation, he might feel the same way. He couldn't imagine watching a baby growing inside a woman he loved and knowing it was another man's, a stranger's.

"That's a tough situation," he told Doug.

Doug's shoulders slumped as he walked back into the cabin and treated himself to another long swallow of beer. "When I get back from this vacation, Kerry and I are going to talk about it. I'm going to tell her I'm against it and I'm afraid she'll hate me for not going through with it. She's already picked out the paint color for the nursery. She's looking at car safety seats and high chairs and bumper pads for a baby crib."

The idea hit Sam all at once, and he didn't even think it over before he blurted it out. "I'd do it. I'd be the father if it would make everything right for you."

"What?" Doug said as if he hadn't heard him correctly.

"I could be the sperm donor. You wouldn't be raising the child of a stranger, and Kerry would never have to know."

Doug stared. "You'd do it? You'd donate sperm?"

"Sure, Doug. I mean, if your resistance to raising a stranger's child is the only stumbling block, I can fix it. Why not let me help you out?"

"Kerry doesn't even like you much."

"Like I said, it could be a secret."

Sam could almost see the wheels spinning inside Doug's head. "Kerry's filled out a profile for the sperm bank. She wants the father to be someone tall, someone intelligent—"

"Someone as much like you as possible, right? And aren't we as much alike as brothers? Didn't people in the Air Force mistake us for each other all the time?"

"Well, sure, but—"

"No buts. It's settled. I make a deposit, her doctor makes a withdrawal, and we keep it a secret from Kerry. It makes her happy, it makes you happy, and I'm probably never going to have any kids, so it makes me happy to know that some of my incomparable DNA will survive in the genetic makeup of the child that you and Kerry will so competently raise.'' He was fittingly expansive. He thought this was a great idea.

"It might work," Doug said with growing excitement. "The guy who is head of that particular sperm bank has been a friend of mine since I moved to Seattle, a golf buddy. We could let him in on the secret if we have to. He's a great guy, very understanding, and he'll probably go along with it."

"So it's done. Let's shake on it."

They'd shaken hands, Doug smiling widely, Sam feeling expansive because he always liked to help out a friend. And after their vacation, Sam had gone directly to the sperm bank and donated sperm, which had been designated for Kerry and Doug's baby.

And several weeks later, Doug had plowed his plane into that mountainside.

So much for the best-laid plans, Sam thought now as he tried to concentrate on where to play a red queen in this solitaire game. Well, maybe things did turn out for the best. Kerry already had enough problems in her life without having to worry about bringing up a child without its father. It was probably just as well that she hadn't gotten around to visiting the sperm bank before Doug died.

Black jack on red queen, red ten on black jack...

Sam made himself concentrate, hoping to banish his thoughts about Doug and the baby that would never be.

Black nine on red ten. Red eight on black nine.

Up in the loft, Kerry blew her nose. His heart went out to her, but there was nothing he could do to help. Except, perhaps, fly them out of here. And that was iffy, to say the least.

KERRY WOKE UP in fits and starts. She kept trying to go back to sleep, but the pain in her finger wouldn't let her. Finally she pushed herself to a sitting position and squinted at the clock. It was three o'clock in the morning.

Only a bit of illumination from the coals in the fireplace below reached the loft. She held up her finger and studied it in the dim light, trying to figure out if it was more swollen than it had been when she went to sleep. She thought it might be.

She wished she could go back to sleep. If she wanted to help Sam tomorrow, she'd need to be well rested.

The pain didn't abate, and after half an hour or so, Kerry gave up trying to doze off. She pulled on a robe and quietly descended the ladder.

Sam was asleep on the couch bed, lying on his back with one hand extended. He was breathing softly, not making any noise, and she smiled at how sweet and little-boyish he looked. She saw that he had moved his pack to the side of the bed near the place where his hand rested. She'd hoped the pack would be close to the door, where it had been before.

She tiptoed close, taking care not to let the floor creak beneath her feet. She had been living in this cabin long enough to know where every protesting plank was located, a fact for which she was grateful at the moment. She hoped she could find the packet of pills in Sam's pack and shake one out without waking him.

She knelt at the side of the bed, reached her hand into the pack. There it was, the envelope of pills, and stealthily she withdrew it. Unfortunately, the motion caused her to lose her precarious balance and fall forward, catching herself on the edge of the bed. The shudder of the mattress startled Sam so that his hand snapped out and grabbed hers.

She yelped, and he bolted upright, holding her wrist in his viselike grip.

The light of recognition flared in his eyes. "Damn! Kerry, what the hell are you doing?"

"I—I—"

He came to his senses and released her. His gaze dropped to the white envelope of pills.

"I was getting these. The pain's pretty bad," she said.

"I'm sorry, I was sleeping so soundly that I acted reflexively. When I'm camping in the bush, I have to be alert to danger, and I guess I forgot where I was. Did I hurt you?"

"Scared me. And I was already hurting." She tried to smile as she rose to her feet and went to get a glass of water.

"I *am* sorry, Kerry."

She poured water from the pitcher at the sink. "Want some water?"

"I could do with something a bit stronger, but since I have to be in top form tomorrow in order to deal with the plane, I'll settle for water."

She tried not to look at his bare chest as she traversed the short distance to the bed and handed him a glass.

"Don't go. Sit and keep me company," Sam said suddenly.

"I don't know," said Kerry, unsure of the wisdom of this.

"I won't be able to go to sleep right away now that I'm awake," he said.

She relented. "All right, but only until the pill starts to take effect."

Sam slid over on the bed. "Here's a pillow," he offered.

Self-consciously she plumped the pillow into the corner of the couch as far away from Sam as possible. She shiv ered and Sam noticed. "It's warmer upstairs," she said in an attempt to explain.

"Makes sense. Heat rises," Sam said, settling a corner of the blanket over her legs. The sheet still covered him, hiding the rest of him from view.

She turned away, resolutely refusing to think about what she was convinced was his nakedness. "It sounds as if the sleet has stopped."

"It was still snowing when I went to bed."

"Snow in September," Kerry said in disbelief.

"This is Alaska. I've lived here all my life and I've learned to expect the unexpected."

"Well, you've had plenty of the unexpected here at Silverthorne."

"It makes life interesting," he said with predictable irony.

She relaxed slightly and sipped her water. It felt comfortable to be sitting up late at night with Sam, although if someone had told her that she would have this sense of ease with him, she never would have believed it.

She stole a glance at him. "May I ask you something, Sam?"

"You'll ask it whether I give permission or not."

This made her smile. "Why haven't you ever married?"

He didn't answer right away. "I never found the right person, I guess. And then as time went on, I figured I never would. With the kind of life I've always led, it seemed best to be unattached."

"You've settled down in the past few years. Doug said so."

"I suppose I have."

"But there've been girlfriends."

"All of them as committed to staying uncommitted as I was. Except for a few who tried to make something out of nothing, to stake their claim when I wasn't at all interested, which is why I ran like hell."

She thought for a moment of these women who had scared Sam away and, to her surprise, she felt pity for them. And for him.

"It's sad, somehow. You'd make somebody a good husband, Sam." She was beginning to feel sleepy again.

"I'm not so sure of that," Sam said before lapsing into silence.

"I was a good wife to Doug," she said.

"I know you were. He said so many times." Sam turned to her, his eyes serious and kind. He paused. "How about you? Have you started dating yet?"

"A few dates, nothing more than that. My heart wasn't in it, and I had more important things on my mind."

Sam seemed to take this in, and in that instant, Kerry wanted nothing so much as to tell Sam about her pregnancy. It would have been wonderful to have someone to rejoice with her, to tell her that she'd done the right thing by going ahead with the insemination.

But she was so sleepy. And when she looked over at Sam, his eyes were closed.

She closed her eyes, too. Just before she fell asleep she told herself that she ought to climb back to the loft, but then her head lolled over and rested on Sam's broad shoulder. And she didn't think anymore about going upstairs.

Chapter Six

Sam started awake in the gloom of the cabin. Kerry mumbled something and settled closer to him, one hand—the one without the broken finger—cupped trustingly on his bare chest. Her hair tickled his chin, and he wanted to brush it away, to smooth it off her forehead in a tender gesture. Would tenderness be out of line here? He had to ask himself that question.

But tenderness wasn't the only feeling he was experiencing. His arousal let him know just how much he wanted her, and he would have liked to act upon it. More than that, he would have liked to know how she felt about beginning a sexual relationship with him. But this wasn't something they had talked about, and it wasn't something that he could bring up after yesterday, when she'd skittered out the door like a frightened little mouse when she thought he might be going to talk about what was happening between them.

He'd give her time. They had lots of that.

Outside it had stopped snowing, but the sky was a dull gray. He glanced down at Kerry. She slept with her mouth slightly open, her full dark eyelashes casting smoky shadows on her cheeks. Her color was good, something that he was glad to see. He wanted, in that moment, to kiss her awake and to see the light in her eyes leap in joyful recognition, but he knew that even if he had the nerve to kiss her, the recognition might not be joyful.

He didn't think he could move without disturbing her, so he lay as still as he possibly could. He didn't know how long they lay there, but after a time she stirred and blinked.

She struggled to a sitting position and pulled the blanket up under her chin. "What time is it?" she wanted to know.

Sam looked at his watch. "Almost seven o'clock."

She swung her feet over the side of the bed. "I didn't mean to fall asleep here," she said briskly.

"Plenty of room," he mumbled, unwilling to hear her protests. He'd liked waking up beside her. He wished he could wake up beside her every morning.

Kerry started toward the kitchen in those ridiculous bulky wool socks she liked to wear, all of which seemed to be wearing thin in the heel or toe and sometimes both.

"I'll get the coffee going, run out to the shed, be back in a minute," she called over her shoulder.

He didn't say anything, but got out of bed and folded it back into a couch. By the time Kerry returned, Sam had already dressed and was standing over the sink shaving, scraping whiskers off his chin as if it were the most interesting pastime in the world.

He spared her a glance via the mirror. "I'm heating water on the stove. You can have it for your bath if you want," he told her. He concentrated on shaving, trying to seem nonchalant when all his energies were vibrating at a higher frequency, and merely because Kerry had walked into the room.

"I think I'll have a quick wash this morning, save a bath for later," she said. "We'll want to be on our way to the plane as soon as possible."

He turned to look at her, his face still half covered with shaving cream. "I didn't say we were going to the plane."

She stared back. "It's not snowing. We have work to do there." She started to brush past him, but he caught her shoulder.

"Even if I go to the plane, I don't want you coming along."

Something changed behind her eyes, flamed briefly and was shuttered when she lowered her lashes. "You need my help."

"I need you healthy and ready for whatever happens, whether we fly out of here or have to walk or—"

"Walk!" Her eyes flicked open, widened.

"It would be my last choice," he assured her, turning back to his shaving mirror because for a minute he'd caught a flash of sheer terror as it flitted across her expression.

"And where would we go?" she said in a tone that was deliberately casual but resistant nonetheless.

"Athinopa," he said. "If we have to."

"Athinopa's sixty miles away!" Incredulity now, and he supposed he couldn't blame her.

"As the raven flies."

"And how far walking?"

He shrugged.

Kerry blew out a long breath. "I don't know, Sam. It's pretty cold out there to go camping."

"We wouldn't have to sleep outside. There are cabins along the way where we could make ourselves comfortable." He finished shaving, dipped water up from the basin and splashed it on his face.

"You seem to know the area well," she said. He understood from her tone of voice that she was considering the idea, turning it over in her mind as a new possibility that might have merit.

"I've been flying over this part of the Country every year as long as Doug and I have been taking our vacations together. We used to hike to a camp on Everygood Creek for the fishing. There's a hut there where we can stay one night, plus I know of some hunters' cabins along the way where we'll find hospitality whether the owners are there or not. And I'm familiar with Athinopa and the people who live there. Ollie Parker is a particularly good friend of mine." Ollie, the village leader, was a Native American and an expert musher who had placed in the Iditarod sled-dog race three years in a row. He usually stopped by the office and talked Sam into going out for a beer whenever he found himself in Anchorage.

"Athinopa's a small Indian village, isn't it?"

"Right. A hundred or so people, a school that doubles as a rec center and an airstrip. That's about it. And a powerful radio that keeps them in touch with the rest of the world."

Kerry wrapped her robe tighter around herself. "I should have made sure there was a snow machine here at Silverthorne. I should have asked Captain Crocker to drop off more food during the summer when he was making weekly runs."

Sam dried his face. "No point in beating yourself up about any of that. You weren't expecting snow in September."

"I feel guilty about it, that's all."

"Well, don't."

She traced a finger along the edge of the counter, lost in thought. When he went to put on his coat, she turned her attention back to him. "Are you going out?" she asked sharply.

"I'm going to check the ice in the river." He zipped the

coat, pulled on his gloves, not looking forward to going out there and learning bad news.

For a moment Kerry didn't speak. Then she said in a tone of resignation, "I might as well heat up a can of hash, scramble some eggs, throw together a few biscuits."

Sam nodded. "I'll be back soon."

He left her standing in the middle of the cabin and looking forlorn. He wished she wouldn't look like that. It grated on his heart to see her so worried.

ATHINOPA!

Sam wanted her to walk to Athinopa?

Well, he hadn't exactly said that. It was more like he was floating the idea for her reaction. Kerry was nonplused because the idea of hiking out of here in the snow had never occurred to her. She didn't know if she could walk sixty miles or not. She was, after all, three and a half—no, almost four—months pregnant. She had trouble keeping food down. The growing baby pressed on her bladder, making it necessary to run to the shed more often than usual. She was tired much of the time.

How could she keep her pregnancy a secret from Sam if they walked to Athinopa?

SAM KNELT on the riverbank and studied the ice formation. The shelf ice was consolidating, and slush was visible further out. It seemed to be stiffening even as he watched. Freeze-up wasn't far off.

Also, this snow was deeper and softer than the last snowfall, almost over the tops of his boots. There would be no walking to the plane today without the aid of snowshoes. Fortunately, there were several old pair, all made years ago of birch wood and moose hide, hung on nails in the shed.

He didn't know if it was worthwhile to think about flying

the plane out. The river was freezing. He still had to reat-tach the prop, repair that strut and do something about the float. He wasn't sure how long any of this would take, nor did he believe that the weather would stay clear. Not that it was clear at the moment. It was cloudy, and the clouds hung low over the mountains. Even if he managed to repair the plane, he wasn't sure he could fly it out of there.

Discouraged, he headed back to the cabin. Under the trees, where snowfall was light, he noticed bear tracks in the snow. Shallow prints, meaning that the bear was in no big hurry. In fact, Sam found a log that had been clawed as the bear looked for grubs. So it was a hungry animal, by this time feeling an urgent need to go into hibernation for the winter. Bears could travel eight miles in one night searching for food; there wasn't any attainable food at Sil-verthorne, and therefore this particular bear probably wouldn't come around again.

Which was the only good thing he could think of this morning. It was also why he decided not to mention it to Kerry. She had enough to concern her without worrying about bears.

"I'M GOING WITH YOU."

"You're not." Sam, sitting on the backless bench near the fireplace, was trying on the snowshoes so he could see if any of the laces needed replacing before he started out on his long trek to the plane.

"Why not?" Kerry crossed her arms across her chest and scowled at him.

He paused in what he was doing and gave her eyeball for eyeball. She wore a wool plaid shirt over a turtleneck sweater and a pair of sturdy jeans that hugged her hips.

He strived to be patient in the face of what he considered misplaced obstinacy. "Because all I'm going to do is take the lumber I've already cut and try to figure out if I have enough time to repair the strut, and if not, I'll be back.''

Kerry pushed her hands down into her pockets and rocked back and forth on her heels.

''You don't want me to go because I fainted last time, right?''

''No, Kerry.''

She didn't say anything, and he found himself staring at the lush contours of her breasts, now more noticeable because she'd thrown the shirt back when she'd tucked her hands in her jeans pockets. He couldn't make himself look away; all he could think about was that she must have beautiful breasts. The speculation was one he'd made before, of course, but never with as much interest as now.

Kerry didn't notice his appraisal, mostly because she was too busy reeling off reasons why she didn't want to waste this day by staying behind.

''I should go with you because first of all, I can help you with the plane. Second, I feel fine. Third—''

''Kerry, what part of no don't you understand?''

Silence sizzled between them, and then Kerry turned on her heel and stalked to the kitchen table. There she proceeded to bang dishes around with great abandon while she cleaned up after their breakfast. Sam watched her in profile and found himself thinking again, *Why, she's gained weight.* His gaze dropped lower, and he saw how the front of her jeans strained across her stomach. Kerry with a potbelly? He hadn't noticed that before, but then he hadn't been looking at her from quite this angle. He'd been surprised to find her so thin when he arrived, and this thickness around her middle seemed at odds with that first impression.

She eyed him balefully. ''Well, what am I supposed to do all day?''

Sam tried his best to sound reasonable. "You could make an inventory of the food here and figure out how many days it will take us to use it up," he said.

"That chore will take fifteen minutes tops. I think I'd be more useful handing you tools or knocking ice off the wings or something."

Sam decided that he'd better be blunt. "Look, Kerry, I know you mean well, but the last thing I need is someone who can't keep up, someone I have to worry about. I have to concentrate on getting the plane back in shape, not on whether you're okay."

"And won't you have to worry about whether I'm okay if we trek out of here?

"That's exactly the point. You need to save your strength for later."

Two spots of color burned her cheeks, and she whirled and went back to the sink. "I'm sorry I'm such a bother. I'm sorry I got you into this," she said hotly.

"You didn't—" But he couldn't say it. She still thought that he'd come to Silverthorne out of some high-minded urge to help her. "Oh, forget it," he said, disgusted with himself for his duplicity. He knew he should have been upfront about his reason for coming here. He should have told her as soon as he walked in the door.

He *could* tell her now and be done with it.

He reached into his parka and withdrew the waterproof pouch containing the papers from the sperm bank. He stared at the pouch for a moment, judiciously considering what opening he might use. Suddenly an idea careened through his consciousness—he could leave the pouch here and be on his way. She would find it while he was working on the plane.

Not a good idea. On the other hand, not a bad one. It would get the whole ordeal over with.

She'd be mad as hell.

But he already knew that.

So what should he do?

Kerry wasn't paying attention to him. "I apologized," she reminded him stiffly.

"Apologized for what?" he asked, drawn back to the moment.

"For getting us into this. The least you could do is acknowledge it."

"Okay, I acknowledge it," he said. Damn! The woman had a way of getting to him.

Suddenly he wanted to be rid of his conscience. He didn't want to have to accept apologies from Kerry who thought he was here for one reason when he was here for another; he didn't want to be the recipient of any kindnesses from her.

He carelessly tossed the pouch down on the table beside the couch alongside Kerry's crossword puzzle magazine where she couldn't help but see it. Curiosity would probably get the best of her. She'd take a look, and then when he got back she'd light into him in a fury.

And that would take care of any possibility that the two of them might get to know each other in the way that he wanted to know her. It would make her dislike him intensely. It might even make her hate him, and then he'd be free to go on his merry way after all this was over. He would never have to think about Kerry Anderson again. Which would all fit in with his well-known method of operation; that is, doing something to undercut every relationship he'd ever had with a woman.

Before he could change his mind, he slid his feet out of the snowshoes, stood up and dragged on his parka. "All right, I'm going. I'll be back as soon as I can," he said gruffly. He slung the snowshoes over his shoulder, already thinking ahead to what he'd do when he reached the plane.

He wasn't prepared for Kerry to rush across the room, nor for the anxiety of her expression. Anger had been displaced by concern, and he saw no trace of the obstinacy she'd displayed earlier. "Here," she said. "Take these." She slid a large packet of saltines and a tin of smoked oysters into his pocket. She attempted a smile, albeit feeble. "At least you won't go hungry," she said.

He'd left emergency rations in the plane, but he was so touched by her concern that he decided not to tell her. Besides, her thoughtfulness made him feel as guilty as hell.

He managed to say, "Well, thanks."

"Sam," she began, but she bit her lip.

He didn't want to hear any soul-baring revelations, didn't want to hear how sorry she was to have been short with him and didn't want to be gazing deep into those marvelous eyes, now fixed upon him in anxious concern.

"I—I just wanted to tell you to take care, that's all."

He couldn't make himself look away. In that moment, knowing he couldn't allow it, he wished she could come with him today. He didn't like leaving her here alone and, worse, he didn't want to be without her.

This realization rocked him to the core. He'd never known a woman that he wanted around him all the time; he liked his space. He also liked his women to be like him: uncommitted. And kind of wild. Kerry was neither of these.

"I'll be all right" was all he said, but he said it quietly and in as reassuring a tone as he could muster.

Suddenly eager to be away so he could think things over, he stepped out into the cold. First he strapped on the snowshoes and walked around in the snow for a few minutes as he grew accustomed to the feel of them. Then, deciding not to use poles, he shouldered the piece of lumber he intended to use for the strut and headed down the slope toward the river.

It was roughgoing on snowshoes, with the snow slipping out from under them like granulated sugar. Sam had to remember to put his heels down ahead of his toes in order to keep the front tips of the snowshoes from collecting snow. This took a lot of energy even though he stopped a couple of times along the way to rest. Eventually he developed a rolling motion of his body, shifting his weight from side to side as he walked, the way his friend Ollie did.

Once he spotted a lone bull moose shambling through a stand of spruce. "I know how you feel, buddy," he muttered under his breath. As he watched, the moose faded ghostlike into the silent woods, barely making a sound. That was more than he could say for himself, he thought grimly as he flailed his way through snow and brush.

When Sam reached the plane it was covered with snow, and he spent some time cutting pine branches to use for brushing it off. He also cleared snow off the tarp they'd left on their last trip as a signal to planes overhead. He took his time repositioning the tarp, placing it so that it might be more visible from the air.

He decided that the river wasn't as slushy here, and as he rebolted the prop, he cast a look at the sky, thinking that he might be able to replace the strut and the float in time to fly out of here if he hurried. He hauled the lumber over to the plane and struggled with numb fingers to adjust it to fit where the strut was supposed to be, cursing at the cold.

He paused only once to eat Kerry's crackers and oysters, resuming work as quickly as he could, jamming the new wooden strut in place. The idea rose in his mind that perhaps, just perhaps, it was possible to return to the cabin and collect Kerry, and maybe, just maybe, he might be able to get this crate off the ground.

He made his mistake right at the end when he stepped out on the float with an eye to scraping ice off the windshield. His foot slipped on the icy metal, and he fell headlong into the river.

KERRY WATCHED anxiously at the window most of the afternoon, sure that she'd see Sam looming out of the forest any minute. When he didn't appear early in the afternoon, she decided that he must be making real progress in the repair of the plane and made herself take inventory of the food that remained on the kitchen shelves.

Afterward, looking for something, anything, to do, she waded through drifted snow to the lodge, but felt too edgy to go to the trouble of lighting a fire in the fireplace so she could work there. She wandered the rooms, hunched into her parka, making herself think of how gratifying it would be to welcome her first guests here next summer, to see them to their rooms all sparkling fresh with paint, with vases of native wildflowers in every bathroom and the newfound paintings gracing the walls.

Usually such exercises in optimism lifted her spirits, but today she couldn't shake her feeling of foreboding. Something was wrong. She felt it.

The only other time Kerry had ever felt the way she did today was on the day Doug died. She'd awakened earlier than usual that morning at their house in Seattle harboring a vague uneasiness. As the day had worn on she'd felt as if a hand were crushing her heart, and for no reason that was readily apparent.

In fact, it had been a happy day: lunch with friends, shopping at Pike Place Market. And because she had been thinking of Doug all day, she'd bought ingredients for his favorite bouillabaisse. Then as she had stepped out of her car, she'd seen officials from the airline waiting on her front porch. The expressions they had fixed on her had been grim, and she'd known. Oh yes, she'd known. She'd dropped the shopping bags and started screaming, and the neighbors had come and led her into the house. That was how she had learned her husband had died.

So now Kerry knew better than to ignore these anxieties. But she didn't know what to do about them, either. She told herself she was making things up in her mind, that she was simply too sensitive to things that might go wrong, that Sam would be fine and that there was nothing to worry about. There was nothing wrong.

Well, that wasn't true. A lot was wrong. They were stranded in a cabin with only enough food to last a few more days, the river was freezing, and the plane might not fly.

She walked back slowly to the cabin, keeping a wary eye on the mountaintop for signs that the weather would hold. The cabin seemed empty, hollow, lonely without Sam's presence.

Kerry slid out of her coat, brewed a pot of tea. "I wish I'd gone with him," she said out loud. Her voice seemed to echo back at her from the very rafters, and after she drank her tea, she climbed up to the loft and lay down on the cot, trying to nap. But even though she closed her eyes, she felt wide awake.

SAM FISHED HIMSELF out of the icy river, soaked to the skin. He lost no time in divesting himself of his wet clothes, but they started to stiffen with ice before he'd even hung them up to dry inside the plane. Shivering so violently that his teeth chattered, he dug behind the backseat of the Cessna and found a spare set of clothing, some things that Vic had left there, probably a long time ago.

With shaking fingers he pulled on the heavy wool lumberman's long johns, thick sweater and jeans, topping it all off with a heavy rain slicker. All the garments were too short for him, and by the time he'd managed to dress, he was dismayed to see a thick ice fog rolling in from nowhere, obscuring the river, the trees, the mountains—everything.

Ollie, his friend from Athinopa, had once shared a bit of Indian lore. "The secret, if you're ever out in the cold and can't get back to shelter, is to conserve your energy," Ollie had said. "One good way to freeze to death is to get exhausted. In a case like that, you don't have enough energy to keep your blood circulating, and without the blood, you die."

Considering this piece of wisdom and the whited-out landscape, Sam decided he'd better not strike out for the cabin after all.

KERRY WAS BESIDE herself when darkness fell and Sam hadn't returned.

She paced back and forth in front of the cabin, breathing out plumes of vapor into the cold night air, even lighting a lantern and setting it on a tree stump near the river trail to light his way back. Doing something constructive made her feel only slightly better, and once it was done she couldn't think of anything else that might help. She wished she'd gone with him. She wished she'd followed him later and surprised him at the plane. She wished...

Overhead something rustled in the treetops, and a large helping of snow dumped on her head.

Realizing that it wasn't prudent to stand around outside in the dark, she retreated to the cabin, peering out the window into the night and seeing nothing but the glow of the welcoming lantern and her own reflection staring back at her.

OTHER ADVICE that Sam had received over the years from Ollie about survival in the wilderness had included digging a trough in the snow and laying showshoes on top, then covering those with a blanket or tarp and climbing under it. Ollie had touted this as a good way to keep warm. But Sam didn't have to do that. He had the plane.

Stuffed into the tail of the plane was a moth-eaten old sleeping bag, but it was made of down and would be warm. Huddled inside, he lit a couple of candles he'd found in the emergency kit. Outside, the fog was so thick that he couldn't see a thing.

He worried about Kerry alone in the cabin waiting for him. He thought about why he had come to Silverthorne in the first place. And he thought about how Kerry would hate him when she found the papers in the waterproof pouch.

Maybe she wouldn't hate him for long. Maybe she'd get over it. He hoped so, considering that he'd once been willing for Kerry to be the mother of his child. No, not his child. It would have been Doug and Kerry's child. It would have been a boy, he thought, with dark curly hair like his and Doug's and eyes like Kerry's, all gold and silver. He thought about Kerry's eyes now, how they could dance in merriment, how they softened when she was talking about the lodge and her hopes for it, how they could snap in anger.

And how if he kissed her the lids would drift slowly closed, casting feathery shadows on her cheeks.

He wanted to kiss her. And more.

Sam punched the sleeping bag into submission and tried

to settle into its depths, warm enough, but not looking forward to a long, cold, lonely night.

BACK IN THE CABIN, Kerry gave the place a thorough cleaning. It only made sense, since if all went well, they'd be leaving it soon. She wiped down the stove, cleaned the kitchen floor, polished the inside of the windows with a mixture of vinegar and water. She dusted the furniture and swept out the loft. Then she straightened things in general, tossing everything burnable into the kitchen stove.

On top of her crossword puzzle magazine lay a waterproof pouch that she didn't recognize. She started to open it, but realized that it must be Sam's and assumed that it would be the sectional charts and logbook that pilots carried with them, so she stuffed the pouch unopened down into Sam's pack and resolved to tell him what she'd done with it when he came back.

SAM HAD A HARD TIME going to sleep in the cockpit. The seat was approximately the size of the one in the Volkswagen bug he'd restored when he was a kid, and it afforded little room for his big frame. When his feet started to go numb, he didn't know if it was from the cold or from lack of blood circulation due to his cramped position. Remembering Ollie's advice, he massaged his legs to get the blood going again. Afterward he tossed and turned and finally fell asleep, dreaming so vividly of a grizzly attack that when the dream woke him, he peered warily out over the plane's wing toward the forest, trying to see if there really was a bear.

He didn't see one. He didn't see anything but the fog drawn around the plane like a shroud.

FOR DINNER, Kerry heated chili from a can and then took refuge under an afghan on the couch. She stayed awake as long as she could, wanting to remain alert so that she'd hear Sam's approach or see his face grinning at her from the window.

But she was so tired that she couldn't keep her eyes open, and her head kept slipping to one side. Finally she gave in to it, pulling the afghan up over her shoulders and letting herself be borne away on a wave of gentle slumber.

She was jolted from her drowsy state by the clatter of metal in the breezeway.

Sam.

She jumped up from the couch and ran to the back door, so sure it must be Sam that she flung it open without a second thought. A blast of cold wind knifed through her, but she didn't stop for her shawl. She rushed through the breezeway and banged on the shed door with her fist, thinking that Sam must be inside.

''Sam?''

She heard the rattle of dry leaves on snow crust. She whirled and just beyond the first trees, but within the pale circle of light from the kerosene lamp inside the cabin, she saw a fat-haunched grizzly bear standing over the big metal-covered container where she stored the cache of dried blueberries she'd harvested from the patch behind the lodge.

The bear seemed as startled as she was. It charged through the breezeway, sending the blueberries flying into the snow, but it soon found itself blocked by the stacks of wood that Sam had so recently chopped. Confused, it stumbled, then recovered.

Kerry broke out in a sweat that chilled her with the icy numbness of pure terror. Her heart began to pound as if it would leap out of her chest. She tried frantically to remem-

ber what she was supposed to do when confronted by a
bear. Run? Curl into a ball? Don't move?

This was an enormous grizzly, bigger than she could
have even imagined. It rose threateningly on its hind feet,
the hackles rising on its neck and its enormous head weav-
ing back and forth. It stood much taller than she was and
must have weighed almost a thousand pounds. Its teeth
were ugly fangs, and its claws were at least four inches
long and looked as if they could use a good manicure.

At least the bear was only standing there looking at her,
not lunging or pawing or doing any of the other things that
bears could do. But she was also mindful that bears had
been said to rip a man's scalp off with one swat and she
had no intention of giving this bear such a chance.

Slowly she inched backward, reaching behind her with
one hand. The bear teetered on its hind feet, beady eyes
intent upon her. Kerry had the impression that things could
go bad in a nanosecond. Her hand met the shed's door
handle, gripped the cold metal and slowly drew it toward
her. The door scraped the ground, grinding into the dirt.
The bear's ears perked, and suddenly it dropped back to all
four feet.

That was when Kerry made a crucial move. She jerked
the shed door open and tumbled inside, pulling it shut behind her and slamming the hasp of the heavy iron bolt
through. She fully expected the bear to come crashing
against the planks.

As she leaned against the door holding her breath, she
heard snuffling around its edges. She stood quaking as she
waited for the animal to attack the shed; she'd heard numerous tales of bears' ill-temper and aggressiveness when
provoked. But nothing happened.

She endured a few jiggles of the door as if the bear were
bumping against it, and then she heard the animal ga-

lumphing toward the woods. After a while, the bear began to rattle the lid of the blueberry container, so maybe it had decided to finish its snack.

Listening to the noises, wishing she had a flashlight, Kerry shivered in the cold shed. When she was sure that the bear was not in an attack mode, she searched by touch until she found a waterproof box of matches. She lit one and located the one-burner kerosene heater that Doug had stored there years ago. It held kerosene, not much but enough, she hoped, to last for a while. After several unsuccessful attempts, she managed to light it.

The flare of another match revealed that Doug's boyhood sleeping bag was stored on one of the shelves above her head, and she fumbled around in the dark until she was able to pull it down from the shelf. She wrapped herself in it and settled down beside the heater for what she was afraid might be a very long wait.

SAM WOKE UP early the next morning feeling stiff all over. His clothes, which had been wet the night before, were so cold that they crackled to the touch. It didn't matter, he could wear Vic's clothes, although he wished he had something warmer to wear than the rain slicker.

He thought about Kerry, knowing that she must have found his pouch with its incriminating papers by this time. All right, so he'd been chicken. But letting her learn on her own about his sperm donation and Doug's complicity might be the kindest way to handle it. This way she'd have her privacy when she found out. This way she could marshal her thoughts before she assailed him with blame and accusations.

This way he felt like a cad.

But still. His purpose in donating to the sperm bank had been to help out two friends who desperately wanted a baby. He hoped Kerry would eventually understand that his offer had been driven by kindness and that Doug's acceptance had been full of gratitude.

He waited until the fog cleared before climbing down from the cockpit and looking around. The sky was still overcast, but pale-pink fingers of light pointed up from the horizon. Rays of hope, Sam thought without much humor.

He studied the river for a long time, uncertain whether it was too slushy to consider taking off even if he finished his work on the plane. Finally he decided that the jerry-built strut could use some adjustment, so he worked on that for a couple of hours. Later he built a fire on one of the boulders and boiled water for coffee, and he also heated up a can of sausages from the plane. After this unsatisfactory breakfast, he turned his attention to the float, and that's when he first noticed large chunks of ice flowing down the river.

This meant that the Kilkit River would be frozen solid before long. And the chunks of ice tooling along in the current would make it nigh unto impossible for the plane to take off. Optimism fizzled, quenched by despair.

Sam did what he could to secure the plane. He emptied it of everything that could possibly be useful to them, devised a makeshift pack from the sleeping bag and tied it to his back. Then, with a heavy heart, he started to hoof it back to Silverthorne Lodge.

Kerry had certainly found the pouch with its incriminating paperwork by this time. He was pretty sure there'd be hell to pay when he got back.

Chapter Seven

When Sam arrived at the juncture of the woods path and the river trail near the cabin, he noticed the lantern on the stump. It wasn't lit, and when he checked, there was no oil in it. He had no idea why Kerry might have put a lamp there.

The cabin looked dark, and no smoke rose from the fireplace chimney. This seemed strange. It was so cold now that Kerry would need to have the fireplace going at full blast in order to stay warm.

He opened the front door.

"Kerry?"

He was cautious, not knowing what to expect. Something was strange. Had she been rescued? Was she sick again?

He'd spent his walk back here preparing himself for a tongue-lashing over those papers. He'd prepared himself to defend himself as well as Doug. He was prepared to cajole, mollify and appease.

He was prepared, in fact, for almost anything except Kerry's absence. She wasn't there.

It was cold in the cabin because the fire in the fireplace had gone out. A pot of congealed chili stood on the stove, and the stove fire had faded to a few glowing coals.

"Kerry?"

No answer from the loft.

"Kerry?" He hurried up the ladder, taking two rungs at a time, and calling to her even as he went.

Kerry wasn't in the loft. The wool coverlet she used for a bedspread was tucked neatly under the cot's mattress, and he could see the concave imprint of her body where she had lain upon it.

"Kerry!" Now he was frantic, worried. Where could she be?

He descended the ladder, rushed to the back door, wrenched it open. To one side was a big heavy container that he'd seen outside the back door of the cabin, and a few berries were scattered through the breezeway and in the snow. Had she been storing blueberries outside where a bear might get a whiff of them? Of all the stupid *cheechako* things to do!

And then he spotted the footprints, bear footprints, the same kind of footprints he'd seen earlier and neglected to mention to Kerry because he didn't want to frighten her. The sight of them pierced him like a knife to his heart.

The shed door flew open and Kerry stumbled out. Her hair was wild, her face pale, and she was wrapped in Doug's old sleeping bag. He thought he had never seen her looking more beautiful.

"Sam, oh Sam, there was a bear, a grizzly bear, and I came outside because I heard the noise and thought it was you, and it stood up on its hind legs, and I didn't know what to do, but I ran in the shed and locked the door and I've been there I don't know how long—"

"You left berries out where a bear could get their scent?"

"I kept them in a covered pot, I didn't know any bear would notice."

"Of all the fool things—"

But he didn't get a chance to finish his sentence before she threw herself into his arms, clinging to him with all her might. In the face of such neediness, his anger evaporated. Whether the neediness was mostly hers or mostly his, he couldn't say. All he knew was that it felt wonderful to hold her close, to feel her heart beating close to his.

"Shh, it's all right, you're fine, it's okay," he soothed, burying his face in her hair and wrapping his arms more tightly around her.

He had to loosen his grip when she pulled away to look at him. "What—what happened to you, Sam? I was so worried when you didn't come back."

He slid an arm around her shoulders. They felt frailer than he expected, and something inside him turned over. Because he had been stupid enough to fall in the river, he'd had to spend the night away from her, and because of that she'd had a run-in with a bear, and he knew bears terrified her.

"Come inside and I'll tell you about it," he said, pulling her close as they walked into the cabin.

As soon as they were inside, his eyes flew to the table where the crossword magazine had been. It was gone, and so was the pouch he had left there. His heart dropped to his toes and swooped up again.

Had she read the papers? Surely not. If she had, she would have mentioned it. Or maybe she was so upset about the bear that she'd temporarily put the papers out of her mind. Whatever the reason, this was a reprieve. Relief washed over him, shocking him with its intensity. He hadn't realized how much he'd dreaded being the focus of Kerry's anger, dreaded having to explain.

He noticed that Kerry was looking at him, really looking at him in the light of the lantern on the table. She drew back in consternation at the sight of his stubbly beard and the dark circles under his eyes. "Something terrible happened to you, didn't it, Sam? I knew it, I knew it!"

He realized then how tired he was, how bone weary. He released her and removed the rain slicker that he still wore for warmth. "It wasn't as awful as being chased by a bear." Where had she put the incriminating papers? He didn't see them anywhere around the cabin.

While telling Kerry about falling in the river and how he'd camped out in the plane all night, Sam got the fire going in the fireplace. As he worked, he kept a sharp eye out for the papers. They weren't on top of the wall cabinet, and he didn't see them in the bookcase or on the floor. That left the most likely place—his pack, but before he had a chance to check, Kerry asked him about his repairs to the plane.

He related how he'd almost finished the repairs, and while he was talking she snickered at the way his knobby wrists protruded from Vic's shirt. Sam was glad that she could find something funny in this situation because he didn't think he could bear to see the devastation on her face when he told her they'd have to hike out.

But she surprised him again, this woman. She beat him to it. "We're going to have to walk to Athinopa, aren't we?" she said as he sat back on his heels and warmed his hands at the fire.

He reached up and took her hand, pulling her down beside him. "Yes, Kerry, we are."

A muscle moved in her eyelid, and that was her only reaction. She didn't cry, she didn't scream, she didn't blame him for anything. She only stared into the flames and said in a matter-of-fact tone, "When do you want to leave?"

"As soon as we can," he said, matching calmness for calmness and taking in the determined set of her jaw, the sweet seriousness of her expression as she turned her head to look at him.

"Tomorrow morning?"

"If the weather holds."

"How long will it take?"

"Depends on how far we can walk in a day's time. Several days, a week. How experienced are you at walking with snowshoes?"

"Doug and I used to go cross-country skiing and snowshoeing sometimes. I should be okay."

"A man in good condition can walk maybe an average of 15 miles a day in this terrain. Snowshoes will slow us down."

"I'll try not to be a drag, Sam."

He rested a hand on her shoulder. "We'll start packing up now. We should leave as soon as it's light in the morning."

She nodded mutely and got up.

"I don't have to tell you not to take more than you need. We don't want our packs to be too heavy."

"I know." She started up the ladder.

"I'll heat up the chili again," he said. He tossed more wood on the cook stove.

Soon he had the chili bubbling on the stove, filling the air with its aroma. Overhead, the wooden floor creaked as Kerry moved around packing.

"That chili sure smells good," she called down to him. Her tone was so matter-of-fact that there might have been nothing wrong. To Sam, waiting downstairs, the whole scene suddenly seemed normal, as if he and Kerry were about to sit down at the kitchen table of a real home like a real couple, basking in familiarity and each other's presence.

But this was anything but normal. They were situated at

the edge of a glacier in a cabin with virtually no amenities and a hungry bear camped on their doorstep. Their food supply was running low. And there was the matter of those papers, which he didn't want to ask her about, and he didn't want to look for them while she might be watching, either.

No, there was nothing normal about any of this. Nothing at all.

IN THE LOFT, Kerry tried to gather her thoughts, knowing that she'd better remember to take everything she would need or risk being a burden to Sam. She assembled her warmest clothes—thermal underwear, utilitarian sweaters, the ubiquitous wool socks. Pants that no longer fit—and there were many of them that had grown too tight in the past weeks—she left in the trunk where she kept her clothes.

While going about this task, she tried to think of what to do about telling Sam that she was expecting a baby. No matter how she looked at the situation, she knew she couldn't tell him now. What if he decided her condition posed too much of a problem and insisted on hiking to Athinopa without her?

Oh, she knew he'd send help later. But after what had happened with the bear, she certainly didn't feel safe here by herself. And Sam shouldn't attempt the long and grueling walk alone. The Alaska wilderness was too dangerous for a solitary hiker—too many predators. Bears, wolves and who knew what else? Not to mention the capricious weather. She'd heard many stories about people freezing to death when they'd undertaken lone journeys in this land where the temperature could drop more than thirty degrees in thirty minutes.

Maybe she wouldn't have to tell Sam about her pregnancy until they reached safety in Athinopa. He'd be furious with her, she knew, but she'd explain. He'd understand. Or would he?

She already knew that the trek to Athinopa would be grueling. Experimentally she ran her hands over her stomach. The bulge in the lower part of her abdomen seemed bigger every day. And her waist was slightly thicker than its normal twenty-four inches. Fortunately, although her shape was changing, she didn't feel ungainly or off-balance. She was athletic and in good condition.

Except for the horrible morning sickness. And the exhaustion that never quite went away.

But some days were better than others. Some days she felt fine.

She could only hope that tomorrow and the next several days would be like that.

WHEN KERRY DESCENDED from the loft, Sam brought two bowls of steaming hot chili over to the fireplace. He had arranged floor and couch cushions in front of the fire and poured two glasses of cabernet.

"Where'd you get that?" Kerry was astonished at the appearance of the wine because she hadn't known there was any.

Sam's eyes twinkled. "Doug and I had a secret cache. I'd almost forgotten about it. Sit down. I've opened a can of fruit salad."

The wine posed a dilemma because she didn't drink alcoholic beverages now that she was pregnant, but Sam seemed so pleased with it that she didn't say anything. While Sam went into the kitchen, she lowered herself to the floor and arranged two of the cushions against the couch.

"And," he announced with a flourish when he returned,

"here's a napkin. Sorry it's only a paper towel. They're all I could find."

"You did well to find these," Kerry told him.

"I almost forgot this." He flicked on the small tape player that Kerry recognized as being from the lodge. The soft mellow sounds of Johnny Mathis filled the air, too loud until Sam adjusted the volume. Kerry had always wanted to play that tape, but Doug hated Johnny Mathis and wouldn't hear of it. That was good because the songs held no prior association for her.

Sam settled himself beside her and dug into the chili. "I thought we might as well pamper ourselves as much as we could, since our meals for the next few days are not likely to be elaborate."

"We have enough food to last several days."

"It should be plenty. Remember, we'll stop along the way, and there will probably be food supplies in the cabins where we'll stay."

"And if there isn't?"

"I know how to survive in the wilderness," Sam said with quiet confidence.

She didn't doubt him. She was on the verge of telling him so when he noticed that her wineglass was still full.

"You haven't drunk any of your wine."

"I'm not in the mood for it," she said, hoping this would suffice as an explanation.

He took it in stride. "Okay, that's cool." He paused. "Let's talk about tomorrow."

"Sure, I'd like to know the plan."

"We'll get a good night's sleep, leave early in the morning," he said. "Is that okay with you?"

"It's fine." It occurred to her in that moment that she was trusting him with her life.

"We'll follow the river, then head overland. Doug and

I hiked to the fishing camp many times, and I figure you and I should be able to make it before nightfall.'' He shot her an unfathomable look. ''You're not worried, are you?''

She hesitated. ''Not now.''

''That isn't what you were going to say.'' His voice was low, certain.

She plunged ahead. ''I could never be more worried than I've already been today. I was so worried, Sam. I was afraid you wouldn't come back.'' She couldn't help it, her bottom lip started to tremble. She set the chili aside, her eyes suddenly blinded by a sheen of tears.

She would have risen and fled to the kitchen on some pretext, but Sam lowered his wineglass to the hearth and said in a low tone, ''Kerry, I was afraid, too, afraid that if something happened to me you'd be here all by yourself.''

''Not exactly,'' she said wryly, blinking away the tears. ''I had a bear for company.''

Sam chuckled under his breath. ''You handled the situation well. I don't know too many *cheechakos* who would have shown your presence of mind with a bear breathing down their necks.''

For some reason, this brought back the tears. This time when she tried to blink them away, one slid down her cheek. Oh God, one of the unaccustomed things about her pregnancy was her roller-coaster emotions. *Up, down, all around, the higher they go, the harder they fall.* No, that wasn't it...what was she thinking?

She was thinking that she wanted Sam's arms around her, his voice comforting her, his breath warm against her forehead.

And then his arms *were* around her.

''Kerry, it's okay, you can cry if you want to,'' he said close to her ear. And though crying had been the farthest thing from her mind only seconds before, she found that she was sobbing against his broad chest, clutching at his shirtfront and reveling at the way his lips moved against her hair.

She didn't know how long she cried, only that it was a catharsis and that Sam was kind, patient and sweet. She cried for Doug, for Sam, for all she'd been through and for their present predicament. She cried for her baby who would never know its father, for herself because she was so distraught, and for the fact that she liked being distraught if it meant that Sam would go on holding her.

"Shh," Sam said close beside her ear. But she didn't *shh,* she only quieted down a little. She became aware that Sam was rocking her and that it was soothing, and she reached up and touched his face. It was wet with her tears.

When she stopped crying, Sam was smoothing her hair. She wouldn't have guessed that Sam had a streak of tenderness. Nothing in his personality had ever given her a clue.

She pulled slightly apart from him. "Oh, Sam, I'm so embarrassed. You'll think I've lost it. Gone slightly nuts. Have I?"

He smiled down at her. "Nope. You deserved to get it all out of your system. Whatever 'it' was."

She laughed shakily. "Oh, um, you wouldn't believe it," she said, thinking that it would be such a relief to get back to civilization if only so that she could reveal her pregnancy to Sam.

"Try me," he said, his face inching closer so that her heart caught, released, started skipping beats.

"I—I—" she said, stammering as she tried to think of something to say, but he wasn't listening anyway. Slowly he lowered his head, bringing his lips to hers. He brushed them lightly, softly, a whisper of a kiss that made every muscle in her body slack with desire.

"Kerry," he murmured, "don't pull away."

She didn't resist. She couldn't. His lips skimmed seductively over hers, caught, nipped. "You taste so good," he breathed, and she started to protest. But then his lips, tasting like wine, found hers again, and the kiss deepened. She felt his tongue and resisted at first, knowing that she should stop this and feeling powerless to do so. She couldn't think, she couldn't reason, all she could do was feel. And feel she did—his lips drawing her into a warm vortex where time and place did not exist, his hands sliding up her back and tangling in her hair, his heartbeat synchronizing with hers.

And all of it was defined by the feelings of utter longing that sprang up somewhere deep within. She tried, really tried to ignore them, but it was impossible with the way he was kissing her, caressing her, pressing her against him as if he would never let her go.

"I've been wanting to do this," he said against her lips, and she realized then that this was what she had wanted, too. But how could she have wanted it? She didn't like him. She'd never liked him.

She certainly liked what he was doing at the moment, however. His hands were cupping her face, his eyes searching hers. "You've been thinking about it too, haven't you?"

She didn't speak, sure that he could read her answer in her eyes.

"Haven't you?" His voice was rough, urgent.

Mutely she nodded, and he closed his eyes for a long moment. He thought about Doug and what good friends they'd been, and he thought about Kerry and the way they'd always been at odds. Something had happened in this cabin, and he couldn't understand what it was. Yes, he had learned to appreciate Kerry, to like her, and even to admire her. And to desire her.

But maybe he needed to think about this more. To turn the whole situation over in his mind before he did something he would regret. He didn't want anything to interfere with their safe journey to Athinopa. He desperately needed Kerry's cooperation tomorrow and for the next couple of days until they were out of danger. He needed her to be strong, fit and able to hike miles and miles through snow.

"Sam," Kerry said, and he looked down at her and melted. She was so beautiful, desirable and sweet, her eyes so dazzling, and her arms were around his neck, her breasts soft against his chest. Just one kiss more, that's all he'd allow himself, with Johnny Mathis singing a wholly appropriate "Chances Are" on the tape.

She lifted her lips to his, and they were moist and slightly parted. He took them, savaged them, captured them. A heat rose in his blood, surged through his veins, pumped through his heart in trip-hammer rhythm. He slid his hands over her breasts, gently, softly, and she moaned low in her throat. The sound was like music to his ears, and in that moment he wanted to touch her in places she'd never been touched, take her places she'd never been.

"Sam, oh, Sam, I don't think this is a good idea."

He had to remind himself that a few minutes ago he hadn't thought so, either. He swallowed, forced himself to focus his eyes on her face.

"You may be right," he said, reluctantly admitting it.

"I—I—" Her eyes were clouded with something he didn't recognize. Doubt? Anguish? And more.

"We'd better get a good night's sleep," he told her, trying as hard as he could to act as if nothing had happened between them.

She seemed to be holding her breath, but then she rose unsteadily to her feet and began to move toward the ladder.

He forced himself to sound normal. "Set the clock for

an hour before sunrise. We'll need that much time to pack up.'' He turned his attention to poking the fire, releasing a drift of bright embers up the flue.

"I'll cook the last of the powdered eggs for breakfast,'' she said. Her tone was flat, and she didn't look at him.

"Good night, Kerry.''

"Oh, by the way, I found the pouch with your flight charts and logbook in it, and I stuck it way down inside your pack if you're looking for it.''

For a moment he didn't understand. Charts? Logbook? Those were already in his pack, safely zipped away in an inside pocket. Then he realized that Kerry must be talking about the pouch containing the papers. She couldn't have looked inside the pouch if she'd thought it contained charts and a logbook.

"'Night, Sam.''

He muttered a reply.

He waited until she was all the way up the ladder before checking his pack. Sure enough, tucked up against the frame next to a clean pair of jeans, was the pouch. The papers inside appeared undisturbed. Sam glanced up at the dark loft where Kerry was quietly preparing for bed.

She hadn't looked. She didn't know. Relief washed over him in a wave that nearly bowled him over. He had to get out of the cabin, had to have time to think what to do next. To wonder why this mattered so much.

"I'm going over to the lodge for a few minutes," he called up to her.

"Why?"

"I have things I need to get for tomorrow. Wire for rabbit snares in case we run out of food. Some other stuff.'' Ammunition. Doug's rifle.

Kerry's answer was indistinguishable, muffled.

Sam felt elated. He'd been given a reprieve. He'd have

another chance. Right now, that seemed like the most important thing in the world.

THE NEXT MORNING Kerry was awake before Sam, bustling around in the kitchen, heating water on the stove, making eggs and heating canned sausages.

She regarded him coolly. "Are you planning to get up anytime today?"

He blinked the sleep from his eyes. "I'm not wearing clothes," he said as apologetically as he could considering that he didn't really think this was anything a person should have to apologize for.

Her mouth rounded into an *O*. "Oh," she said.

"Turn around." She did, and he threw aside the blanket and pulled on a clean pair of long johns from his pack, followed by his jeans. "There," he said.

"Well," she said briskly, "I'm ready to go. Is it time to douse the fires?"

Douse the fires? Oh, yes, he thought that was a jolly good idea, especially the fire she'd lit inside him. But he knew she meant the ones in the fireplace and the cookstove.

He told her that it was and he helped her do it. He remained pensive, quiet, but if Kerry had any trepidations about the trek on which they were about to embark or regrets about leaving Silverthorne, she didn't voice them.

He busied himself strapping his leather knife sheath on his belt while she handled last-minute cleanup chores. She did a double take when she saw the rifle protruding from his pack.

"We might need it," he said.

The implications of this statement were not lost on her, but she made no comment.

She prepared the pack she would carry, Doug's old one,

and hardly spoke at all. He wondered if she was thinking about last night. He certainly was.

Things lightened up a bit when they left the cabin, and he noticed that she didn't lock the door.

"Now that you've learned to adapt to the hospitality requirements of the Country, you're not a *cheechako* anymore," he told her. She grinned back at him, clearly pleased.

They started out along the creek, turning north at the fork. After a few missteps, Kerry began to manage walking on snowshoes well. Sam didn't like to use poles with showshoes, never had. Kerry did, but he was glad to see that she could maneuver them well despite a slight awkwardness due to her broken finger. Sam, breaking trail in front of her, deliberately kept their pace slow in order to conserve Kerry's energy. He had no doubts that he would be able to reach the first overnight stop without any trouble, but he wasn't sure about her.

Fortunately it was a sunny day; only a few high clouds adorned the distant sky on the other side of the mountains. As they penetrated deeper into the bush, they passed whitened moose antlers protruding from the snow. For a while, a band of caribou foraged ahead of them, eventually drifting into a willow thicket alongside the creek. Once an eagle with a seven-foot wingspan soared overhead, catching a thermal that carried it out of sight across the mountains.

"I've always admired eagles," Kerry observed.

"Me, too. They're such beautiful birds. But have you ever heard their cry?"

Kerry shook her head.

"They sound like hysterical chickens."

"You're joking."

"No, I mean it. This is how they sound," and he commenced to cackle like an eagle, which made her laugh.

"Seriously? That's what an eagle sounds like?" Her eyes danced.

"It's true. I once met a movie director who told me they have to splice other birds' cries into the sound tracks because the moviegoing public would never accept the way eagles really sound."

Kerry attempted the eagle's cry, and before long they were laughing together. It felt good to be enjoying each other's company, and the time passed quickly.

They stopped early for a lunch of moose jerky as well as a rest. By this time, snow was melting in places where the sun could reach, and there was no wind. If a wind sprang up, Sam told Kerry, they would be protected because their route, the furrow of an old dog-sled trail, scraped circuitously through a valley; the wind would be cut by the mountains rising on either side.

"I wonder what this trail is like in the summer," Kerry said, stretching her legs out full length and raising her face to the sun.

"It's wonderful. In fact, some of your guests might enjoy hiking up here for the fishing. It'd be a good day trip."

"I'll keep it in mind. I'll need to be able to plan a week's activities for my guests because I hope they'll all choose to stay at least that long. That reminds me—Josiah Crocker only makes his run once a week, and I hope to be able to fly guests in and out so that the ones who can't stay a whole week will be able to come and go according to their schedules. Any chance Harbeck Air would be interested in the route?"

"Sure. We could plan midweek flights or charters, whatever suits."

"We should talk about it, Sam, and come up with a plan. That way I'll be able to include the information in the brochures I'll be sending out this winter."

"We'll sit down and map it out when we get to Anchorage, okay?"

Kerry stood up. "Great, I'll take you up on that. Oh, Sam, finally everything is coming together, and I'm seeing the light at the end of the tunnel. Fixing up the lodge has been more work than I ever imagined." She looked excited and pleased all at the same time.

As they strapped on their packs, Sam thought that he and Kerry were remarkably easy with each other, considering what had happened between them last night. He glanced at her surreptitiously, wondering if she had thought about it or if she'd put it out of her mind. He couldn't. He couldn't stop thinking about the way she had looked up at him, mouth parted, eyes sultry. And his heart—but he didn't want his heart to play any part in this.

They stopped more frequently in the afternoon, and he couldn't help but notice that Kerry needed lots of rest breaks. She'd loosen her pack, drop it on a rock or a log, and disappear into the woods long enough to take care of what she had called "certain needs" when they were back at the cabin. He made no comment even though this slowed them down.

To Kerry's credit, she managed to keep up with him, her energy flagging only in midafternoon. When he noticed, he made sure that they stopped for a short break. At Kerry's insistence, they set out again after only a few minutes, re-energized by handfuls of the dried fruit-and-nut mixture called gorp.

"It's getting late," Kerry said as encroaching shadows began to define the spaces between the mountains on either side of them; it was four-thirty, the time when light began to fade. "Are we almost at the place where we're going to stop?"

"Just over the next ridge," he told her. "Tired?"

"No way" was all she said, and he knew that even if she were, Kerry would never admit it.

Halfway up the ridge, she fell, rolling over a few heart-stopping times until she came to rest against a large boulder. Her poles landed out of reach below her. In those moments, time seemed to still, and everything switched into slow motion. All he could see was Kerry, her legs akimbo, snowshoes in danger of tangling with each other, and all he could think of was that she might break an arm or a leg. He rushed forward, terrified that she might have injured herself.

"Are you hurt?" he shouted before he even reached her. She surprised him by sitting up immediately, laughing.

"I'm so well padded by my parka and thick clothes that all I did was go with the flow," she said.

He gave her a hand up and retrieved her poles for her, and she brushed herself off and fell in behind him to resume their upward passage.

Sam was glad that he was walking ahead of her so that she couldn't see how shaken he was. The sight of her rolling over and over in the snow had brought his heart to his throat, and his reaction to the mishap rammed home to him how much her well-being meant to him.

When they topped the ridge and she first saw the primitive shelter where he had planned for them to stay, Kerry looked dismayed. "I thought it was a real cabin," she said, sounding disappointed.

The hut, surrounded by brambles, was only about eight by ten feet in size and leaned precipitously sideways toward the nearby creek. The metal roof that gleamed so dully through its mantle of crusted snow appeared to be composed of flattened gasoline cans. There was one window, grimed with smoke and grease, but no kitchen, no fireplace and no sanitary facilities.

"It's shelter," he said stoically. "And we're desperate."

Kerry said nothing, but traipsed doggedly down the incline behind him and waited apprehensively while he creaked the sagging door open. He wished he had thought to warn her earlier about this place; it simply hadn't occurred to him. Now he affected an old codger's accent and said, "It sure ain't much, Miss Kerry, but we call it home," which elicited something like a smile from her. When he motioned for her to follow him inside, she did, but she wrinkled her nose at the beaten-earth floor. "Smells musty in here" was all she said.

He took a whiff. "Smells like moose," he told her.

In almost no time they had a fire going in the barrel stove, which like many Alaskan heating stoves was nothing more than a modified oil drum with a flue leading out one of the walls, and since the stove took up much of the hut's interior, it warmed the place considerably. They unpacked some of their gear, changed to dry socks, and soon the odor of wet wool replaced that of moose.

For supper, they perched on the wooden shelf that was slung low on the wall and served as a bunk. They ate a couple of cans of hash and a handful each of dried apples, a meal that they both found satisfying enough. Afterward they played a desultory game of cards by the light of a candle, losing interest before anyone won. Kerry was yawning widely by the time Sam had bundled the cards into a rubber band and replaced them in his pack.

"I'll sleep on the floor," he told her when he saw that she seemed unsure about what to do next. "You can spread your sleeping bag on the bunk."

She unrolled her sleeping bag, but appeared hesitant. "Maybe we should toss a coin and see who gets the bunk. Although I think the floor might not be as hard."

"Well, take your choice."

"The bunk, I guess. Fewer creepy crawly creatures there, maybe."

He cleared his throat. "Kerry," he said. He didn't know how he would summon the delicacy to say what needed to be said, but he had to say it.

"Hmm?" She unzipped the sleeping bag, bending over it so that her jeans outlined the neat curve of her hips.

"When you need to go outside, I'd better go with you. I don't want you to meet up with any of our less unsavory wildlife." He didn't mention bears although they were a possibility, and so were wolves.

She sat down on top of the sleeping bag and drew her feet up until she was sitting cross-legged, her face illumined by the single candle they were using for light. Her eyes were bright and they seemed enormous.

"I might have to get up more than once during the night to go outside," she said haltingly. "I mean, it happens."

Sam spread an insulating pad on the floor and arranged his sleeping bag on top of it. "You'll have to wake me up. Every time."

She made a little gesture of futility. "I'm sure I'll be fine if I have to go out by myself," she said all in a rush. "I won't have to wake you. In fact—"

He stopped what he was doing and eyed her with what he hoped was an implacable expression. "Wake me up, Kerry. Every time you have to go out."

She gazed up at him, and he sensed a desperation behind her eyes. "Sam—"

"Don't argue. Now let's you and me catch some z's."

She drew in a long breath. He happened to notice—and he didn't know why he noticed—that she'd clasped her hands so tightly that her knuckles had turned white.

Something inside him turned over and then stilled into a moment of calm. Somehow he knew that what she was about to say was of great import. He didn't know how he knew, but he did. And it was clear that Kerry was having a hard time saying it, whatever it was.

She twisted her fingers together, then looked at him, her eyes searching his face. "There's something you need to know, Sam." She looked him straight in the eye.

He lifted his brows, a question mark.

"I'm pregnant, Sam. Almost four months."

Chapter Eight

He tried to force air into his lungs. He couldn't breathe. Her words hit him hard in his gut, sinking in with all the force of a two-fisted punch. He stared at her, his mouth hanging open, unable to speak.

All kinds of thoughts jangled through his mind. She couldn't be pregnant. Kerry couldn't *get* pregnant. But her infertility hadn't been due to any deficiency on her part. It was because Doug had a problem.

"Anomalies of the sperm," Doug had told him. So this baby, the one Kerry said she was going to have, must be someone else's baby. Not Doug's at all. But Sam knew that Kerry hadn't been with anyone else since Doug died, and he was as sure of that as he was of his own name.

Kerry couldn't be pregnant. That was all there was to it. Unless—

Oblivious to his shock, Kerry kept talking. "That's why it's so important to me to have Silverthorne in operation by next summer. With the baby coming, I'll need the money. And running the lodge is good wholesome work, Sam, and I won't have to worry about day care for the baby because I'll be able to keep it with me at the lodge. So I stayed on at the cabin longer than I should have and now I wish I hadn't. And I don't want to slow us down."

Still in shock, Sam sank down on the bunk beside her. "You're going to have a baby. Why didn't you tell me before?"

She took her time answering. "I want to pull my weight. I don't want you to make exceptions for me just because I'm pregnant. I've been feeling pretty good for the past day or so, I'm sure I'll be able to hike the whole distance to Athinopa." She gazed at him, anxiety apparent in the furrow between her eyes.

"You should have mentioned the baby. I never would have let you come with me if I'd known. This can't be good for you, Kerry. Or for the—the child."

Her chin shot up in a familiar gesture of defiance that he knew all too well. "I'm used to walking a lot and I'm in good physical condition. I get a little more tired than usual because of the pregnancy, but that's not so serious. The morning sickness hasn't been too bad for the past couple of days. Yesterday and today I didn't feel any."

He passed a weary hand across his face. "Morning sickness, a little more tired than usual—we shouldn't have tried to hike out, Kerry. I shouldn't be putting you through this." Now he knew why her jeans had looked so tight. They *were* tight. She was pregnant.

She slid around to face him, her eyes imploring. "I knew if I told you before we left that you'd make me stay in the cabin at Silverthorne by myself. I didn't want to be alone there, not after the bear. And I know it's safer for you if you have someone with you. It's not a good idea to go traipsing around this wilderness by yourself."

"So you made the decision without consulting me." He was beginning to be angry now, really angry.

"Sam," she said, but he didn't want to talk to her anymore. He stood up abruptly, his mind whirling with what he knew. Things he couldn't tell her. Things he might never tell her.

He stared down at her for a moment that stretched into eternity. Her eyes were wide, almost all pupil, and her cheeks were bright with two spots of color, and her hair gleamed in the candlelight. She was so beautiful that his heart rose in his throat, and he wanted to gather her into his arms and hold her tightly, to smooth her hair, kiss her eyelids and trace her mouth with his fingertips.

But he couldn't. He was still too flattened by her revelation. He needed to think and he couldn't do that with her so close by.

So without a word, he hauled on his parka, clenched his fists and slammed out of the little hut.

SHE WISHED she hadn't told him. She'd only made things worse.

Kerry huddled miserably in her sleeping bag on the hard bunk and waited for Sam to return. The candle burned to a stump, flickered and went out. She stared into the dark, listening. She thought she heard a wolf howl in the distance.

Suddenly every sound seemed magnified—the protest of the boards beneath her sleeping bag, the crackle and snap of the wood burning in the stove, the creak of the metal stovepipe as it expanded with the heat. She wondered why, as tired as she was, she couldn't stop thinking about Sam and go to sleep. She wished she could forget how he'd looked when she'd told him the news.

What was keeping him?

Oh sure, he'd been baffled. She had read it in his eyes, his consternation, his shock and something else—pain? Worry? She couldn't exactly blame Sam for feeling any or all of those things, the sum of which added up to something more. But what? They'd been getting along so well, and she'd thought it would be okay to tell him, and it hadn't been. Considering his reaction, it was probably the last thing she should have done.

Now she needed to make an urgent trip outside. And Sam had been firm about wanting to stand guard when she did. But Sam wasn't around, and she couldn't wait. She'd go out without him whether he liked it or not.

She slipped out of her sleeping bag, pulled on her boots and parka, and opened the door. The night was nippy, but unbelievably clear; the stars above seemed hugely magnified. She had no trouble picking her way into the woods. She saw no sign of Sam. Maybe he had gone down to the stream. Maybe he was so angry he wouldn't be back until much later.

When she arrived back in the clearing where the hut hunkered low against its skirt of brambles, she heard a rustle. Startled, she wheeled around. It was Sam.

She could only see him in outline, but the sight of him unnerved her nonetheless. He said, "Kerry. I told you to let me know if you had to go out."

She pulled herself together. "You weren't around."

"You knew I wouldn't be far away."

"I knew no such thing." She began to pick her way across the clearing. She'd convinced herself that last night's tenderness, the kisses and caresses, had been a fluke, a mistake. And nothing had happened today to make her think that he wanted to expand upon the kisses they'd shared last night. On their last night in the cabin at Silverthorne, their last night of relative safety, they'd been two lonely people, and she'd been scared, and Sam had comforted her. That's all there was to it.

But now Kerry didn't want to look at him. She didn't want to talk to him. She didn't even want to touch him.

Evidently he felt differently. He stepped into her path, blocking her way. And then his arms were around her and his head was against the top of hers, a warm hug that she felt from the top of her head all the way to the tip of her toes. It wasn't sexual, that hug. And yet it wasn't entirely platonic.

"I'm sorry," Sam said. His lips and breath were warm against her temple. "Really sorry."

This fervent apology, offered for no apparent reason, made her snap to attention. She repositioned herself so she could look up into his brooding eyes. "I want this baby. Doug and I wanted it."

She expected him to acknowledge that this was true, to accede the validity of her statement. But his eyes were deep, sorrowful. She had the idea that he just didn't understand. Well, what had she expected? This was Sam, Sam Harbeck. Understanding was not his strong suit. He was looking at her with—what? Was it pity? Or was it something else?

She didn't know what else to say. Even though she thought she knew where he was coming from, she remained nonplused that he wasn't happy for her. People were always happy about babies. And this one was going to be such a blessing. She inhaled a steadying breath of the frosty air.

"Look," Sam said suddenly. His face was turned toward the sky.

It was the aurora borealis, the northern lights, and they were arrayed across the sky in all their glory. Kerry had seen them before, but never had they been so lively, the multicolored streamers seeming to dance on the wind.

"Sometimes I think I can hear them, out in the bush. They crackle."

"Let's listen," she breathed, but all they heard was the gentle soughing of the breeze in the trees.

"So beautiful," Kerry said, and Sam said, "Yes." But when she glanced at him, she knew he wasn't talking about the northern lights.

"I think we'd better go inside where it's warm" was all she said.

Inside the hut the air was damp with evaporated moisture from their drying socks and coats. Sam didn't bother to light a candle, but proceeded to pull off his boots and his coat in the dark. She did, too. Then they each crawled into their separate sleeping bags.

She didn't know how long Sam lay awake, but exhaustion finally caught up with her and she fell into a deep and profound sleep.

KERRY WOKE in darkness to see Sam silhouetted against the window in the starlight.

"Sam?" She elbowed herself to a sitting position. "What are you doing up?"

"I heard something."

"Like what?"

"A noise. A wolf howl." He turned, and she couldn't see his face. She couldn't see anything about him except his shape.

"I thought I heard one earlier."

"Well, there's no sign of any wolves now." His tone was brusque.

"What time is it?"

"Around midnight." He opened the door of the stove and shoved in a piece of wood. "That should keep us until dawn." The small square of flame lit his face. Kerry thought he looked sad, unsettled. The corners of his mouth were drawn down, and for the first time since she'd known him, he'd lost that jaunty devil-may-care quality.

After he'd slammed the stove door, Kerry pulled the

sleeping bag up and around her shoulders. "I'm wide awake," she said.

Sam eased himself down onto his sleeping bag and plumped his parka into a pillow. "So am I."

They didn't speak for several minutes, just listened to each other's breathing. All she could see of Sam was his dark silhouette against the small window. He didn't lie down.

Kerry didn't get any sleepier. If anything, she felt more wide awake.

"Sam?"

"What?"

"I know you're angry with me."

Sam let out his breath in a giant sigh. "I'm not angry with you," he said quietly.

"I wish you could be happy for me."

Happy for her? Sam said nothing. A knot of guilt wrapped itself around his gut, and that was all he could feel at the moment.

"Did Doug ever talk to you about our problems? About the fact that we couldn't have a baby?"

This put him on the spot, but he decided that there wasn't anything he could do but be truthful. "He told me," he said.

"I wanted children—we both did—more than anything in the world."

"Well, looks like you're getting your wish," Sam said gruffly.

"We had already made arrangements with a fertility center. I was going there to be inseminated in the next couple of weeks when Doug—when his plane crashed. Naturally I had a lot of second thoughts in the months after he died, but I decided to go ahead with the insemination four months ago. I think that's what Doug would have wanted."

Sam rubbed his eyes with the thumb and forefinger of one hand. In his present crisis of conscience, he had no idea how to reply to this.

"Don't you think so, too, Sam? Don't you think I'm doing the right thing?"

In that moment all Sam could think about was Doug's relief when he, Sam, had volunteered to be the donor. And how happy Doug had been that Kerry would get her baby. And how they'd made a vow of silence never to reveal to her that Sam was the true father of the child. "I'm sure Doug would approve," Sam said. It was the best way to answer such a loaded question. He wasn't sure Kerry had done the right thing, but he couldn't tell her that because then she'd demand to know why. And now that there actually was a baby, now that the destruction of that vial of his sperm was no longer relevant, his lips must remain sealed out of loyalty to his best friend and the vow that they had made never to reveal to Kerry the child's true parenthood.

"I hope you'll eventually be glad that I'm happy," Kerry said in such a lost voice that Sam stood up and walked back to the window. He couldn't look at her.

But he couldn't *not* look at her. The hut was so small that he couldn't help seeing her out of the corners of his eyes, and he noticed the way her hair fell softly to her shoulders, the way the sleeping bag was pulled up to her neck and the determined set of her chin. And more than that, the sweet curve of her jawline, the winging of her brows. The parting of her lips.

It was getting too warm in here by far. He shouldn't have put that last log on. It was heating the hut into an oven, and maybe he'd better go open the door, let fresh air in for a few minutes until the temperature normalized.

Kerry must have thought the same thing because she was

shaking her shoulders free of the folds of the sleeping bag, exposing her shoulders and her breasts, but she had on clothes, red thermal underwear that molded to her slight frame and left little to the imagination. He turned to go to the door, but as he did, she slid fluidly out of the sleeping bag and came to stand beside him at the window.

He took in the gentle rounding of her belly, her swollen breasts, the slope of her shoulders, her long, long legs. The top of her underwear had a deep V neck, and he thought about how good it would feel to bury his face in the hollow between her breasts.

He turned, thinking to go to open the door, but in the process he brushed up against her and her arm slid up and around his neck. He couldn't believe it; he hadn't expected this. He caught his breath, not daring to believe this was really happening and afraid to hope.

"Hold me, Sam," she whispered. "Just for a minute."

He caught her other hand, the one that no longer wore Doug's ring, and placed it against his chest. His heart speeded up, and her hand rested there for a moment before it slid upward to join her other one. In that moment Sam knew that he no longer considered her Doug's wife. By now, Kerry was the mother of his child, *his* child! And that made everything different—every look, every nuance, every wish he'd entertained since he first laid eyes on her.

The tender and passionate feelings he felt for her in that moment sprang from the bottom of his soul. He closed his eyes, certain that she could read these things in their depths and not at all sure that he wanted her to. He gathered her close, reveling in the smoothness of her cheek, the warmth of her body against his. She was going to have his baby. That made her all the more precious to him.

Kerry had never been overtly seductive, but she was so sensual and so devastatingly beautiful that he couldn't have helped desiring her from the very first night he had spent in the cabin with her. All this time he had been wanting, waiting, and he didn't want to wait any longer. He wanted her with all the pent-up longing a man could feel. He wanted to kiss her breasts, her hair and her eyelids. He wanted to lie beside her in the cold dark night and warm her with his body. With his heart.

He slid his hands down to her buttocks and ground her tight against him, so tight that she uttered a little gasp. He released her immediately. "I didn't mean to hurt you," he said.

But, surprising him, she only laughed low in her throat. "It didn't hurt. I'm strong as an ox, Sam. You should know that by now."

He should, but he didn't. Her bones beneath his fingertips felt so fragile and delicate. He explored them, moving his fingers down her vertebrae one by one, along her arms to the elbows, then back up again and under her arms to her ribs, then down to her hipbones. He avoided the area where the baby was. He was reluctant to touch her there because he thought it might hurt, but she seemed to sense his curiosity and cupped one of his hands over her abdomen.

"That's what it feels like," she said softly. "Not too scary, is it?"

He shook his head, speechless because he knew that beneath the palm of his hand, floating in its own special world, was a major miracle, his child.

She smiled at him tremulously, her eyes shadowy so he couldn't read their expression, but somehow he knew what they were saying and he replied in the best way he knew, which was to crush her mouth beneath his, her luscious mouth, exploring her in excruciatingly passionate detail— tongue, teeth, lips, all of it. And when he had finished, although he thought he would never be finished, must return to drink of her kisses again and again, he drifted his mouth downward to her neck and twined his hands in her bountiful hair, his lips exploring the cool hollow of her throat, the shadow between her breasts.

His hands slid under her long-sleeved knit underwear. She wasn't wearing a bra, and his hands molded to her breasts as if made to fit. The nipples puckered at his touch, were hard against his fingers. He was surprised, but then not surprised, when she pulled the top up and over her head in one swift motion and tossed it on the bunk. She tugged at his shirt. "Now you," she said.

Moments later he was glad that he hadn't opened the door after all, because the temperature in the hut was toasty warm and comfortable for two people who stood before each other wearing nothing, absolutely nothing at all.

Kerry felt suddenly self-conscious and shy. She'd wanted this to happen, and now, paradoxically, she was apprehensive. She wasn't sure whether her desire was born of loneliness, desperation or a need for reassurance. And maybe it was something else, an unexpected thread of emotion that curled up from somewhere deep inside her.

She studied the dark whorls of hair on his chest, refusing to lock her eyes with his in those long moments when she thought that this might be a terrible mistake. He curved his hand to her waist, urged her toward him, and she thought that of all the ways she had come to know Sam Harbeck in the past few days, this was the most momentous. And then she couldn't think at all.

He held her carefully at first, like he might hold a carton of eggs, but she nestled up against him and said, "I won't break, Sam."

He chuckled into her hair, and it was an exultant sound, and it made her feel happy. Happy that they were doing this. Happy to be with Sam.

He kissed her then, nothing restrained about it, and his hands cupped her breasts and played across her nipples until she thought she'd go mad with the wanting of him. Her own hands strayed downward, down, down, until she touched the nest of curls there, and he was ready for her, all ready, but she thought she needed more time.

"Over here," she whispered, and she led him to the bunk where her sleeping bag cushioned the narrow ledge, and she pulled him down on top of her. His weight was welcome, hard, and he kept kissing her, and she kissed him back, and he kissed her up the slope of her jawline to her ear, leaving a damp trail, and she hid her face in his neck and wanted to say his name over and over, but didn't.

After spending the past few days together, the smell of him was achingly familiar, and so was the shape of him even though she had never explored it with her hands before. Now she did, as much as they could when she was pressed up against the wall that was so cold against her back.

He began to move against her, slowly at first, carefully supporting himself above her so she wouldn't be hurt. There was no question of lying side by side or any other way except one on top of the other, and with Sam on top she was so comfortable, felt so overwhelmed by him that she had no thought of wanting it to be any other way. Her hands skimmed his back, the muscles tensing there, and the ones lower. He levered above her, his face working with emotion, and said, "Am I hurting you?"

She shook her head, pulled him fiercely down upon her, guided him into her softness. He murmured indistinctly against her hair, and she gasped at the utter strangeness of him inside her, and then they found a rhythm and silently pursued it. It was so quiet, so still, that the sound of their own breathing seemed magnified, so much so that soon there was only sensation and their breathing, each one containing the other. And because the bunk confined them so closely, Kerry couldn't tell where Sam began and she ended. And then passion took over, became paramount, and she gasped against his cheek, saying his name over and over until it became her breathing, her pulse, her everything.

When it was over, when their breathing had slowed to normal, Sam sat up and pulled the edge of the sleeping bag over her. He wove a strand of her hair between his thumb and forefinger, smoothing it, and then he let that one go and did the same thing with another one. "You are very beautiful, Kerry," he said.

She smiled at him, replete. "I'm glad you think so," she said.

He looked as if he might want to say something else, but he didn't. He leaned down and kissed her lightly on the cheek. "Time to go to sleep," he said. "We have another long walk facing us tomorrow."

She didn't want to think about that now. She didn't answer. She didn't want to be apart from him on this night. She wanted to sleep safely enfolded in his strong arms.

He stood up and went back to his sleeping bag, scuffed his fallen clothes out of the way.

"Wait, Sam, I'm coming along," she said, and then she got up and dragged her own sleeping bag down to the floor.

"Wouldn't you be more comfortable on the bunk?" Sam said, wrinkling his forehead at her in that utterly charming way of his.

"Not on your life," Kerry said firmly. "Help me zip these bags together." The bags, once connected, made a snug nest on the floor.

"Well, I didn't suspect that one of those creepy-crawlies

on the floor that you referred to earlier would be me,'' Sam said as they both climbed inside.

She laughed and snuggled close. Sam wrapped his arms around her, tucked her face against his shoulder, and the last thought she had before falling asleep was, *This feels so right.*

RIGHT OR WRONG? was what Sam thought as soon as he woke in the morning.

He was a believer in situational ethics. That is, he preferred to let the situation dictate morality. Oh, there were certain absolutes—stealing was always wrong, and kindness was always right. But the gray areas in between could be handled in whatever way seemed appropriate at the time. However, in all his life, Sam Harbeck had never slammed up against a situation remotely like this one. Nor had anyone else he'd ever known.

He gazed down at Kerry, her body curved to fit his, her hair rioting across his chest. She had been so passionate last night. So loving. So—needy? No, he wasn't sure that would be the word. This was an independent woman, but at the same time she wasn't afraid to show her vulnerability. For him, that made the utmost difference. He'd never come across a woman who was strong enough to let him see who she really was in her most defenseless moments.

The morning's light looked gloomy and gray. He woke Kerry with a kiss, and she opened her eyes and smiled at him. Her smile was like sunshine on such a dreary day.

He boosted himself out of the sleeping bag first and went to the window. A low-lying cloud cover brushed the top of the trees.

"How does the weather look?" Kerry wanted to know. She reached for her long underwear and pulled on first the bottom, then the top, staying inside the sleeping bag where it was warm.

"It doesn't look good." He glanced back at her. He liked the way she looked with tousled hair.

"Then we'd better start right away." She scrambled out of the sleeping bag.

"Maybe we should stay here. I'll go out and take a look around, bring back some water from the creek to heat for washing."

"Good. I'll use yesterday's water to start breakfast." She was already tearing the tops off packets of oatmeal.

Sam donned jeans, a T-shirt and a heavy wool shirt. He kept sending covert glances in Kerry's direction, studying the way she looked in that red underwear. She had a great figure, and you could hardly detect the bulge in front. Last night during their lovemaking he hadn't thought about it at all. She was a woman who left no room for thought. With her, it was just feelings—mental, physical and emotional.

He cleared his throat. "Kerry, about last night. It was—"

"An exception," she said briskly. "Don't worry. It won't happen again."

That wasn't what he had started to say. His word of choice would have been *wonderful.*

He felt surprised, flattened, hurt by this dismissal. He spared her a curt nod. Then he went out into the cold damp morning.

As soon as Sam left, Kerry sank down on the hard un-padded boards of the bunk and buried her face in her hands. If Sam had said anything negative about last night, she didn't think she could have borne it, and that was why she hadn't given him a chance. She'd spoken first. She'd wanted to let him believe that their lovemaking had been no big deal. She wanted him to think of her as a sophisticated woman of the world who could take his attentions in stride. Sam had told her about the women who had tried to make a claim on him where none existed, and the last thing she wanted was for him to think she was like them.

Sam couldn't possibly know that her experience in matters of love and sex had been confined to only one other man—Doug, her late husband. He was the only man she'd ever cared about, the only man she'd ever known in an intimate way.

But last night had been exceptional. Sam was an attentive lover, careful to make sure that she found pleasure in the act. He was strong, tender, caring and—well, he was perfect. And she didn't want him to be perfect. She needed Sam Harbeck to be the kind of man she could walk away from once this experience was over. She needed the kind of man who could be there for her now and who would leave her alone later.

Alone to have her baby.

She dressed quickly, went to the window and gazed out toward the creek. She saw the bright blue of Sam's parka through the trees and she wished he'd come back. Soon she would need to go out and she'd promised him last night that she'd never go without him, and the whole thing was so embarrassing, but there was nothing she could do about it.

He came back in carrying a bucket of water, which he placed atop the stove. While the water heated, she went outside and tended to business while Sam stood on the other side of a brush pile and rocked back and forth on his heels. As embarrassing as this procedure was, at least he didn't make any comments.

When they went back in the hut, Sam washed first, shaving quickly. They didn't talk much. While Kerry combed and bundled her hair into a scrunchy, Sam dealt a game of solitaire, not paying a whole lot of attention to her, and she was glad because she felt as if his presence while she bathed and smoothed her hair into submission was an invasion of privacy. Then she snickered out loud at the thought—how could she be embarrassed in front of Sam after last night?

"What's so funny?" Sam wanted to know.

She told him, and he made a noise that didn't communicate anything more than acknowledgment. She was at a loss to deal with the kind of tense watchfulness that seemed to direct what he said and did this morning. She wanted things to be like they were before, but last night had apparently made it impossible. All right, so she shouldn't have slept with him. She'd known it might not be a good idea. Was she sorry? No, not at all. But it wouldn't happen again.

They ate oatmeal with raisins and drank the coffee that Sam had brewed woodsman-style. Then, grateful because the sky cover seemed to lift, they struck out on the trail again, Kerry dutifully following close behind Sam. Their conversation was stilted now, and neither of them mentioned her pregnancy. Kerry found herself longing to talk about it, about the baby and her plans for it, but one look at Sam's mouth riveted into a tight line made her think better of it. As the day progressed, she was glad not to feel any pressure to converse because she knew silence would conserve energy, and she would need it. Today's trek was slightly longer than the one the day before.

They passed through an old ghost town, the remains of two log cabins and the sites of several other cabins, now torn down because their lumber was a coveted item in this land where such things had to be freighted in at great expense.

"This was a thriving place back in the old gold-rush

days,'' Sam said. Kerry found it hard to imagine even though the old concrete vault, once surrounded by a bank building, still stood. They stopped and ate lunch shortly after leaving the ghost town behind, shivering in the cold and eager to be on their way again.

It was getting on into the afternoon, around two o'clock or so, when they heard a faraway whine. High in the sky they spotted a blue-and-white speck floating toward them. They exchanged a look of incredulity and then hope as the whine became the drone of an engine and the speck became a plane. They couldn't believe it could really be a plane; the old dog-sled trail was not located below any established flight path.

"We'd better hurry to the top of that ridge!" Sam shouted, and they began to traverse the rise. Kerry lagged behind, but Sam was there as the plane passed slightly to the north and he started waving his arms and shouting.

"Damn Vic Parnell, he should have kept emergency flares in his plane," Sam said as Kerry reached him.

Kerry jumped up and down and waved, too, and Sam used the mirror in his survival kit, hoping that its reflection would catch the pilot's eye. But as they watched in dismay, the plane circled slowly and gained altitude without any answering waggle of wings.

Kerry, worn out from her mad dash up the ridge, sank to the ground. "Do you think they were specifically searching for us?"

"I couldn't read the identification number—the sun was glaring on it. But that sure wasn't a Search-and-Rescue plane. It wasn't a plane from Harbeck Air, either. I don't know if the pilot was looking for us. Probably not. No one knows we're out here."

Sam looked almost as disappointed as she felt. Impassively she handed him a bag of gorp, and they each ate several handfuls for energy before resuming their hike.

"How much farther is it?" she asked after a while.

"See those trees down there?" Her gaze followed the line of his forefinger, and she nodded. "The cabin where we're going to stay is on the other side."

It wasn't so far. And suddenly she couldn't wait to be there, to be warm and snug inside. "Race you down the hill," she hollered, and she would have done it, too, except that Sam grabbed her arm and insisted on a more sedate pace.

He dropped her arm as soon as she agreed not to race, but Kerry felt a sharp pang of regret as his hand fell away. She wished he hadn't let go. It was the first time he had touched her all day.

Chapter Nine

The only available bed in their new lodgings was a double bed. They both saw it as soon as they entered the door; it was the biggest piece of furniture in the sparsely furnished cabin. After the first glance, they both self-consciously avoided looking at the bed as if to do so would bring up the subject of where they were going to sleep. Neither of them felt ready to tackle that, at least for the time being.

Aside from there being only one bed, the accommodation was excellent, and the owners had extended hospitality in absentia, as Alaskans were wont to do for strangers. Kerry found a penciled note on the brightly painted table in the middle of the cabin.

Use what you need and leave the cabin as you found it.

"Who owns this place?" she wanted to know.

Sam heaved his pack off and onto the floor. "A couple named Stanchik. They live in Fairbanks, come here once a year. Both husband and wife like to hunt moose."

"Do you know them?"

"No, but it's okay. I'll have some food delivered to replace what we use."

At least this cabin was clean. It was built of yellow cedar logs, pleasingly fragrant, and the owners had left an ample supply of split cedar kindling. Sam started a fire, and soon the cabin was warm.

They ate well that night. They found frozen moose meat in the outside cache, which was built up high on sturdy legs to protect it from predators, and they thawed moose steaks hastily over the fire in the cook stove, which was the sole way of heating the cabin. Sam cooked, and they ate the steaks with rice from the Stanchiks' store.

Afterward they played cards again, another lackadaisical game. The cabin never heated up, and Kerry wrapped her down sleeping bag around her legs to keep them warm. As the game wore on, it was apparent that they were avoiding looking at each other. The bed sat unmade in the corner, a silent sentinel to their denial of its presence. Finally, when the tension had grown so thick that Sam could have cut it with a slash of his hunting knife, he slapped his cards down on the table and stood up.

"Look, Kerry, I know what you're thinking."

She gathered up the cards, straightened and stacked them. She pretended she didn't understand. "Oh?"

"We don't have to sleep in that bed." He gestured with his head toward the offending piece of furniture.

"No, of course not," she replied.

He stalked to the table, leaned forward on his fists. "But I want to."

"Sam—"

He straightened. Agitated, she stood up and faced him over the expanse of the table.

"Sam, it's okay. We can both sleep in the bed. We don't have to—well, do anything we don't both want to do."

He looked deflated. "Of course we don't. Absolutely not."

"In fact, we should simply accept that we need to sleep in it for warmth and forget about it."

"For warmth," he affirmed.

She walked toward the bed. "So why don't we just make up this bed with the sheets we saw in the cupboard and get in it?"

"Good idea." He went to the cupboard and tossed a top and a bottom sheet on the bed, also two pillow cases.

Kerry unfolded the sheets, which smelled slightly musty but not unbearably so. She fluttered the bottom sheet up over the lumpy mattress, and Sam caught the corner of it as it floated past. They busied themselves with making the bed. Kerry leaned across the mattress to tuck in the far corner, and when Sam brushed past her and she felt his hip bump against hers, she lost her balance and fell against the mattress.

Sam made a wild grab in her direction, missed, and she fell against the headboard, whereupon one corner of the bed came separated and the mattress crashed to the floor, taking Kerry with it.

She fought her way out of a welter of sheets to find Sam reaching for her.

"Are you okay? Here, I'll help you up."

She held out her hand, he took it. And as she started to wedge herself upward, a second corner of the bed frame parted and the mattress lurched downward. So did Sam. He landed on top of her.

He knocked the wind out of Kerry.

Almost as soon as the dust settled, Sam was rolling sideways, kicking away the entangling sheets and swearing under his breath. Kerry couldn't speak. She merely looked up at Sam, who was leaning over her, the roughness of his palm against her arm, one leg thrown across one of hers. If she angled her head oh so slightly, it would be in perfect

line for him to kiss her on the lips. Or she could slide a
hand up the rough wool of his sweater to the place where
his collar ended and hook her hand around his neck and
pull him down, down…

"Kerry?"

"I'm okay," she said, which wasn't entirely truthful if
she considered that she wasn't breathing right, her heart
was thumping and all the muscles in her body seemed to
have gone limp.

Something in his eyes, those glacier-blue eyes, shaded
from concerned to intense, and his head cocked slightly,
quizzically. "Are you sure?"

"I—I—" There was something so disarming about
Sam's concern and caring that she could hardly speak. But
she didn't want him to care about her. It was ridiculous to
think he could, anyway.

She struggled to pull herself upright, bracing herself
against Sam on one side and the upraised side of the mattress on the other.

"Not so fast," he said, his eyes burning into her. His
arm snaked around and pulled her close.

"We have to get up," she said.

"Why?"

"Because we have to fix the bed."

"Why do we have to do that?"

"So we can get in it."

"Seems to me we're already in it," Sam said in that
laconic way of his that she'd always found so infuriating.

"You know what I mean, Sam. Now either get up or
help me."

"Oh, I'll help you up in a while. But for now—" and
to her dismay she felt his lips grazing her temple "—we
might as well enjoy this."

This totally unnerved her. "I thought we were going to—no, I mean I thought we weren't going to..."

"Well, we weren't. I'm not so sure how I feel about it now."

This was dangerous. It was dangerous because she didn't want to think about last night and how good it had felt to surrender to the powerful feelings that had so overwhelmed her. She wanted to be angry with him the way she had been in the old days. She wanted to rage at him for tempting her, for making her forget that she was almost a mother. No, she was a mother already. The mother of her child and Doug's, and Sam was an interloper, someone with whom she'd dallied away a cold night during which she'd been miserable and unsure about a lot of things. Not the least of which was Sam himself.

Sam was running his finger down the slope of her neck, nibbling on her earlobe, threading his other hand through her hair. His breath was hot upon her skin, his beard stubble rough upon her cheek. She couldn't think while he did these things.

And then his mouth was on hers, and the bed was still tip-tilted and might thud the rest of the way onto the floor at any moment. But his kisses were so adept, so smooth, silky and altogether delicious. She opened her mouth to his, wanting to taste him, to devour him the way he was devouring her, and she wanted to slide her hands up under his T-shirt against his bare skin. She not only wanted to, she was actually doing it. And she didn't want to stop.

"I thought you were tired," she breathed against his neck, and he laughed low in his throat.

"I was. Not now."

"This is not a comfortable position," she said with as much dignity as she could.

He kissed the tip of her chin. "You might be right about that. But you gotta admit it's warmer this way."

"Sam, let's get up. Help me."

"Ah, Kerry, why can't you enjoy this? Give in to it."

She blinked at him. "It doesn't feel right."

"On the contrary, it feels wonderful."

"Well, not tied in knots like this. Not on a topsy-turvy mattress all tangled up in bedclothes." She pushed him away and managed to sit up. She braced one hand against the bedstead, one hand against Sam's knee, and heaved herself upright. She stood looking at Sam, who was lounging amid the tumbled sheets, smiling up at her with that old impudent grin of his.

"I'll repair the bed. You can get ready to get in it."

"I can? Well, thanks." She tried to sound miffed, but failed.

Sam started to wrench and jerk the mattress around, and she turned her back on him. She tugged things out of her pack: clean long johns, her toothbrush. By the time she turned back around, Sam was putting the finishing touches on making the bed. The sheets were smooth and white, and the pillowcases still bore creases from being folded. After today's long hike, it looked immensely appealing.

"Do you want the side next to the wall or the outside?" Sam asked.

"Oh, um, the inside. I guess. Unless you do." She was back to being over-polite again.

"I'm going outside for a few minutes. While you—" and he angled a thumb toward her neatly folded long johns "—get ready for bed."

"Maybe we shouldn't sleep in the same bed," Kerry said on a wave of doubt.

"Maybe we shouldn't. It's your call." He lifted an eyebrow and walked to the door, opened it and went out.

Kerry stared after him. Sam made this so difficult. She didn't want to want him. She didn't even want to think about wanting him. And that was all she seemed to be thinking about.

When he came back in, Kerry was already in bed with the covers pulled up to her neck. Her eyes, big in her face, were solemn, wide.

He went to the bed and stood there, still wearing his parka. "Kerry, I just want to say one thing. And that is that I want everything to be all right for you. And for the baby."

"I thought you disapproved of the baby."

He felt weighed down beneath the gravity of all he could not tell her. "It's not that. Believe me, it's not that. I know you want a baby. I was surprised that you're pregnant now, that's all. Now that Doug is gone, I mean."

"Maybe that's why I pursued it," Kerry said.

Her earnestness, her sincerity and above all her innocence frustrated him. He felt a surge of anger against Doug for getting him into this mess, but it faded immediately as he admitted that he was equally to blame for the scheme. He had volunteered. Doug hadn't exactly dragged him kicking and screaming to the sperm bank. He had been glad to do it. It was a favor for a friend, nothing more, until he'd been confronted with Kerry and all the feelings he had for her.

"You haven't taken off your parka," Kerry reminded him gently.

He took off his parka and draped it over a chair before turning down the wick in the wall sconce.

"Sam? Could you leave the light on? Just a little?"

"Sure," he said, but the light was so dim that his eyes didn't adjust right away. He started to undress, almost removing his long johns before he remembered that he'd better leave them on. On the way to the bed he tripped over something in the half dark—Kerry's boots.

"Are you all right, Sam?" Kerry's voice was drowsy, muffled.

"Yep," he said, little more than a growl.

He sat on the edge of the bed, enduring the protest of the temperamental bedsprings as he slid the rest of the way under the covers. Beside him, Kerry breathed quietly. He had the idea that she was alert and waiting to see what he would do.

Well, *he* was waiting to see what *she* would do. They lay side by side in the dark, each trying not to roll into the depression created by the other's body in the knobby old mattress, each thinking silently about, Sam would wager, the same thing. Last night.

God, she'd felt so good. So soft, warm and giving. It had been a long time since he'd been with a woman who knew how to do anything but take. And the giving had made him more willing to give to her, had made him want to. He'd thought less about his own pleasure than hers. Which meant that he really cared about her.

He turned over on his side, pretending to close his eyes, but studying her profile through his lowered lashes. She lay motionless, relaxed but not resting. He wished she'd go to sleep. That way he could sleep, too.

"Sam?" She spoke softly.

"Yes?"

"Do you think there's any chance that plane will come back?"

"I don't know."

She didn't say anything more. Sam waited, tense, wanting so much to touch her, but afraid that she didn't want him to. He made himself close his eyes to shut her out of his sight, and even though he didn't drowse off, he thought maybe she was already asleep. After a while—maybe fifteen minutes or so—he opened his eyes again. At first he stared up at the unfinished timber rafters, hardly daring to look at Kerry. When he did, he noticed a trickle of dampness sliding slowly down her cheek. Her eyes were wide open, staring at the ceiling.

He reached his hand over and touched the spot of wet. Tears. She was crying in silent anguish, all the more disturbing because he had been lying right beside her and hadn't known what she was feeling.

"What's wrong, Kerry?"

At first he thought she wasn't going to answer him, but she said in a kind of choked whisper, "Sometimes I get so afraid."

"Of bears? You don't have to worry about them. We have the rifle."

"Not bears. Of everything. Of death. And life."

"Oh, Kerry," he said helplessly. All he knew to do was to reach for her, take her in his arms, dry her tears with the corner of the sheet.

"I mean, now I'm responsible for the baby, not just me, and I've endangered it by being a stupid *cheechako*," Kerry said against his chest.

"You didn't mean to," Sam said.

"Of course not, but now you're in danger, too."

"We'll be all right. We'll get out of here." He amended this in his own mind, thinking *I'd be fine if it were just me. But it's harder when I have to look after Kerry. And the baby.* He recalled belatedly that Kerry still thought that the reason for his visit to Silverthorne had been to check on her. Well, she'd have to go on thinking that. He thought about those papers in the pouch in his pack. They'd never see the light of day now.

"I thought everything would be all right when the plane

flew over today. I thought we'd probably get rescued.'' She nestled her head trustingly into the hollow of his shoulder, and he wanted to kiss her, but didn't dare. She clearly didn't want a sexual relationship with him; what had been started between them was not important to her.

Which gave him a bleak feeling.

Well, sometimes the things you couldn't have were the things you wanted the most. He wanted Kerry Anderson. But she didn't want him.

He distracted himself by thinking that once they got back to Anchorage he'd look up that little redhead, Jolie somebody, he couldn't remember her last name. He tried to picture her in his mind and failed utterly. He'd met her at a party and asked for her number after Marcia left, but he'd never called her. He didn't even really like her much.

Kerry had fallen asleep in his arms, and he tightened his arms around her. He wanted to tell her that he'd take care of her, that he'd do anything for her, that he wouldn't let any harm come to her or their baby. *Their baby,* product of the union of his sperm and her egg, and she didn't know and never would.

The thought brought tears to his eyes. He blinked them away in the dark and stroked her hair, thinking that this was all he would allow himself, this small intimacy, that he must deny both of them the greater intimacy. She sighed deeply and adjusted her curves to his.

He wondered if she would hear if he were to whisper that he was falling in love with her. He was sorely tempted; he wanted to say the words. But he didn't say them. He didn't dare.

IN THE MORNING, they dressed and left the cabin, leaving behind a note with their names and addresses for the owners. Sam didn't like the way the air felt. He thought it carried hints of bad weather.

"I hope you're wrong," Kerry said fervently.

"Me, too," he replied.

But they had only been on the trail for forty-five minutes when a dark gray bank of clouds swept across the mountains, soon obscuring their peaks and much of the lower range. Sam stopped and stood, hands balanced on hips, as he watched the weather front moving in.

"What's happening?"

"Storm front," he said.

"Maybe it's only passing through," Kerry said doubtfully.

"Well, it's a humdinger."

"Looks like it," she said. She glanced at Sam, trying to read his thoughts.

"I'd planned for us to make it to the closest shelter, a forest service cabin."

"We'd better get going." Kerry adjusted the straps on her pack and dug her poles into the snow to move forward.

Sam spoke curtly. "No, Kerry, we're not going anywhere."

She stopped and halfway turned to face him.

"What do you mean?"

"We're going back to the Stanchiks'. I'm not taking any chances that we could be caught outside in that."

"Sam—"

"Don't argue. You won't change my mind."

One look at his face showed her the truth of his statement, and it was with a sense of discouragement that she followed Sam back to the cabin. She was beginning to feel despair over their whole situation, and that may have contributed to the fact that later she couldn't eat lunch, even though it was onion soup made from a dehydrated mix. And she usually loved onion soup.

"Why can't you eat?" Sam demanded to know as he sat across from her and her untouched bowl at the table in the Stanchiks' cabin.

"My stomach is upset." Kerry didn't even like to talk about how nauseated she felt. Talking about it made it worse.

"You need to replace all those calories you've used up walking. You have to eat," Sam said patiently as if talking to a child.

All his cajoling did no good. At a loss, Sam sat down at the table and ate his soup as well as hers, glowering at her all the while. She finally retreated to the bed, huddling under a pair of blankets until Sam said he'd better go split some firewood outside before the storm hit.

She listened to the sharp rhythmic thwack of ax against wood, closing her eyes against the nausea that swept over her in waves. She wished she'd never heard of Alaska, that she'd never decided to open Silverthorne Lodge, that she'd stayed in Seattle. She had no business here, and as for Sam, they were thrown together in this situation, which was her fault. But it was so hard to maintain her distance when all she wanted was to snuggle up against him and make love.

She realized that the sounds of Sam splitting wood had stopped. He came back inside as the storm hit, snow blowing down off the mountaintops, wind sweeping through chinks in the little cabin. Despite the fires in the fireplace and cookstove, it grew colder and colder inside as the wind snorted and scuffed outside.

Sam tried to entice her to eat.

"I can't eat," she said truthfully as she burrowed deeper beneath the covers, and Sam retreated to a corner where he sat on a stool sharpening the ax without speaking. Once or twice she attempted conversation, but Sam was taciturn and uncommunicative.

It was storming so hard that if it hadn't been for her wristwatch, Kerry wouldn't have been able to tell night from day. She insisted on rousing herself from bed long enough to prepare moose meat for dinner. Sam ate enough, she ate very little, and, cold and discouraged by the day's events, she slid back into the warm bed at eight o'clock.

Sam rearranged his pack, puttered around the cabin, set out his clothes for the next day and spared Kerry long covert looks when he thought she wouldn't notice. Finally she was exasperated.

"For heaven's sake, Sam, stop it! Come on to bed."

"No need to shout," he said with extreme patience.

"Who's shouting?" she hollered. She immediately felt contrite.

"If you can yell, you're obviously feeling better."

"Maybe so. I don't know. I wish things were different, that's all."

Sam came over to the side of the bed and stood staring down at her. "Different how?"

"In every way. Just get in bed. It hurts my neck to look up at you."

Sam removed his boots, his socks, his heavy shirt, his turtleneck. His hands lingered on the snap to his jeans.

"Oh, go on. We know each other pretty well by this time," Kerry said, wondering why she was lashing out at him and knowing why even as she drew the next breath.

"Yes, I suppose we do," Sam said. He snapped open the fly of his jeans and unzipped them. Kerry averted her eyes, though it probably wasn't necessary.

He climbed into bed beside her, immediately warming her with his presence. The storm still raged outside the cabin, a terrible ruckus.

"I hope this experience doesn't make us hate each other," she said in a small voice after he blew out the candle.

He considered this. "I don't think I could ever hate you," he said at last.

"That's good," she said.

She stayed on her side of the bed, and he stayed on his. After a while she shifted her position and her bare feet grazed his. Her feet were cold.

"Sorry," she mumbled.

"Are your feet always that cold?" They'd felt like individual blocks of ice, each toe an icicle.

"No. I don't think so. It's just that I'm closest to the wall and the wind whistles through."

"Let's switch places," he said.

"I'm fine."

"Why don't you put on some socks?"

"All the ones I brought are wet." She sounded miserable.

In the dark Sam couldn't see her. He knew how she looked, though, and he pictured her now. In his mind she wasn't huddling as far away as possible on the edge of the bed trying to keep warm, she was walking on a beach, Malibu perhaps, wearing a bikini and laughing up at the man beside her, who happened to be him. He'd take her to Malibu when they were out of this and—

No, he wouldn't. She had other priorities, one of which was his child.

He thought about that child and recast the image in his mind to include a baby. Kerry was walking on the beach, a small boy holding her hand, and he was holding the child's other hand. They looked so happy together, a lovely family.

But they weren't a family. This was as close as he would probably ever get to knowing what it was like to be a father.

Now he rolled over on his side to face her, wanting to drink her in, wanting to experience this feeling to the fullest. To his surprise he felt peaceful and fulfilled, and that was from only thinking about forming a family with this woman and her child. *Their* child.

"Are you asleep?" he asked quietly.

She waited a few seconds before answering. "No, my feet are too cold."

He could either get up and find her a dry pair of socks in his own pack or warm her feet some other way. "We can fix that," he said, and he wrapped his legs around hers so that her feet were tucked between them.

For a moment she stiffened, but then it was okay. She relaxed, and soon he heard her regular breathing and knew that she had fallen asleep.

Tentatively he reached out and slid his arm around the curve of her waist. She sighed, and he fully expected her to wake up and object, but then she leaned in closer to him, and soon they were molded together like spoons in a drawer. He fell asleep then, too, and his last thought was that with any luck, maybe they wouldn't be able to leave here for a couple more days.

Kerry woke once during the night and when she first realized that she was sleeping so close to Sam, she instinctively tried to insert space between them. She didn't want to wake him, though, and he murmured something in his sleep, something Kerry didn't quite catch, but in her half-waking state she at first thought he'd said, "I love you."

But, of course, he hadn't. It was only her imagination.

IN THE MORNING, it was still snowing lightly, though the blizzard seemed to have blown itself out. A new soft blanket of snow covered everything, blunting angles and falsely rendering the reality of their situation much less harsh than it was. Kerry was sick to her stomach with the worst morning sickness so far.

Sam felt helpless against such a miserable symptom, but it also left him in awe of what expectant mothers had to endure. He brought her wet cloths for her forehead, seethed because she had run out of the saltines she used to quell morning sickness and silently cursed himself for his part in the whole thing.

"I apologize," Kerry said over and over, but he wished she wouldn't. He should be the one apologizing and he was heartsick at the thought.

He insisted that she lie in the bed, but after a while she curled up there and said, "Talk to me, Sam. It makes the time pass faster."

"Talk to you about what?" he said.

"I don't know. Oh, I take that back—how about Sybilla?"

Sam had to laugh. Kerry wouldn't give up on Sybilla.

"You wouldn't be interested. It was nothing much," he told her.

She considered this. "I'd be interested in anything that would take my mind off things."

He thought about this. "How about a joke?"

"I always like to hear a good joke."

"I didn't say anything about a good joke. We're better off with the stupidest jokes I can think of at this point."

"All right. I'm game."

"What do you get when you cross a frog and a dog?"

"I don't know. Sybilla?"

"Nope, not Sybilla. I told you I'm not talking about her. What you get when you cross a frog and a dog is a croaker spaniel."

"That *is* stupid. I know a stupider one."

"Shoot."

"How do you stop a bull from charging?"

"No idea."

She grinned as close to a malevolent grin as she knew how to grin. "Take away his Visa card. You're next."

He had to think a minute. "What's black and yellow and goes zzub zzub?"

"A bee flying backward! I've heard it before."

"I'm out of stupid jokes."

"So am I," she said.

"It's probably just as well."

"I don't feel so sick anymore, Sam. Maybe the jokes worked." She sat up and smiled at him, swinging her feet over the side of the bed.

He smiled back. "I wouldn't count on it, and besides—" He stopped talking and listened intently. They exchanged astonished looks as they heard an alien sound, one that they weren't accustomed to hearing.

"Damned if that doesn't sound like an iron dog," Sam said on a note of incredulity.

Kerry jumped up, ran to the door and looked out into the flat light of midmorning. The sky was lambswool gray, too overcast to lend shadows to the trees, and the landscape undulated toward the mountains, white and spare. As she watched, a snow machine roared around a copse of firs, breaking a groove in the fresh-fallen snow of the trail, and it was followed by a dog-sled team running full tilt.

Sam was right behind her, and she tried to ignore his hands gripping her shoulders.

"It's Ollie Parker from Athinopa! My old friend!"

"How can it be?"

"I don't know, but that's who it is, all right. Ollie!"

Sam released her and opened the door, walking out and

waving his hands. Soon he was lost in a sea of wagging tails and embracing his friend enthusiastically. Kerry didn't join them. Suddenly she understood that Ollie's arrival signaled something she hadn't been willing to think about. True, her long trek with Sam was over, and they would soon be safe. This was good for her and good for the baby, and presumably it was good for Sam, too.

She should have been able to summon a feeling of joy or even relief. But all she felt was a sinking feeling and a dull pain somewhere in the region of her heart because she knew that for her and Sam Harbeck, this was the end of the trail.

Chapter Ten

A month later

Kerry faced into a cutting wind on the street where Emma lived, a pleasant residential neighborhood in Anchorage. With her head down, she didn't see Mr. Lagunoff on the sidewalk until she ran right into him.

"Oof," he said, but his small plump figure was well padded by his down coat, and he regained his balance immediately. His grocery bag, however, went flying, and cans and bundles landed in the mound of snow piled at the edge of the sidewalk.

"Oh, I'm so sorry," Kerry said, horrified at the damage she'd caused. She scrambled to pick everything up.

"No problem, no problem," Mr. Lagunoff told her. "I'm glad I ran into you." He indulged in a hearty laugh at his own attempt at humor while Kerry dropped the retrieved items into his bag.

Kerry wrapped her scarf tighter around her neck. "Well, I'll be on my way. If you're sure you're not hurt."

"I'm fine, but a man was asking about you this morning."

"A man? What man?" *Sam,* she thought to herself. She'd thought he'd put her out of his life.

"Oh, he was tall and nice-looking. A prosperous kind of fellow. Drove a black Mercedes."

Sam. Her heart lightened at the thought of him.

"Was there a message?"

"No message. He said he'd get in touch with you."

"Oh. I see." Disappointment settled in. Well, that's what she deserved for building up her hopes.

Mr. Lagunoff's eyes twinkled behind thick glasses. "Nice to see you, Kerry. Come next door and enjoy a cup of tea with me. You're probably lonely with Emma gone."

Kerry made herself smile. "Thanks, maybe I will," she told him.

He continued on his way with a jaunty wave, and Kerry hurried up the walkway to Emma's house.

She took the mail inside out of the cold before riffling through it. Today's take was mostly advertising circulars and correspondence for Emma, but one envelope was addressed to her. It was from her mother.

Dear Kerry,

I'm sending snapshots of Dad and me on Halloween. He's promised me never to drag me to the neighborhood Halloween party again.

Dad's so excited. We won four tickets to the Rose Bowl game! Charlene's coming from Seattle for Christmas, and she'll stay over for the game on New Year's Day. Please tell us you'll be here, too! I worry about you up there in the cold and snow, and it would be wonderful if you could come for an extended stay—maybe until after the baby's born?

We love you and miss you and I'm ready to pamper you to your heart's content.

Much love,
Mom

P.S. Charlene says she's tried to call you a few times, but you haven't been there. She worries about you, so please give her a ring when you get a chance.

The enclosed pictures showed her mother and father dressed as Beauty and the Beast for Halloween, her mother poised and pretty in a long flowing gown, her father decked out in some kind of furry getup that made Kerry smile. Suddenly she felt overwhelmingly nostalgic for the good times they'd all had together when she and Charlene were growing up. Spending the winter holidays with her family was an option that she hadn't really considered because of the long distance involved, but it was warm in California. She knew that most of Alaska would be an icebox from now until May or June. In December, Anchorage would be lucky to get five and a half hours of daylight in a twenty-four hour period.

She didn't have to decide about La Jolla right now. She'd think it over and discuss it with Charlene when she called her.

Since her return to Anchorage, Kerry had occupied the spare bedroom in Emma's house, and Emma, a hospital administrator, was on assignment in Fairbanks for the next month and a half, performing unspecified financial tasks at a down-and-out clinic. That left Kerry on her own, which was okay, but she was getting tired of eating grilled-cheese sandwiches by herself. Maybe she really would take Mr. Lagunoff up on his offer of tea sometime.

As she hung her coat in the closet, she caught a view of herself in the hall mirror. Bemused, she pivoted for a full frontal view. She looked—well, like one of those Teletubbies on TV. Soon she would have to start wearing maternity clothes. Her oversized sweaters and leggings would not accommodate the growing baby for long. If Sam could see her now, he wouldn't be the least bit attracted to her. She felt fat and, even worse, ugly.

If Sam could see her now... But he wouldn't be seeing her. And that was a depressing thought.

If they were still weathered in at Silverthorne, *if* they had been forced to stay longer, they'd be sitting down at the scarred old table right about now making a meal of whatever they'd managed to scrounge together. Sam would be teasing her about something, and she'd be trying not to let him know that she was amused by it, and later they'd settle down in front of a roaring fire with mugs of hot chocolate. And after that, maybe they'd make slow, sweet love, making it last because they had nowhere to go and nothing to do but be with each other.

But, of course, none of that would be happening, not really. The whole lovely scenario was only a dream, a wonderful dream that Kerry sometimes slotted into her thoughts to make herself feel better when she missed Sam so much that she couldn't stand it. When her heart ached and hung like a lead weight in her chest and when she longed to feel his arms enfolding her and his heart beating next to hers. When she contemplated life without him, because she understood all too well, all too unhappily, that that was the way her life was destined to be—without Sam.

She felt a stinging sensation behind her eyes and blinked to ward off the tears that were always all too ready to flow these days. She didn't want to indulge in a pity party and she might as well accept reality. She'd be without Sam, all right, but she still had the baby. The baby, whom she pictured as an adorable round someone with chubby cheeks, dark hair and a winning grin. Just thinking about the baby cheered her, and she made herself unwrap the crib sheets that she'd bought today. They were printed with droll yellow teddy bears and they'd lifted her spirits considerably when she'd spotted them in the department store, so much so that she'd bought them at full price. Ever mindful of unpaid bills, she usually waited until she found a good sale to buy the things she wanted.

And now that she was thinking about bills, today she'd pay the ones she could, figure out what kind of brochures she needed for Silverthorne, and after that she might as well call her sister, Charlene, to reassure her that she was happy and doing well.

Was she really happy?

A difficult question. *I want this baby,* she told herself. It was true. She did want the baby. But it seemed to her that happiness had eluded her since that day when Sam's friend Ollie mushed up to the cabin and bore her and Sam away on his sled. Kerry had been stunned when rescue happened so quickly, so stunned that she barely remembered the long jolting ride through the backwoods by dog sled, the creak of the harness as the dogs strained against it, Ollie's shouts, the steaming vapor of her own breath curling back over her shoulders as they made rapid headway toward what passed for civilization in those parts.

Athinopa had been a tiny village with an airplane runway running parallel to the main street in the manner of such outposts. But the village had a shortwave radio, and that's how Ollie had heard that two people might be stranded in the snowstorm near the Stanchiks' cabin. Ollie hadn't had any idea who the two people were and, when he'd arrived at the cabin, he had professed amazement that one of them was his good friend Sam Harbeck.

"That guy in the airplane—he was a young *cheechako,* a student pilot from the Lower Forty-eight on one of his first solo flights. He didn't know to waggle his wings to let you know he'd seen you. He only knew to go back to the airport and tell someone he'd spotted two people out there.

By the time someone radioed me, it was storming. I left the village as soon as I could, but I had no idea that one of the people I'd be rescuing would be my old friend Sam,'' Ollie had told them.

Kerry and Sam had spent the night after their dramatic rescue in Athinopa, Kerry sharing a bed with Ollie's teenage daughter, Sam in his sleeping bag on the floor of the Parkers' small living room amid drying dog booties and harnesses. When the Search-and-Rescue helicopter had come for them the next day, Kerry had carefully kept her expression blank because she didn't want to cry in public. And that's what she'd wanted to do—cry until she couldn't cry anymore. She hadn't, though, not a tear. But her heart had been breaking.

Her parting with Sam had been strained and awkward.

"Well," he'd said as they stood near the helicopter, its blades stirring up new fallen snow around them. "It's been real." It was a pretty lame thing to say, considering, and judging from his expression he knew it.

She could forgive him that. She'd gazed up at him, memorizing his ruggedly chiseled features, that funny little scar in the middle of one eyebrow, the way the groove in his upper lip seemed deeper when he was serious. He was serious then, his eyes all pupil so that they didn't seem blue anymore. Unfathomable, that's what they were. Somewhere in their depths, she thought she detected a remote sadness— if that's what it was. With Sam, it was hard to tell.

"Thank you. Sam. For everything."

"Kerry," he'd said. Just her name. And for a moment she'd thought he might kiss her goodbye, but the helicopter blades had been making a racket overhead and people were milling everywhere. The pilot stuck his head out and asked if they were ready, and then she was suddenly being boosted out of the chaos on the ground and into the helicopter by Ollie and Sam. And Sam was climbing in, then they were lifting off, villagers below waving to them, dogs running around excitedly, and Kerry's stomach turning flip-flops.

The flight to Anchorage had been uncomfortable, disorienting and miserable. Sam had sat next to the pilot, she'd sat behind him. It was all she could do not to reach forward and ruffle her fingers through his hair one last time.

She'd spotted Emma right away in the crowd at the airport.

"Kerry! Kerry, I'm over here!" Emma, long-limbed and slender, had rushed forward. While her friend had oohed and aahed over Kerry's plight in the wilderness, over the hollows in her cheeks and the circles under her eyes, Sam had quietly slipped away. Disappeared. And, not surprisingly, Kerry hadn't seen or talked to him since.

So why, a month later, had Sam come to Emma's house? Kerry couldn't imagine. He was history.

AT THE CORPORATE offices of Harbeck Air, Sam marched out of his inner sanctum and barked at his administrative assistant. "Get me the file on Kerry Anderson."

She stopped scrolling through the document on her computer screen. "You mean the file on *Doug* Anderson?"

"No, I told you to start one on Kerry." For convenience, Sam kept file folders on all his friends, and that's where he filed information pertinent to the friendship—invitations, Christmas cards, and if there was something he wanted to discuss with a friend next time he saw him or her, he dropped a reminder to himself into the file folder.

"I don't remember your mentioning it."

"Well, I'm mentioning it now."

"If you don't mind my saying so, you're been awfully crabby since you came back from your vacation."

This gave him pause. He scowled. "I do mind your saying so."

"Then cancel the thought."

"All right, all right, but I'm not canceling the request."

"File on Kerry Anderson. Right." Ann Blyler scribbled a reminder to herself on a stick-on note and tacked it to her computer screen. She'd been Sam's assistant ever since he'd taken over Harbeck Air from his father, and she was efficient in the extreme.

"And Ann?"

"Yes?"

"Bring Kerry's file into my office as soon as you can."

"Of course."

Sam wheeled and strode back into his inner sanctum, where he stood at the wide plate-glass window and surveyed his domain, which consisted of a fleet of float planes, another of planes with skis or wheels, several runways, and a brand-new hangar. It was satisfying to take stock of the empire he'd built in such a short time. Usually he felt good about it. Today he didn't. He felt empty.

He'd anguished over seeking Kerry out for the past month, ever since their precipitous departure from Athinopa. He was slightly acquainted with her friend Emma, whose telephone number was unlisted; so he didn't have a clue about how to reach Kerry by phone, but at least he knew where Emma lived. The house was an attractive green clapboard structure nestled between fir and spruce trees, and he'd driven by twice before actually stopping at the curb. He'd knocked and knocked on the door, but had managed to raise no one but the bespectacled little man next door who had peered at him myopically through the curtains at his kitchen window and finally emerged on the porch to ask what Sam wanted.

Kerry, was what Sam had said, meaning it in more ways

than one, but the man said he'd seen her leave earlier. Sam had thought about dropping his business card in the mailbox, but decided that it wouldn't do any good. Kerry wouldn't call him anyway.

"Mr. Harbeck?" Now Ann stood at the door to his office.

He turned around, morose and sure that he looked it. In fact, Ann wrinkled her forehead.

"I've put the Kerry Anderson file on your desk."

"Thanks."

"Will that be all?"

"For now. Oh, by the way, you wouldn't happen to know anyone named Jolie, would you?"

"Jolie?"

"Right." He managed to look disinterested. Well, he was. He didn't really want to call this Jolie, whose face he couldn't remember. He did remember Kerry's face, however. It haunted his dreams, bedeviled his days, had impressed its bright image on his very soul.

"No, I'm afraid not. I know a Julie—several, in fact—but no Jolie." He thought Ann was looking at him strangely.

Time to put this to an end. It wouldn't do for Ann to think the boss wasn't tending to business.

"Get Carlin on the line. He wants to talk to me about buying some planes."

"Yes sir." Ann went out and shut the door behind her.

Sam picked up the folder she'd set on his desk. KERRY ANDERSON, read the label. After a moment's thought, he slid the envelope containing those papers from the sperm bank out of his desk drawer. He read them over carefully, thinking he might as well throw them away. They were of no earthly use now.

But for some reason, he couldn't bring himself to toss

them. They were a link to Kerry and the time they'd spent
together, and it was all he had of her except, of course, his
memories. He tucked the papers into the folder and slid it
under a pile of others on his desk.

Ann buzzed him. "Mr. Carlin is on line one," she said.

He scooped up the phone, glad of the distraction. He
didn't want to think about Kerry anymore. He didn't want
to, but he knew he would anyway.

IT WAS WHEN Kerry was putting the Silverthorne brochure
together that she ran into trouble. She needed to include
information about how to get to Silverthorne, and she and
Sam had informally agreed that Harbeck Air would be the
charter airline of choice for her guests.

Should she call him?

She'd rather not. She didn't trust herself because she
knew that hearing his voice would make her want him even
more.

Absently she went to the phone and stared at it. If only
it would ring and it would be Sam! But it didn't ring. It
seldom rang for her, only for Emma.

If she had been home when Sam dropped by yesterday,
she could easily have broached the subject of flights to
Silverthorne. She mulled this over, wondering if that was
in fact the reason that he had visited.

As she sat there, she felt a flutter of movement in her
abdomen. She thought it might be indigestion, but her
stomach felt fine. She felt it again, placing her hand over
the spot. When she finally realized what it might be, she
jumped up and ran for the book she'd bought about expectant motherhood. She found the page she was looking for,
scanned it quickly and sank down on the couch in awe of
the moment. She'd just felt the baby, her baby, move for
the very first time!

She felt the little ripple again, and without warning, tears began to stream down her face. She had no one with whom to share this tender moment, and she'd never felt so alone in her life, not even on that horrible night she'd spent in the shed with the bear waiting outside to gobble her up.

After a while, she dried her tears and decided that it was time to visit Mr. Lagunoff, who might not be at all interested in the fact that the baby had moved, but could probably be counted on to quote snatches of Robert Service's poems about Alaska and to provide a steaming cup of Earl Grey.

Some days, that was good enough.

SAM COULDN'T help it. Somehow that afternoon his car drove itself through the neighborhood where Emma lived, and it stopped in front of her house.

Again, no one was home. You wouldn't think an expectant mother would want to go out in the cold weather so often, he thought grumpily. Like Ann said, he'd been grumpy a lot lately, and never so much as today. Too bad he was supposed to go to a gallery opening tonight, something for which he could muster no interest.

This time before he left Emma's house, he slid his business card under the storm door.

The gallery opening was as boring as he'd expected. Shortly after his arrival, he managed to shunt himself off into a small side gallery, where he gazed moodily at several paintings hung there. They had a vaguely familiar look, something about the subject matter. Or was it the colors? He moved closer to inspect them more carefully.

"Nice, aren't they?"

He turned around blankly. A man was standing in a doorway, leaning on it casually. He wasn't dressed for a party.

"I think I've seen this artist's work somewhere," Sam said.

"Oh, you won't find the artist's signature, although those paintings have been authenticated. These are some of her very early works, completed before she realized that her paintings would have value. Elise Anderson is the artist's name."

"Elise Anderson," Sam repeated. He remembered that dark little closet in the attic at Silverthorne, the paintings that had escaped destruction by Doug's grandfather's second wife. He remembered sharing his first kiss with Kerry in that closet and—

"Yes, Elise Anderson died much too prematurely. Her works are selling for astronomical prices. We paid ten thousand dollars for that small one in the corner."

"Ten thousand!" The figure jolted Sam out of his reverie.

"It's true. Amazing, isn't it?" The man sauntered over to look at the largest painting. It was, Sam was sure, of the bend in Chickaback Creek. The colors were strong, the strokes bold.

"If someone had an Elise Anderson painting, do you think you could sell it?"

"Sure, especially if it's signed. They're hot right now. In fact, I'm in the back room researching Elise Anderson. Did you know that she planned to create an artists' colony somewhere in the back of beyond, I think it was called Silverthorne—" He prattled on, but Sam didn't listen.

He was sure that Kerry had no idea that those paintings in the lodge were worth so much money. Knowing how much she worried about finances, he should call her and tell her about it.

But he couldn't call her. He didn't know her phone number.

He could write her a note, then. Tomorrow, first thing. Deliver it to her house personally.

He made his way back into the main room of the gallery and pushed through the crowd toward the front door. He was already framing his note to Kerry in his mind. What if he managed to catch her at home and could tell her in person? What if he went over there tonight, say, and her eyes lit up, all silvery and golden, when she saw him?

Lost in thought, Sam was more surprised than anyone when his name was called out from a dais in the front of the room. He stopped stock-still, stared blankly, accepted congratulations that made no sense until a bubbly matron descended upon him and pressed a carving of some sort into his hands.

"You've won the door prize!" she enthused. "It's Inuit! Carved by Inuits in one of their villages! By a master craftsman!"

Sam, in the middle of a bunch of gawking strangers, stammered his thanks, thinking that all he wanted was to get out of there. He looked down at the carving. Even though he liked Inuit art as well as anybody, all he could think about was that Kerry would enjoy it. The carving depicted a bear scooping a salmon from a river, and he thought it might make Kerry laugh. That is, if she were to see it.

He retraced his steps toward the door and he had almost escaped when he heard someone behind him say, "Well, hello, stranger!"

He turned, stared blankly.

"Remember me? Jolie?" The redhead smiled up at him, her face plainer than he recalled.

She wouldn't listen to his protests that he had something else to do. She led him away to meet her friends, all of whom wanted to see the carving. While he was smiling and saying all the right things, he realized that it was too late to drop in on Kerry unannounced. She might be sleeping. She might not even be there.

Just for a moment—one wishful moment—he wanted to see Kerry walk through the door, her hair golden in the glow from the track lighting overhead, her smile just for him.

Knowing that it couldn't—wouldn't—happen, rocketed him to the depths of despair.

"Come to dinner with us," Jolie was insisting, and Sam didn't want to. But he did. He didn't know what else to do with himself. He didn't want to go home. No, that wasn't right. He didn't want to go home *alone.*

And tonight maybe he wouldn't have to.

KERRY FOUND Sam's card when she came back from having tea with Mr. Lagunoff. So he'd been around again, and she did want to talk to him.

After a night of tossing and turning and wondering if calling him was the right thing to do, she hesitantly phoned Sam's office the next morning. The woman who answered the phone told her he was out. Kerry hung up, feeling deflated even though she wasn't sure she'd wanted to talk to Sam anyway. It would feel so different, hearing his voice over a phone line, and she couldn't remember how his voice sounded anyway. Or maybe she could, but didn't want to think about it.

She should have asked the woman on the phone if there was anyone else at Harbeck Air who could help her set up regularly scheduled flights to Silverthorne.

Well, she didn't have to include flight information on the brochure, but she did need the brochures right away so that she could mail them before Christmas. People liked to plan their summer vacations early when they were traveling to Alaska, and she could accommodate only so many guests.

As snowflakes began to drift slowly out of the sky again, she stood at the window and thought about her parents in La Jolla. For the first time, she thought she might take them up on their offer of a plane ticket. She was tired of being cold. And she was tired of being alone.

SAM WOKE UP early the morning after his encounter with Jolie nursing a humongous hangover. He made his tortuous way into the kitchen and poured himself a cup of coffee, wondering where Shwano was. Shwano, his housekeeper, was a brand-new father and proud of it. Sam had an idea that he was in his home behind Sam's house marveling over the new baby.

Not that Sam cared. More power to Shwano, who could at least acknowledge his own child. Who had a lovely wife who adored him. Who wasn't invited to go to gallery openings where he would meet women who wanted to sleep with him.

That's why Sam was so hungover this morning. He hadn't wanted to go home with Jolie or, worse yet, to invite her to his home. So he'd stayed out late drinking, dragging Jolie to one bar after another until she'd finally said she was tired and would go home with friends.

End of Jolie. End of evening. And almost the end of him.

He picked up the phone and punched out the number of his office.

"Ann?"

"Yes, Mr. Harbeck."

"I'll be in a little late. Hold my appointments until eleven o'clock, will you?"

"There's someone here to see you, and—"

He sighed. "Okay, okay, I'll be right in." This was exasperating, but his visitor was probably Weeb Carlin, who was pestering him about buying those planes. It wasn't a bad deal, but Sam didn't want to think about it now. Only thing was, he'd put it off long enough, and Carlin was impatient.

He drained his coffee cup and hurried back upstairs to shower and shave.

KERRY PERCHED on the edge of a leather couch in the ante-room to Sam's office and sneezed. Someone was waxing the hall floor, and the odor of the wax seemed awfully strong.

"Are you all right?" The woman behind the desk, identified by the nameplate on her desk as Ann Blyler, was instantly solicitous.

"Oh, it's the smell of the wax, it tickles my nose," Kerry told her. She was beginning to regret her split-second decision to stop by here on the way to the printer's, which was only a few blocks away, but she'd thought she'd catch Sam in his office, have a quick and impersonal conversation about flights to Silverthorne and then be on her way. Unfortunately, Sam wasn't around yet. She glanced at her watch. It was already ten o'clock.

As the drone of the buffing machine drew closer, Ann stopped what she was doing and aimed a sympathetic glance at the bulge under Kerry's coat.

"How far along are you? Oh, I'm sorry, I shouldn't ask such a personal question, but I just had a baby a year ago." She smiled at Kerry.

Kerry didn't mind talking about the baby. In fact, it seemed to her that there were too few people in Anchorage with whom she could discuss it. "Almost five months," she said.

Ann rose from her desk, moved closer to talk over the

sound of the machine. "There's no reason why you can't wait in Mr. Harbeck's office. I can close the door, you won't smell the fumes, and he'll arrive in a few minutes. Do you think you'll be here long?"

"No, I doubt it. I only need to ask him about scheduling flights to Silverthorne Lodge, and we've discussed it before." Kerry waved her brochure materials under Ann's nose.

"Well, come with me."

This was a relief; Kerry had begun to feel the familiar stirrings of nausea from the fumes. She followed Ann into Sam's office, which she remembered from previous times she'd been there with Doug. The scenery outside the window was all wide and blue with a view of snowy Mount Susitna in the distance, and she sank gratefully into the plush chair near the corner of Sam's desk.

"There," said Ann. "You'll be more comfortable here." She went out and closed the door behind her.

A runway was directly in her line of vision, and for a while Kerry watched planes taking off, tucking their landing gear and disappearing into the sky, but when that grew tiresome, she began to look around Sam's office. He had eclectic taste, that was for sure. A sealskin robe, probably an antique, was draped across a couch. A modern mobile swayed gently in the air from a heating vent. A model airplane that looked as if it had been built by a child sat on the corner of his desk. Perhaps Sam had built it himself. That seemed likely, and captivated by the idea, Kerry leaned closer for a better look. That was when she saw her own name on a file folder.

Why on earth would Sam have a file folder with her name on it?

She stared at the folder, its manila surface blank and innocent except for her name typed neatly on the label. She leaned closer and saw that the folder held several papers and an envelope. At that point curiosity got the better of her, and she edged the folder out from under the others in the stack. Surely she had a right to know what Sam thought important about her. Didn't she?

That question didn't seem at all relevant when she saw to her astonishment that the papers were typed on the letterhead of the Oliver Fertility Clinic in Seattle. She shuffled through them, scarcely believing her eyes. There were donor applications, signed by Sam, and appointment sheets for Sam, and a summary of the fertility clinic's services. *Now that's peculiar,* she thought, but it seemed to her like nothing but the oddest of coincidences, and in no way did she comprehend what she was seeing. She certainly didn't think it had anything to do with her.

It wasn't until she saw the envelope with her name on it that she felt a tremor of shock running down her spine. KERRY, it said in Sam's bold handwriting.

But why would he put an envelope addressed to her in a file folder with documents showing that he'd been sperm donor at the clinic where she had become pregnant?

She didn't have to think twice about the ethics of snooping; in her opinion, it wasn't snooping if an envelope was addressed to her. With trembling fingers she withdrew packet of papers from the envelope and unfolded them. She read quickly, her eyes scanning the lines of print, scarcely believing what she saw. A release form, meant to be signed by her so that the clinic would destroy vials of sperm. A letter from Doug to Sam, thanking him "from the bottom of my heart, good buddy" for donating to the cause—namely, what was to be Doug and Kerry's baby.

She was so engrossed in the damning evidence that she didn't even hear the door open. Footsteps behind her made her look up, and she expected Ann Blyler to be there. Instead it was Sam standing there, one lock of hair falling across his forehead in that way that she found so endearing.

When her eyes locked with his, a panoply of emotions played across his features, among them astonishment, shock and a sudden sickened look when he realized what she'd been reading.

The papers slipped to the floor in a flurry. Sam's gaze followed them down and then moved up again to her face.

"Kerry, I want to explain," he said, taking a step toward her. His voice sounded gruff, tense.

"I don't believe any explaining is necessary," she said. "I read the documents. Doug should have told me that you and he—"

"Doug didn't want you to know."

A dull ache throbbed across her forehead. "But why?" She was bewildered, confounded, totally at a loss.

Sam walked around his desk, tapped his fingers on its surface, looked up at the ceiling and blew out a long breath. "I don't feel right telling you," he said.

"Doug and I were husband and wife, and he kept a secret from me! You'd better spill, Sam."

He looked stricken. When he spoke, it was as if he was weighing each word. "Kerry, Doug didn't want to tell you this, but he couldn't stand the idea of raising a stranger's child."

"He didn't want to tell me? Why not?"

"He didn't want to disappoint you. You both wanted a baby and you were already choosing baby clothes and crib bumpers by the time you'd decided to go the artificial insemination route. He wanted you to be happy, and I volunteered when I realized how he felt, and—well, it was supposed to be a good deed. You were never supposed to find out."

"I was *never* supposed to know the donor's name. That

much is true. The clinic always keeps it a secret, revealing it is unethical or something, I'm sure of it. So I never would have known that you and Doug—that—oh, I can't even say it.'' She felt dizzy with this new knowledge. How could this have happened? How?

"That Doug and I planned for me to be the father of your child,'' Sam said in an even voice. His eyes never left hers. "Things *didn't* go as planned. I never expected you to go ahead and get pregnant after Doug died. I thought that signing the papers permitting the clinic to destroy those vials was merely a formality.''

"You didn't come to Silverthorne to make sure I was okay?''

"I came to Silverthorne to ask you to sign the release. I had no idea. You have to believe me, Kerry. I had no idea that you'd gone ahead with having the baby. And after you told me, well, I'd promised Doug I'd never tell anyone that I was the baby's father. That was okay with him. That's the way he wanted it.''

Kerry's eyes flashed. "And what about what *I* wanted?''

"You wanted a baby. You got a baby.''

"I'm pregnant with your baby,'' she said, the words falling into the room like stones. "*Your* baby.''

"My baby. That's right.'' Sam made a conciliatory move toward her.

She spun away from him, blinded by tears.

"Don't touch me,'' she said. "Don't even think about it.'' She was carrying Sam's baby and she didn't know how she felt about that. Didn't know how she was *supposed* to feel about it. Didn't think that any woman on earth should be in this situation.

"Kerry—''

"I don't want to talk to you. I don't want you to talk to me. I hate you!''

She yanked the door open, and again her nostrils were assailed by the pungent odor of floor wax. She wanted to throw up.

"Kerry, don't go like this. Can't we talk?" His eyes implored her, but in that moment she wished she'd never laid eyes on Sam Harbeck, much less slept with him. She felt hurt, betrayed, furious—and nauseated.

When she spoke, she was half sobbing with rage. "I'm out of here. I'm going to La Jolla to be with my parents. I never want to see you again as long as I live."

She slammed out of his office and past the wide-eyed Ann Blyler, who said, "Excuse me, is there anything I can get for you?"

"A barf bag would be nice," Kerry flung over her shoulder, but she didn't wait around.

Chapter Eleven

With the sound of the slammed door pounding on his hangover and reverberating in his ears, Sam closed his eyes and cautioned himself not to run after Kerry. Anything he did at this point would only make things worse.

"Mr. Harbeck? Mr. Carlin is here." Ann stood in the doorway and she was looking at him strangely.

He reached for the bottle of aspirin in his desk drawer. He didn't know how he was going to make it through another hour of Carlin's blather, but he'd have to. One thing for sure, the secret he'd been forced to keep would no longer burn a hole in his heart. He'd get rid of Weeb Carlin as soon as possible and then he'd go and find Kerry, make her understand that he'd never meant to hurt her.

Somehow.

KERRY RAN most of the way through a softly falling rain to Emma's house, sucking in the strong salty scent of the sea as if it was a magic elixir that would make everything right. She clutched her stomach because it hurt so much, and tears and rain froze on her face in the crisp wind from the inlet.

She thought she spied Mr. Lagunoff's concerned face in the window next door as she fumbled in her purse for the front door key, but she let herself in before he came over to inquire what was wrong. Her coat fell on the hall floor, she bent to slip off her boots, and, since she was awkward with the increased weight of the baby, she lost her balance and sat down abruptly on the hardwood floor.

It was then that the tears really started. They coursed down her cheeks in mighty torrents, dripped onto her blouse, clogged up her nose. She sobbed, crying for Doug and his mistake in setting her up for this, for herself for not suspecting that something was amiss and for Sam.

He would never know his own child.

Running all that way had given her a stitch in her side. Kerry dried her eyes as best she could on the sleeve of her blouse and hauled herself to her feet. Only she didn't quite make it all the way up, she fell back to her knees and gripped the legs of a nearby chair. Panic rocked her; was this achy feeling in her back normal?

She waited to see if the pain abated, and when it didn't, she reached for the telephone and tried to recall her obstetrician's phone number.

SAM DECIDED that he would take Kerry a peace offering. The Inuit sculpture of a bear might make her laugh, might make his perfidy easier to accept. Not that it would make everything all right. Things would never be all right between them again. If only she wouldn't go to her parents', maybe they could patch things up, but he doubted that she'd stay in Anchorage; he'd been burned by that familiar fire of resolve in her eyes before.

Well, Harbeck, you're true to form, he told himself. He had sabotaged this relationship, too. And Kerry was the most beautiful, the brightest, the best woman he had ever met. So why would a woman like that be interested in the stupidest guy who ever lived? His eyes glazed over with tears, and he blinked them away.

Kerry Anderson was the only woman who had ever been able to make him cry.

Ann walked in, and he had to turn his back to her to conceal his sorry emotional state.

"Mr. Harbeck?"

It was with great difficulty that Sam controlled his expression. When he turned to face Ann, he was holding the sculpture in its box.

"Would you please wrap this for me, Ann?" he blurted.

"Certainly. Will that be birthday wrap?" she asked.

He tried to think. He didn't even know when Kerry's birthday was.

"It doesn't matter," he said finally. "Make it something nice."

Ann favored him with a puzzled look before she bore the box away to wherever she did such things. After half an hour or so during which Sam took a vigorous walk and made every effort to vanquish his mounting despair, the box reappeared on his desk adorned in silver-and-white paper and topped with a silver bow.

"I hope that's satisfactory," Ann remarked when he left.

"So do I," he said fervently.

"GET THAT IV GOING STAT," barked the doctor. From the gurney where she lay, Kerry tried to stop the holes in the acoustic-tile ceiling from spinning into dizzying patterns. She struggled to raise herself on her elbows.

"No, dear, don't do that," said the friendly emergency-room nurse, pushing her back down again.

"Is the baby okay?" Lying flat on her back, Kerry couldn't see the monitor and she was terrified that harm would befall the baby.

"So far, so good," the nurse said briskly. "Is there somebody you'd like me to call to come to the hospital?"

Kerry closed her eyes. She couldn't think of anyone. Emma was far away. She didn't think Mr. Lagunoff would be much help. And she had no other friends in Anchorage.

Sam.

No, she couldn't. She wouldn't.

"Mrs. Anderson? I'll be glad to call someone for you."

She opened her eyes and looked into the concerned face of the nurse.

"There's no one," she whispered and turned her face to the wall.

FOR THE THIRD TIME in two days, Sam parked his car and walked up the sidewalk to Emma's house. Damp brown leaves had blown across the porch and stuck to the railing, and the curtains were drawn across the windows. He knocked at the door. When that didn't produce Kerry, he rang the bell. Nothing happened. Could she have left for her parents' so soon?

He stamped his feet impatiently on the wooden boards of the narrow porch, looking around, wondering if he'd see her coming down the street toward him, her hair wisping around her face. Or in braids, like the second day at Silverthorne when they'd walked to the plane. He smiled faintly at the painful recollection. She'd looked so pretty with her hair tied up in blue satin bows.

He wasn't aware of anyone behind him until he heard someone clearing his throat. He whirled to see the man next door, the same guy he'd noticed peering through the curtains yesterday, standing there with his hands thrust deep in his coat pockets, hunched against the wind.

"Hello, I'm Serge Lagunoff. Are you looking for Kerry,

by any chance?'' The tone was polite, the eyes behind the glasses curious and penetrating.

"I'd hoped I'd catch her at home," Sam said.

"Oh, no chance of that. Not after the ambulance."

"Ambulance?" A frisson of alarm shot through him, zinging every cell in his body into alert mode.

"An ambulance came. Took Kerry away. I didn't get over here in time to find out what was wrong, but I hope it's not because of the baby. Kerry really wants that baby."

"Where did the ambulance take her? Where is she?" Sam felt panicked, scared, as if he'd had his feet knocked out from under him. Kerry in the hospital? It was unthinkable.

"They took her to St. Francis Hospital. I know that much because I saw the writing on the ambulance. I wonder if I should try to reach Emma. She told me how to contact her in case of emergency."

"Maybe you'd better," Sam called over his shoulder as he made a dash for his car, but he wasn't sure Serge Lagunoff heard him.

THE HOSPITAL STAFF wasn't cooperative.

"Kerry Anderson. She was admitted this afternoon."

The sour-faced receptionist ticked a few keys on her computer keyboard and squinted at the monitor screen. "There's no Kerry Anderson here at the present time," she said.

"Damn it, I know she came here in an ambulance! I want to talk to your supervisor." Sam was steamed and didn't mind showing it.

"Very well, sir, but I'm telling you, there's no one here by that name." The woman was snippy, one of those maddening people who glory in finding themselves in a position of authority, however minor, because it ensures that they can repeatedly put the rest of the world in its place.

"Is there some problem?" An older woman, buxom, motherly and with the mien of an administrator, appeared in a doorway. The snippy one, looking miffed, got up and marched away.

Sam started over. "I'm looking for Kerry Anderson, she was admitted this afternoon, she must have been, it was an ambulance from this hospital." He couldn't help running all his words together. He was so terrified that something had happened to Kerry that he was on the verge of incoherent.

"Anderson, you say?" The woman sat down gracefully at the computer and typed in a few characters. "No, I'm afraid there is no Kerry Anderson. Do you know why she was admitted?"

"No. Maybe a—a miscarriage. Maybe—I don't know." In his frustration, he wanted to strangle someone. Not this kind person who was trying her best to help, but someone. Anyone.

"Perhaps she's on the maternity floor. I can double-check." She watched intently as another chart unfurled on the screen. Sam thought, *What if something terrible has happened? A slip on the ice, a fall, a disease, a coma?* All the ramifications of Kerry's being brought to this impersonal place crashed in upon him. He prayed that nothing would happen to her. *Had* happened to her. He prayed for the baby.

"I'm afraid I can't find a Kerry Anderson, but we did admit a Barbara K. Anderson this afternoon."

Relief hit him then. He recalled that Barbara was Kerry's first name, and she'd always gone by her middle name, which was her mother's maiden name. When Doug had teased her, he'd liked to call her Barbie Doll, which made Kerry mad.

"That's it. The initial *K* stands for Kerry. May I see her?"

"There's no notation about limiting visitors. I assume it will be all right. She's in room 208. The elevator is to your left." The woman smiled at him.

"Thanks," he managed to say before taking off at a sprint.

Sam was the only person on the elevator and he cursed out loud at its slowness as it began its ascent. Once on the second floor, he burst into the corridor, read the sign on the wall that pointed toward her room. He reeled through the hospital miasma of alcohol and antiseptic fumes until he reached the nurse's station. He clutched the counter as though it would impart strength. "Kerry Anderson? Room 208?"

"Right down the hall."

He rushed there, only to come to a skidding stop when he realized that someone was in the room with Kerry. The man looked up when he saw Sam and scribbled a quick notation on a clipboard.

He walked toward Sam, a tall, robust figure in a doctor's coat, and closed the door quietly behind him. "You're a friend of Mrs. Anderson's?"

"Yes. What's happened?"

"I'm her doctor, Ned Wellerman. She's had some cramping."

"Is she all right?"

"We hope it's not serious, but we've started intravenous medication to stop it. There's no bleeding and no dilation of the cervix, and those are good signs. She's asleep now. She needs her rest. She can go home tomorrow if all goes well."

"The baby? The baby's okay?" It was his baby, and he couldn't bear the thought of anything happening to it. Or to Kerry.

"The baby looks fine so far."

Sam's knees went weak with relief. "May I go in? To sit with her?"

The doctor hesitated.

"Please? I don't want her to wake up and find herself alone."

Something in Sam's manner must have made the doctor decide to let him stay; perhaps his earnestness, or maybe it was the nameless fear in his eyes.

"Okay, you can go in if you like. Just make sure she gets as much sleep as she can. It's a marvelous healer, sleep."

Sam opened the door a crack. The curtains were closed, and in the dim light he saw Kerry lying on her back with her eyes shut. Her face was white and drawn, her cheekbones prominent beneath the shadowy circles under her eyes. Her arm was extended across the white coverlet, and a tube dripped medication into a vein. At the sight of her so still and pale, he felt a lump growing in his throat. He couldn't swallow around it.

He realized with some surprise that he was still clutching the box containing the Inuit carving. He set it down on a table and moved closer.

Kerry stirred and opened her eyes. She blinked as though she couldn't quite believe what she saw.

"Kerry," he said. Sam was afraid in that moment that she would order him from the room. That she didn't want him anywhere near her. That she really did hate him.

She only looked at him.

He cleared his throat. "I went by Emma's. Serge Lagunoff saw the ambulance. He told me—"

"I'm so scared for the baby," Kerry whispered, her eyes wide and dark with emotion.

"The doctor said the baby's fine."

"Sometimes they don't tell you anything. Sometimes they don't want you to know."

"He said maybe you can go home tomorrow."

"He said that? Really?"

He forced a smile. She sounded like a little girl. But she wasn't a little girl, she was a grown woman, and that's why she was in here threatening to miscarry. "Yes, really," he said.

She seemed to be thinking about this. "If I lose this baby because of something stupid I did, I want to die, too, Sam."

He sat down in the chair beside the bed. "You're not going to lose the baby."

"I keep thinking that if I hadn't stayed at Silverthorne, maybe this wouldn't be happening. If I hadn't done all that walking and snowshoeing, if I hadn't fallen down the ridge, if—"

"I don't want you to lose this baby, either, Kerry." His mind overflowed with all the things he'd like to say, but he knew this wasn't the time to say them. Bottom line was that he had to keep her feeling up, not down. He had to let her know that she wasn't alone in this, that she would never be alone, that he would always be there for her. But he was sure that she didn't want to hear it.

"Oh, Sam" was all she said, and she began to cry then, soft little sobs that broke his heart.

He reached for her hand, gripped it between his, knew that they were irrevocably linked, whether she liked it or not, by the fact that she carried his child in her womb.

"You'll be all right. Everything will be fine," he said helplessly. To his surprise, she squeezed his hand. At first he thought he was imagining things, but she maintained the pressure.

"I'm glad you're here, Sam."

"So am I."

She drew a deep breath. "Maybe I can blame hormones for that crying jag," she said.

"Maybe. But you're entitled to emotion, you know. This can't be easy."

"That's for sure." She hitched herself higher on the bank of pillows. "What's in the box?"

"Box? Oh, I brought you a present." He'd almost forgotten.

He set the box on the bed beside her free hand, and she ruffled the ribbon. "Will you open it for me? I can't move around much with this IV."

He pulled off the ribbon and wrapping and lifted the lid of the box. He took out the carving of the bear and set it on the table beside the bed. "It's an Inuit carving. Valuable, I think."

Kerry stared at it and began to laugh. For the life of him, he couldn't figure out what was funny.

"I hate bears, Sam. But it's a lovely carving."

How could he have been dumb enough to forget that she didn't like bears? That she'd been scared out of her wits by a grizzly? At that moment, he felt like an idiot, a clumsy and inconsiderate idiot.

"I didn't think," he said slowly. "I wanted to cheer you up, and I thought this might help."

She smiled at him, her eyes luminous and wide. "Well, it has cheered me up. And I don't hate *this* bear. Actually it's kind of cute."

"Do you want it? I'll take it back, exchange it or something."

"Oh, Sam. Of course I want it. It will remind me of—well, it'll remind me, that's all."

"Of our time at Silverthorne?"

"Of our time together."

It surprised him that she would say this. He didn't think that their time there had meant anything to her. And as the realization dawned on him that it *had* meant something, that she still felt something for him, he knew that everything—*everything*—was going to be all right. Kerry might not be over her anger, and he might not know what to do about it, but things would work out between them. This time, with this woman, he was going to be the Sam he wanted to be, not the Sam he'd been in the past. He wouldn't withdraw from Kerry and this baby—*his* baby. He'd be there for them, no matter what.

"Don't leave me, Sam. Stay with me?" Kerry's eyes, a complex dazzle of gold and silver, implored him.

He didn't hesitate, only leaned over and tenderly kissed her on the cheek.

"You bet," he told her.

THE STREETS OF Anchorage slipped past as Sam drove Kerry from the hospital to his house the next morning.

"I wish you would let me go home to Emma's," she fretted, twisting a loose button on her coat.

"Emma's isn't your home. You might as well be where I can take care of you."

"I don't want to be a burden. Just put me on a plane so I can be with my parents in La Jolla, that's all I ask."

He shot her an exasperated look. "There's no need to go right away, is there? You might as well rest for a few days first. What if the cramps start again while you're on an airplane over the Pacific?"

Kerry had to admit that Sam had a good point. But there

was a lot unspoken between them, and she was still angry with him. And with Doug.

"Emma was all set to come back from Fairbanks. You shouldn't have told her not to come."

"She's trying to finish up that job before Christmas. And if she were to fly home, she wouldn't be able to."

Kerry sighed. She'd tried to get out of moving in with Sam, but he wouldn't take no for an answer. At this point, she reminded herself, she needed to make decisions based solely on what was best for her baby.

Sam had been so sweet all last night, holding her hand, getting her ice for the water pitcher, calling the nurse when the IV was running low. Once she'd opened her eyes and seen him staring unblinkingly at the meter that measured the baby's heartbeat. As long as the numbers kept bouncing up and down on the monitor, the baby was okay.

This baby has to be all right, Kerry had thought to herself, and she hadn't even realized that she'd whispered the words out loud until Sam replied with a catch in his voice, "He will be."

She'd drifted away into sleep after that, wondering how Sam could be so sure.

"Do you really think the baby is a boy?" she said now as Sam turned onto the street where he lived. His house rose ahead of them on the cliff, a big architecturally significant structure with enormous glass windows.

"What makes you think I think that?"

"You said last night that *he'd* be all right. You distinctly referred to the baby as male."

He was quiet for a few seconds. "I suppose every man hopes that his first child will be a son."

This admission rattled her, though she tried not to show it. It was hard for her to think of this baby as Sam's, though it was. In her heart the baby had always been Doug's. She felt torn about this and she wasn't at all sure that she was actually better off knowing the truth. Pulling that manila file folder across the desk yesterday had opened a Pandora's box, all right.

A garage door in the base of the rock opened as if by magic, and the Mercedes glided in.

"Don't get out yet," Sam cautioned. "I'll help you."

She opened the door on her side. "Don't be silly, Sam, I'm perfectly capable of navigating on my own."

He was around the car before she could swing her legs out. "Don't take chances with our baby, Kerry," he said, and then he swept her up in his arms. It was so unexpected that she didn't protest, and anyway, she knew he was right. Besides, it felt wonderful to be cradled against Sam's wide chest, to be able to rest her head on his shoulder and feel safe and secure.

A small elevator carried them upward to a wide hall. Sam strode through it to the living room with its vista of cliff, sea and sky, and there he set her down on a couch. He pulled an ottoman over for her feet and draped a warm hand-knit wool afghan over them.

"Don't move," he said sternly. "Not even one inch. I'm going downstairs to get your suitcase."

"There's not much in it," she said. "It's just an overnight bag that I packed for the hospital."

"No matter, we can send Shwano's wife to shop for you."

"But—"

"Don't talk. Don't do anything. For the baby's sake."

She could have smiled at the worried expression on Sam's face, but wisely refrained.

"Okay. I'll sit here and do nothing. I promise."

With one last cautionary glance, Sam wheeled and left. Kerry leaned her head back and surveyed her surround ings. This was a lot different from the cabin at Silverthorne and the places where they had stayed on their trek toward Athinopa. Spaces in Sam's house were defined by swooping curved walls designed to maximize the view, and everything seemed to be leather, burled wood or fluffy carpet. She wondered where Sam slept. She wondered where she would sleep.

This question was answered when Sam arrived with her suitcase in hand.

"I've asked Shwano to fix you a cup of hot herbal tea, and when you've rested a bit, I'll show you to your room."

She bit her lip.

"It's around the corner from mine," he said evenly.

"I didn't ask."

"But I answered anyway." He grinned at her.

Schwano, a squat swarthy man with a bright smile, arrived with the tea.

"My wife will be glad to help you," he told Kerry. "She just had a baby, so she knows all about it."

"Thank you," Kerry said gratefully. All of this—the magnificent house, the view, the house servant, even Sam himself—all of it seemed unreal. Her life had taken on a dreamlike quality, and she could hardly take it all in.

She sipped her tea, and Sam sipped something much stronger.

I wonder what Sam expects of me, she thought.

The baby stirred inside her, gladdening her heart. She stroked her stomach, to reassure the baby that she would do whatever she had to do to ensure its survival.

I wonder what Sam expects of us, she silently asked the baby.

WHEN KERRY was resting in her room, which was huge and decorated in blue-and-white toile accentuated with bright touches of lemon-yellow, Schwano's wife arrived in her room with armloads of shopping bags. Nicki was a giggly little Athabascan who had married Schwano on the reservation and followed him to town when he went to work for Sam. She loved Schwano, she loved her new baby and she loved shopping.

"Sam, he gave me money, he said go buy clothes and everything Kerry would need. I said, how do I know what size? Sam, he said she looks like this—'' And Nicki sketched an ovoid shape in the air. At this, Kerry couldn't help dissolving into laughter, and Nicki laughed with her.

The clothes Nicki brought were beautiful and expensive, and they fit much better than the stretched-out leggings and oversized sweater that Kerry had been wearing when the ambulance bore her away to the hospital. Nicki carried her old clothes away to be washed, and Kerry, who realized that she could not pay for the new clothes herself, inspected herself in the full-length mirror on the wall. She looked great. The top she wore was a carnation-pink fluff of angora and wool, and the pants were wool and dyed to match. The color was perfect for her.

But Sam had spent more on these two items of clothing than she would feel comfortable spending on a month's worth of groceries. She squared her shoulders, went down the hall to the closed door of Sam's room and rapped smartly on the door.

He opened it and seemed mildly surprised to see her there.

"I thought you were supposed to rest," he said as she swept past him into the room. The walls were upholstered in dark blue fabric, the big bed covered with a plaid quilt. A fire crackled in the fireplace, warming the room with its glow.

She drew a deep breath. Sam was wearing a soft burgundy shirt, the collar thrown open at the throat. He still didn't look like the Sam she'd known at Silverthorne, but he was certainly a very handsome Sam.

"Sam," she said, "I can't accept the clothes. Too expensive. I'll never be able to pay for them, and—"

He interrupted. "I'm paying for them. I can well afford it."

Kerry let out an exasperated sigh. "Look, Sam, I'm certainly grateful for your getting me out of the wilderness and I appreciate your coming to the hospital. And even though I could have gone home to Emma's, it was nice of you to bring me here. But you don't need to spend money on me."

Outside, it was getting dark, the way it usually did by this time in the afternoon, and along the cliff, lights were winking on in houses as car headlights snaked along the road. Kerry was momentarily distracted by the scene, so much so that she was surprised when she realized that Sam had moved and was standing close beside her.

"Did you ever consider," he said slowly, "that I would like to provide for my child?"

When he was standing so close, it was hard for her to think. Or at least she wasn't thinking about what he'd said, she was thinking about that night in the Stanchiks' cabin when he had held her in his arms and let her sob. It had felt so good to give in to her feelings, and he had been kind and understanding. He had known then that she was pregnant with his child, but he hadn't spoken of it. What had changed? Why was he speaking of it now?

"You don't have to provide for me or for this baby. I will do that," she said in a low tone.

"You don't understand. I want to."

Slowly she lifted her gaze so that she was looking straight into his eyes. They were calm, steady and sure. But sure of what? She didn't know, but she was surprised and she knew she showed it.

"Sam, you didn't ask for this. When you and Doug decided to take destiny into your own hands, you didn't expect to ever have to be a father."

"No," he said. "I didn't." He paused, then said, "I've never told you why I decided to do it."

She blinked at him. "I'm not sure I want to know, Sam."

"You should or you'll never understand. Doug was my best friend, Kerry. We were Air Force buddies and we became like brothers. He saved my life once."

"I didn't know that!" Kerry stared at him.

"It was before he knew you, and Doug was so modest that he wouldn't take credit for being a hero. We were shot down in the desert during a clandestine operation in the Middle East, and I got a nasty blow on the head. I was pretty much out of it, but Doug kept telling me not to give up, that he would get us out of there. He carried me on his back until we found shelter in a cave, gave most of our skimpy supply of water to me, kept me alive until local tribesmen rescued us. It was a national security matter, didn't make it into the press. I've never talked about it and neither did Doug."

Kerry knew that Doug hadn't cared to talk about some of his military experiences, but she hadn't realized that he'd ever been shot down.

"So anyway, after that, whatever I could do for Doug, I would have done. No matter what. And becoming a sperm donor was something I could do, you see. It would make him happy, and you would get the baby you wanted, and everything was supposed to turn out right." Sam shrugged, a forlorn gesture.

Kerry couldn't stand looking into Sam's face, his dear face, for one more minute. She whirled and marched to the window, where she stood with her arms folded across her chest above her swollen belly.

"You should have told me about your agreement, you and Doug."

"No. There would have been no point. It would only have made things awkward for the three of us. It was a secret, Kerry. A secret between best buddies."

"I wish I'd never found out."

"So do I, in a way. And in a way I'm glad you know. I don't want secrets between us ever again. And now I can be up front about taking care of you and the baby."

"You don't have to feel sorry for me!" The words were impassioned.

"Sorry for you? Kerry, you've got it all wrong. I'm the one to feel sorry for!"

Stunned, she swiveled to face him. She couldn't believe he'd said that. "You?" Her sweeping gesture took in the view, the furnishings, the paintings on the walls. "You're a man who has everything! No one in this town feels sorry for you, Sam Harbeck!"

His hands gripped her shoulders, holding her immobile. His face was inches from hers, his eyes blazing.

"I have everything a man could want, it's true. Everything, Kerry, except the love of a good woman."

Her gaze faltered. She couldn't speak.

"And that's what I want more than anything," he said evenly. "That and a child would make me the happiest man in the world."

"You're not the type to settle down. You always found a way out of every relationship. You said so."

His hands on her shoulders relaxed, but he didn't release her.

"That was before I knew you. Before I realized how

well-suited we are. Before I knew how much a helpmate would mean in my life, before I fell in love with you.''

Kerry's knees felt weak. ''It's because of the baby. You feel responsible and you *are* responsible, and now you want to make it up to me. That's all it is.''

''Stop babbling, Kerry, and kiss me.''

''You said you love me,'' she said unevenly. ''You can take it back if you want. I'll give you ten seconds to take it back. One, two, three—''

''You are the most stubborn woman in the world. I don't want to take it back. I wouldn't change anything, not ditching the plane in the river, not the time at Silverthorne, not our trek through the wilderness. I wouldn't change being the father of your baby. *Our* baby, Kerry. I'm totally and completely in love with you. What would convince you?''

''Well, that kiss for starters.''

She let herself be drawn into his arms, enfolded in his embrace, and she felt her head tilting back and her lips opening to meet his. He kissed her, his mouth moving masterfully against hers. She was marginally aware of his hands sliding through her hair, of her growing arousal and of his.

''If you weren't barely out of the hospital, woman, I'd carry you off to my bed and have my way with you,'' Sam growled into her hair. ''But as it is, I suppose I'll just have to carry you off to a justice of the peace instead. Do you think your broken finger has healed enough to wear my wedding ring?''

''Wh-what?''

''I'm asking you to marry me, Kerry Anderson. Until death do us part. As long as we both shall live. Whichever comes first.''

''Marry you,'' she repeated slowly and clearly so that there could be no mistake that she'd heard him right. ''You can still take that back, Sam. I'll count to ten. One, two—''

"Please stop procrastinating. I just proposed to you."

She swallowed. "You really mean it?"

"As much as I've ever meant anything," Sam told her fervently.

"Sam, I think I'd better sit down."

"Are you all right? You're not feeling any cramping, are you? Should I call Dr. Wellerman?"

She laughed then, laughed through her happy tears. "No, I think three in a bed is quite enough."

"Kerry, what are you talking about?"

"I'm saying that I want to get in bed, just the three of us, you and me and this baby of ours, and the doctor would just be in the way."

"I think I just asked you to marry me," Sam reminded her.

"I think I want to say yes. But I want to do it in your bed. My knees are shaking, Sam."

"Oh, my love," he said, and he picked her up and carried her to the bed. He laid her down carefully, and she patted the quilt beside her.

"You belong here," she said.

He lay down beside her and wrapped his arms around her until her head was pillowed on his shoulder. Outside it was dark now, and a fog was creeping in from the inlet.

"I take it this means yes?" he asked as he nuzzled the hollow in the base of her throat.

"A very blissful yes." She stiffened, and Sam drew away.

"Is anything wrong?" he asked in alarm.

She smiled at him in the dark. "Give me your hand."

She guided his hand to her abdomen where the baby was performing gymnastics. "Your son moves," she whispered.

"That's the baby? That? And that?"

"It feels like bubbles," she said.

"That's *my* baby! It feels wonderful. Miraculous." He took his hand away, curved it around her breast.

"I love you. And our son," he said.

"Could be a daughter."

"It's a son. Trust me."

"We'll see," Kerry told him.

He cuddled her close. "When do you want to get married?"

"Tomorrow. Tonight, if you can arrange it."

"Tomorrow. Because I want to hold you in my arms all night long."

"I want you to hold me in your arms all *life* long."

"You got it, kiddo."

They lay quietly, listening to each other's breathing.

"Kerry?"

"Hmm?"

"I don't think Doug would mind."

"Nor do I."

"I'd like to name our baby after him. What do you think?"

Kerry didn't even have to think about it. "I'd like that."

Kerry fell asleep then. She dreamed of Silverthorne and of filling it with happy laughing children, and she dreamed of Sam and of growing old with him, and she dreamed of making this big house on the cliff a home for the two of them. And for their children, lots of children.

Sam dreamed, too.

They were flying to Silverthorne, he and Doug, just as they had every year. Doug was the pilot, and he, Sam, was the copilot. They could see all the way to Denali, the highest peak in North America.

"You know," Doug said, "it looks like clear skies ahead for you."

"Yeah, well, you never know."

"Sam. You and Kerry, you're good together."

"It took me a while to figure it out."

"I always said she liked you."

Sam thought this over. "I didn't believe you."

"You do now. That's what counts. You'll be a great dad, Sam."

"I'm going to give it all I've got. I love the baby. Never knew how much it would mean to have a son."

"I wouldn't count on its being a boy, Sam."

"Well, a father knows things like this."

Doug laughed at him then, a long hearty laugh. "Not always. But you know what? This daughter of yours is going to grow up to be a crackerjack pilot. A chip off the old block."

And then Doug faded away, leaving Sam alone in the cockpit flying the plane.

"Doug, wait," he called, and he felt so frantic about his friend's disappearance that he woke up.

Woke up to find Kerry in his arms. Still, the dream was disturbing. If he could have, he would have gone back to find out what Doug meant about his daughter's becoming a crackerjack pilot. But you couldn't ever finish dreams.

Or maybe you could. After all, waking up to find Kerry in his arms was a real-life dream come true.

Epilogue

"Look, Ellie! There's a plane!"

The dark-haired baby in the high chair on the front lawn of Silverthorne Lodge regarded the object overhead with an expression of glee. "Dada," she said with great certainty.

Kerry scooped the baby into her arms and blotted at her drooling six-month-old daughter's mouth. "Won't Dada be surprised that you've finally got your first tooth?"

"Dada!" Ellie squealed. It was her first word, and she was proud of it. She also loved her father very much, which pleased Kerry to no end.

It was quiet at Silverthorne Lodge today, the last group of tourists having flown out earlier. Sam was ferrying in another contingent this afternoon, and more would arrive on Captain Crocker's *River Rover* by nightfall.

They'd fallen into a routine. On Saturday mornings, Sam would arrive, flying in anyone who wanted the thrill of sightseeing Williwaw Glacier from the air. He'd stay as many days as he could until business demanded his return to Anchorage, but so far this summer he'd managed to arrange his schedule so that he could spend most of his time at the lodge.

The lodge was successful beyond Kerry's wildest dreams. Every room had been reserved since before Easter, and reservations were already pouring in for next summer. Guests liked to hike into the valley, fish in the streams and feast on fresh tuna grilled with Kerry's special honey marinade. She and her staff provided wholesome activities for children and pure relaxation for adults.

The float plane coasted to the dock, and Sam was the first one out, running full tilt up the slope from the river. Kerry hurried to meet him, and Ellie gurgled in joyful recognition.

"Dada!"

"How are my girls?" He gathered them both into a big heartfelt hug.

Kerry kissed him. "Ellie's got her first tooth!" she told him.

He took Ellie from her and tickled her neck with his nose until she started to giggle.

"Hmm," he said. "And a fine tooth it is, too. Say, is that another one I see peeking through?"

"She's an early teether and an early talker. I bet she'll walk early, too."

"Good. When do you think her feet will reach the controls of a plane?"

"Not till she's a teenager. Mom's rules." Kerry slid her arm through Sam's. "Emma's coming for a visit next week, don't forget. She's planning to bring Serge Lagunoff. He used to prospect for gold around here, he says, and he wants to explore the territory. And the art dealer in Anchorage wants to buy two of Elise's paintings—if I can bear to part with them."

"So much going on, as if you don't have enough to do

here! Of course I'll bring Emma and Serge with me next Saturday, and as for that art dealer, do whatever you like. Now what do you say we put our dear little Elise Anderson Harbeck to bed for a nap, and you and I work on making another little Harbeck? A son next time, right?''

"Right. But Ellie doesn't seem very sleepy right now."

"Well, of course not. I may have to play with her until she can't keep her eyes open any longer. And then I'll get to play with her mommy. The next Harbeck in this family is going to be conceived in the usual way. I got cheated out of the fun last time. Oh, I almost forgot. I brought Ellie something."

Sam shifted the baby back to Kerry's arms and pulled a package from his jacket pocket. "A cousin of Schwano's makes wooden toys, and I commissioned this from him."

It was a beautifully crafted little floatplane, the finish smooth as silk and all edges rounded so that they wouldn't pose a threat to a baby.

"She can even play with it in the bathtub. It floats," Sam explained.

"What does it say on the side?" Kerry reached for the plane and turned it so she could read the writing on the fuselage. "'Sybilla?'" She regarded Sam with a puzzled frown.

"Well, maybe you don't really want to know," he said.

"Sam."

"There's no point in getting into it."

"Now that we're married, you should be able to tell me everything," she said slyly.

"Now that we're married, I'd rather do something else besides talk." He patted her bottom lightly.

Kerry shot a scandalized look over her shoulder at the passengers disembarking from the plane. "Sam! Someone might be looking!"

"And they'd see a man who is totally in love with his wife and who wants to get her in the sack as soon as possible."

Kerry handed the toy back to Ellie. "All right. I might as well accept that I may never find out who Sybilla was. And I guess, in the total scheme of things, it really doesn't matter."

"Some things just have to remain secret. What matters is that we're happy. Aren't we?" His face was gilded by the last golden rays of the sun sinking behind Williwaw Glacier.

"Happier than I ever thought I could be," Kerry murmured with a kind of wonder.

"What do you say to that?" Sam asked their daughter.

"Dada!"

"And I guess that's kind of what started the whole thing," he said.

Kerry laughed, and he slid his arm around her shoulders, and they made their way, the three of them, up the rise of land to the lodge.

Looking For More Romance?

Visit Romance.net

Look us up on-line at: http://www.romance.net

Check in daily for these and other exciting features:

Hot off the press

View all current titles, and purchase them on-line.

What do the stars have in store for you?

Horoscope

Hot deals

Exclusive offers available only at Romance.net

Plus, don't miss our interactive quizzes, contests and bonus gifts.

COMING NEXT MONTH

Visit us at www.romance.net

CNM0300